THE LIBRARY
AT HELLEBORE

THE
LIBRARY
AT
HELLEBORE

CASSANDRA KHAW

NIGHTFIRE

TOR PUBLISHING GROUP
NEW YORK

This is a work of fiction. All of the characters, organizations, and events portrayed in this novel are either products of the author's imagination or are used fictitiously.

THE LIBRARY AT HELLEBORE

Copyright © 2025 by Cassandra Khaw

All rights reserved.

Endpaper and interior art by Shutterstock.com

A Nightfire Book
Published by Tom Doherty Associates / Tor Publishing Group
120 Broadway
New York, NY 10271

www.torpublishinggroup.com

Nightfire™ is a trademark of Macmillan Publishing Group, LLC.

The Library of Congress Cataloging-in-Publication Data
is available upon request.

ISBN 978-1-250-87781-9 (hardcover)
ISBN 978-1-250-87782-6 (ebook)

Our books may be purchased in bulk for promotional, educational, or business use. Please contact your local bookseller or the Macmillan Corporate and Premium Sales Department at 1-800-221-7945, extension 5442, or by email at MacmillanSpecialMarkets@macmillan.com.

First Edition: 2025

Printed in the United States of America

0   9   8   7   6   5   4   3   2   1

*For Farrell, who is not mine but a good cat
and has been his whole life.*

*And for Sebastien Fanzun, scholar and cat person
and my first friend in Zurich.*

THE LIBRARY
AT HELLEBORE

BEFORE

When I woke up, my roommate, Johanna, was dead.

This was neither the first time I'd come to with a body at my feet, nor was it even the first time I had returned to consciousness in a room transformed into a literal abattoir, but it was the first time I woke up relieved to be in a mess. The walls were soaked in effluvium. Every piece of linen on our beds was at least moderately pink with gore. The floor was a soup of viscera, intestines like ribbons unstrung over the scuffed wood; it'd been a deep gorgeous ebony once, but now, like the rest of our room, it was just red.

Carefully, I reached for Johanna's outflung arm, the one desolate limb to have survived what happened to her, and folded it over her chest, closing my hands over her knuckles. She was still here. There were even parts I could recognize. When it struck me, I thought I'd wake up and none of what I did would have mattered, that her body would be missing. But she was still here. It wasn't much but it was something. I'm not religious in any sense of the word. Far as I'm concerned, dirt's the only holy thing in the world. It can make roses out of even the worst losers: in death, we achieve meaning. I stared at the mess. While I could give a dead rat's rotten lungs about divinity, I had a lot more compassion to dole out when it came to the dead—especially when the deceased in question was someone I'd *just* achieved character growth with.

It wasn't fair.

Being sad, however, wouldn't rewrite the past to give us a platonic happily ever after, although I imagine if I got her necromantic situationship involved, that might change things. Part of me thought about it. Let's be clear about that. Part of me did think about looking for Rowan, about demanding that he see if there was anything that could be done. Johanna had been nothing but kind to me, after all. The fact that she was weird and codependent about it was beside the point. Even in my worst moments, she had cared.

Pity she needed to die. Pity she needed to stay dead. Pity all that was as inevitable as what was coming next.

"Alessa?"

I turned to see a lithe young man at the door. Rowan was thin in the way most smokers eventually became, gristly and lineated with veins, his skin already like a piece of dehydrated leather. But there was an unconventional appeal to his Roman nose, his mobile lips, the eyes like flecked chips of lapis. His expression was affable, unbothered. You'd think he would look more troubled. Johanna *was* kind of his girlfriend.

Then again, this was also Hellebore. But we'll get to that.

"Good morning," I said. "I can explain."

"Is that so?" said Rowan, his gaze making a circuit across the mess, a single line indenting the space between his fluffy eyebrows. Mine felt matted with blood but it didn't feel like it was appropriate to check. "I'd really like to hear it."

"Yes, well." I took a breath. A glob of something lukewarm traveled down the bridge of my nose. "Actually, that's a lie. I can't really explain it. Scratch that. I was asked not to explain it. So, that makes things . . . difficult."

"More difficult than being caught committing homicide?" The lanky boy crossed the room to where I stood beside Johanna's corpse, one of my hands still clasping hers. A smile crept up to his mouth, wary as a beaten animal.

"Lots of judgment from someone who was just a fuck-buddy." His sanctimoniousness drew an unexpected venom from me. "I thought you didn't care about her."

"I cared about her as a person."

"If you did, you'd have left her alone." Cruelty was like riding a bike: it became ingrained in you, became muscle memory. There was no losing the trick of it. You never forgot how to drive a knife in and *twist*. "She loved you, you know."

He flinched like I'd punched him.

Good, I remember thinking, a tang of bloodlust slicking my tongue.

"If you knew what I knew, you'd have treated her better. I take that back. If you knew what I knew, you'd have stayed the fuck away and left her alone." I spat the last word. "You used her."

Rowan stopped about a foot from the steamer trunk in front of Johanna's bed, his knee bumping into the verdigris lid, and tipped one hand at me, turning it palm up. He was the very image of good faith, earnest and smiling. He looked like I'd just anointed him with compliments; there was something almost coy in the way he peered at me through long black lashes.

"Be that as it may," he said. "That doesn't change the fact you killed her."

"Well, I didn't *want* to."

It wasn't a defense. I knew that. Neither was the shrug I offered up, my gaze falling again to Johanna's remains. Even defiled thus, her golden hair was somehow unmistakable. Same with the perfect curve of her jaw, dislodged as it was from the rest of her skull. What surprised me though was how much it hurt to see her dead.

"There is gunk coming down from the ceiling," said Rowan after a minute of obtrusive silence.

I looked up. As it turned out, there was.

"That wasn't intentional."

"Alessa, just tell me what happened."

The coppery, sweetly fecal smell of death was beginning to intensify.

He reached out with a gloved hand, desperation pushing up against that smiling facade, the nonchalance faltering, cracking under the pressure of what I could assume to be grief. For a second, I was witness to the fatal loneliness at the core of that grinning, jocular, often inappropriate boy—to the child who must have spent his early life up to his ears in protective gear so as to prevent him from rampant manslaughter. They say that babies can die from touch starvation. I wondered what Rowan had had to kill to be standing here now, what he had had to give up, all to be too late. I wondered if some part of him had died at the sight of Johanna's remains, knowing there laid butchered most likely the only woman who'd ever look at his deficiencies and still see him as enough.

"Please," said Rowan.

Before I could say anything, another voice broke through the air.

"*What* did you *do?*"

We turned in tandem to see a figure stumbling fawn-legged toward us, pausing at intervals to flinch at the charnel, the color bleeding from a face already arctic in its complexion. Most people would call her a beauty and they'd be right any other day. There and then, however, she was a car crash in slow motion, that long, drawn-out, honeyed second before an explosion. She was a corpse that hadn't caught up to the fact that her heart had been dug out and eaten, dripping like a fruit. In her face, a kind of obstinate hope somehow. Like if she lived in this incredulous grief for a little longer, it'd grant Johanna a Schrödinger's immortality: keep her not necessarily alive, but not dead either.

"What did you *do*?" Stefania screamed.

A little to my surprise if not Rowan's, she arrowed straight toward him, literally serrating as she did: every limb began to split into outcroppings of teeth, skin becoming stubbled with molars, speared through with expanding incisors. Her face bisected and then quartered, petaling, each flap lined like the inside of a lamprey's mouth. When she screamed again, it was with a laryngeal configuration that had no business existing even here in the halls of Hellebore: it was a choir, a horror, a nightmare of sound.

"You," she said in all the voices those new mouths afforded her. Tongues waved from every joint. "You fucking bastard."

Rowan threw his hands up, backing away, even though I was the one smeared with a frosting-thick coat of gore. "First of all: fuck you. Second: how dare you? *The visual evidence alone,* Stefania. It's clear—"

Whatever else he might have said was swallowed by an obliterating white light. The incandescence lasted only for a second but it filled the room, burning away all features. Then it winked out and as our sight returned, we discovered collectively there was now a fourth member of our little tableau.

Standing before us was the headmaster herself, bonneted and in a cotton nightdress ornamented with smiling deer. Though the style was cartoonish, it did little to dull the absolute horror of the sight: ungulate faces were never meant to stretch that way. The headmistress blinked owlishly at us, her eyes magnified by the lenses of her horn-rimmed spectacles. I froze at the sight of her. I knew what was behind that doddering facade.

"Children." Her voice when she wasn't orating was high and breathy, a bad idea away from being babyish, like a sorority girl courting the quarterback's attention. It was particularly weird coming from someone who looked and acted the way the headmistress did: namely, *old*. "What are you doing?"

"What," said Stefania, devolving back to her usual shape, a process that involved more slurping noises than I would have preferred. "Headmaster?"

"This is terrible behavior."

"They *killed* my friend," exhaled Stefania, and the helplessness in her voice was worse than her rage, a note of keening under those panted words. "Headmistress, please—"

"There is a *soiree* waiting for you," continued the headmaster, putting undue emphasis on the word *soiree*, dragging out the vowels, turning them nasal, exaggeratedly French. "You should be dressing up. You should be putting on makeup." Her eyes darted to Rowan. "Better clothes. Why aren't you working to look delicious?"

In movies, it is always clear when the villain slips up with a double entendre. The music score changes; the camera pans in on their faces. It is a narrative design, a conspiratorial glance at the audience: here is the signage marking the descent into mayhem and here too, the strategically positioned lighting, placed just so to ensure no one ignores the moment. But with the headmaster, it was clear the use of those words was deliberate. She did not speak them in error. This wasn't Freudian. This was her *telling* us that she *expected* us to look pretty on a plate. The audacity left me speechless, but not Rowan.

"I'm afraid I taste terrible," he said, flapping his hands.

"Like, absolutely rancid. Between all the smoking and drinking, it'd probably be awful. Just awful. Can I help with the drinks instead?"

"You're insane," said Stefania. "I refuse to be part of this."

The headmaster didn't even look at her. Instead, she said sweetly, "In that case, I suggest you hang yourself."

"You mean it," I said after a drawn-out moment. "You're actually planning to eat us."

"I said make yourself look delicious," trilled the headmaster, twirling a mauve-veined hand at me. "You're the one coming up with questionable conjecture."

But the look in her eyes said everything, as did her delicate smile. Rowan swallowed the rest of his rambling excuses, his jaws clenched so hard I heard the scrape of enamel as they ground together, and Stefania stared at the floor with a furious, indiscriminate hate. I studied the headmaster, wishing I had a rejoinder that didn't make me sound petulant. My only consolation was that the epiphany of this impending cannibal feast had both Rowan and Stefania at least temporarily distracted from the ugly business of our dearly deceased mutual friend.

Her smile deepened. She knew as well as the three of us did that there wouldn't be opting out of the situation.

"You can't make us go," said Rowan.

"Actually," said the headmistress, voice losing its chirping lilt. She spoke the next words in what I'd come to think of as her real voice: smooth and bored, unsettlingly anodyne save when her amusement knifed through the surface like a fin moving through dark water. "I can."

Before any of us could object, the world spun and, sudden as anything, we were in the gymnasium. Each and every one of us were in formal raiment, a mortarboard jauntily set at an angle on each of our heads. We were as pristine as if we'd spent the day in frenzied ablution: hair shining like it'd been oiled individually, faces beautiful. We looked like we were waiting backstage for our turn on the catwalk—like sacrifices, or saints waiting for the lions.

The air had an odd crystalline shine to it like it had been greased somehow. That or I was in the throes of a migraine. It was hard to be sure. I'd been plopped next to Gracelynn, who was sat between Sullivan and me, with Kevin on my opposite side. Bracketing us was a pair of twins I'd only seen occasionally but knew by reputation, the two notorious for the ease with which they procured reagents for whoever had the money to pay: they could get anything so long as what you wanted came from something with a pulse. A few familiar faces were past them to the right: Stefania, Minji, Eoan, and Adam, who slouched almost entirely out of his seat.

"What is going on?" Kevin hissed to me.

"We have to go," I said in lieu of an answer, standing.

The world stuttered.

I was back on the metal fold-out chair I'd been sitting on, like my muscles had changed their mind midway to rising. Except I hadn't *felt* myself sit back down. Instead, it was more like the seconds had rewound, had flinched back from my decision like it was a hot stove. I tried again. This time, I felt it: reality slingshotting backward through linear time, not far enough to leave me discombobulated, but enough to have my ass on the cold, cheap steel. It hit me then that I was trapped. All my efforts, all those months spent trying to get out, and here I was with no place to go, a bunny with the hounds gathered all around.

The doors of the gymnasium opened, allowing our headmaster entry. She drifted down the aisle, splitting the crowd of so-called graduates, resplendent in a fawn-colored suit, the majesty of which was spoiled by the fact that her white hair was still in curlers. A clipboard was tucked in the crook of her left arm. She checked something off as she passed each student, her smile as it always was: slightly too wide for her face.

When she finally reached our row, she only said, with an effervescent giggle:

"Ah. It's time for a speech by the valedictorian!"

Sullivan took her hand when she offered it. I couldn't help the "No, *stop!*" that wrestled out of my mouth. I groped for Sullivan's arm, the motion entirely reflexive. He and I, we weren't close, but some animal instinct roared past all my other sensibilities. I knew unequivocally that if he went with her, he would be dead.

"Sullivan—"

He unbraided my fingers from his wrist, a suicidal gentleness in his eyes as he said, "It's okay." His eyes shifting to Delilah—his light, his lamb, his death. She wouldn't meet his gaze, stared instead into her palms, more statue than girl.

It definitely wasn't.

BEFORE

If you're reading this, there's a small chance you're another student, frightened senseless (been there) by a waning belief (sorry, this book won't make this better) that you are in a safe place; but more likely, you are an incumbent in the Ministry, and therefore are already aware of what the Hellebore Technical Institute for the Ambitiously Gifted is (fuck you very much, if you are). On the off chance that you're neither, that you're a bystander who found my journal in an antique store, or someone raiding the evidence locker for novelties, I want to set the stage before we get any further.

Magic is real.

I want to assert that I know you probably know this already. We do both live in a world where even governmental bodies have acknowledged magic's existence. But we reside as well on a planet where the efficacy of medical science is questioned and media personalities argue whether a clot of cells has more value than a woman's life. To put it another way, these are unutterably stupid times, so I'm not taking chances.

Now, while magic has always been real, there was a period when it thrived. For better or worse, people were once steered by folklore—cultivating gods, curating herbs based on their value in rituals, the works. Back then, population density was low enough that myths could breed in dreams and spring like

Venus from the peasant's skull, ready for mischief. It was the best and worst of times.

That went away with the Renaissance period when society began mass-producing these tender, inquisitive souls: scalpels draped in skin. All they wanted to do was cut the cosmos open and see what was inside. Their joyous and relentless curiosity led to such a revolution in human thinking. We went from soothsayers to science, gods to generating electricity. Our lifespans grew; childbirth stopped being a macabre lottery. We sanded the dark down to a manageable threat; everyone still knew to be cautious when out walking at night, but they were no longer afraid of ghosts, just one another.

Those years of frenzied development, interspaced with decades of war, kept mankind so preoccupied we didn't notice magic receding from us. One day, it was there. The next, it was entirely fictive, all illusions and sleight of hand, cold reading and con men: nothing a rational person would believe in, let alone practice with any kind of seriousness.

But about a hundred years or so ago, it started coming back. And chaos immediately ensued.

Like, *immediately.* Faith healers discovered their snakes now had opinions, many of which were kinder than their own. Relics were demanding their burials, along with a share of what wealth had been accrued through illegal use of their matter. The graveyards woke with barghests and *gwisin.* Rat kings whispered through the walls. The housing market collapsed as hauntings drove tenants to paranoia. Psychiatrists were initially delighted by the prodigious business but then discovered that their clientele weren't all human and weren't all there for simple conversation. Statues wept; no one would sleep for months.

As was customary, the authorities did very little until this plague of global re-enchantment led to a decimation of the workforce. Unable to rest, unable to eat without worrying if their salad would consign them to a lifetime in a fae lord's service, unable to distinguish loved ones from doppelgängers, people began choosing the ledge, the pill bottle, the train tracks, the gun. Suddenly, it was a problem that needed immediate solving. Capitalism was unsustainable without bodies to feed the machine.

So the nations of the world slammed their figurative heads together, and concluded there was only one recourse available: bureaucracy. Magic was legislated. Foreign entities were subjected to hastily drafted but impressively thorough immigration laws, and municipalities came up with techniques for zoning cursed territory. Within a generation, there was something comparable to order so long as you were willing to squint real hard—and to blame any deviancy on the education systems now instated across the globe.

Everyone, and I do mean everyone, no matter age or nationality, who was gauche enough to show even a mote of magical talent was instantly freighted to the nearest available school for proper processing. The Hellebore Technical Institute for the Ambitiously Gifted is one such academy. In fact, you could argue it is *the* premier college for such things. Enrollment isn't guaranteed by proximity. You have to be a specific kind of someone to be inducted here, have to have the type of bona fides that the front page obsesses over and the op-eds love to dissect. Yes, every member of the student body is—how do I say it delicately?—someone with the potential to destroy the world three times over, and still have time for a good long brunch. (Which you'd know, if you were working for the Ministry. I've heard the rumors: you handpicked us for the butcher block.)

Here in Hellebore, we are all Antichrists, all Ragnarök

made manifest. We are those who are destined to break the chains binding Fenris to his boulder; we are Kalki come riding on his pale horse; the death of Buddha; the vectors of apocalypse, avatars of the end, world-eaters; memetic violence distilled into bodies with badly underdeveloped prefrontal cortexes, like the world's least impressive tulpa.

Some of us came by our designations through honest means. Take poor dead Sullivan Rivers (How did he die? You'll see; have patience), for example. Because Sullivan was the first son to be born in fuck-knows-how-many generations, he had found himself the imminent host of the deity his foremothers had dutifully screwed since prehistory. Sullivan had practically flung himself through the doors of Hellebore, hoping they'd save him from the cicada voices scratching at the inside of his eyelids. I wonder how pissed his gods were when his skull was trepanned from every direction. (And his family. I bet they loathed losing, if not a son, then a commodity, a prize; he was their fortune, a bargaining chip, something they could leverage. The powerful never like letting go of such things.)

Admittedly, Sullivan's kind was a rarefied group. Very main character, if you'd like to be colloquial about the subject. Most of the students in Hellebore are more like me. Freaks. Accidents of circumstance. People who might have led innocuous lives if they hadn't turned the wrong corner at the wrong time. Unfortunates who woke up one day indelibly different for no reason at all, their appetites like a cancer gnawing through their skin, growing until it erupted through their gums as a forest of new maws. Girls who were hurt and who discovered they could *really* hurt their abusers in return. You'd be surprised how many of us there are in that last category.

(Or not, depending on who you are.)

The first time I learned I had powers was when my step-daddy decided that the ring on his finger was the master key to every entrance in our household. He slapped me when I said no, unable to contend with the notion that my sense of autonomy precluded his need to be inside where he damn well shouldn't be. I remember my ears ringing, and his hands locked around my wrists, raising my arms above my head. I remember his mouth along the nubs of my spine, his knee trying to spread my legs wide, and thinking, *I need you to hurt.*

So I rent him in half: lengthwise and real fucking slow, suspending him in the air so his guts sheeted down on me like a porridgy red rain. I didn't let him go gentle into that good velvet night, and I took as much time as I'm sure he'd wanted to with me. He squirmed and moaned for hours, begging me for respite throughout, going, *Please, Alessa, let me die, let me die, this hurts.* When I got bored, I made him amputate his tongue with his teeth and choke on it like a cock.

He was the first man I killed and, as you might have guessed, not the last. Though in my defense, the subsequent deaths were less acts of intentional homicide and more (to put it with some modicum of decorum) the consequences of fatally efficient self-defense. One or two of these cases were definitively punitive in timbre, but the victims were deserving. *No* should have sufficed as an answer. *No* should have been taken without interrogation, accepted without need for wheedling or attempts at coercion.

Since they wouldn't listen, I didn't either.

Anyway.

I was told by Hellebore's guidance counselor that such murder sprees were common with girls like me. She was a Swedish woman, lean, small-breasted, often attired in starchy suits in the same sodium white of her hair. She smiled like the expression had been taught to her from a manual, and looked like the first abandoned draft for what would become Tilda Swinton. According to her, what we did was natural instinct, a response engendered by a lifetime spent being waterboarded with systemic misogyny: we were angry and we were *acting out.*

Hellebore could teach us to be better than our impulses, or so student services claimed. It was what the Ministry guaranteed the world. If you forced me to say one nice thing about Hellebore, I'd give it this: the marketing for the institute is award-winning. Everything that has ever been written about Hellebore suggests it is a place of redemption, a place where the unwanted become the coveted. People dreamt of enrollment. It was the highest possible honor.

No one, of course, said anything about the fact Hellebore sometimes kidnaps its students. My salvation was put into motion with neither my awareness nor my consent. I'd mentioned earlier there were students for whom Hellebore represented escape, an alternative to the killing chute of their lives. But not everyone *chooses* Hellebore. Many were apparently enrolled the way I was. *Conscripted,* really. One night, I went to sleep in my shitty tenement in Montreal's Côte-des-Neiges. The next day, I woke up in the dormitory, primly dressed in plaid pajamas, my hair brushed to a gloss. The bed I occupied was the largest I'd ever slept on, a California king with a wrought iron canopy strung with fairy lights and muslin. The duvet was a stiff enamel jacquard subtly inlaid with gold leaf, the sheets themselves a plain and sturdy cream-colored cotton, and there were more pillows than reasonable, like someone had wanted to build me a cairn of goose down and pewter silk.

None of my belongings survived my transit into Hellebore's vaunted ranks. Instead of my things, I found steamer trunks—I should have run when I saw the scratched-out name, the *B* carved over and over into the wood, the mottling along the leather straps; I should have known what they were, the discolorations, the corroded grisailles of dried blood, and *run*—under the skirts of my bed. Inside were uniforms; Peter Pan–collared dresses (the school had an archaic concept of gender expression) in what turned out to be the school colors, jasper and emerald and oxidized silver; well-tailored suits in the same palette; winter gear inclusive of fur-trimmed capelets; modest heels, walking boots; demure underwear; hats; textbooks; alchemic tools; and magical paraphernalia. Every single item was embossed with Hellebore's heraldry: fig wasps and the school's namesake threaded through the antlers of a deer skull, its tines strung with runes and staring eyes.

The first words out of my mouth when I'd inventoried the mess were, "I guess I'm a wizard then."

I remember laughing myself sick.

What a fucking idiot I was.

Like I said, I should have started running right there and then, and maybe I would have. Maybe I'd have clawed out of those flannel jammies, put on shoes, and bolted amid the chaos of orientation if the situation were even infinitesimally different. If I had been alone that day, with no one but the buttery morning light to bear witness to my escape. But I wasn't.

A full minute after my histrionics, a timid female voice to my right said, "I guess that makes me one too."

BEFORE

A small white hand hooked around a fold of my bed's drapery and began to pull. I caught it by the fingers before it could complete the motion; the skin under my palm was clammy, unnaturally hot, as if a furnace burned under the surface.

"Who?" I began. It wasn't just the owner of the hand who was fever-warm, but the room itself: the heaters were on at full blast. I could hear steam chatter and clank through a maze of pipes, hissing like a cornered animal. "The fuck are you?"

The hand slid out of mine. A white girl of similar age to me shouldered through the canopy and sat herself on the edge of my new bed, hands set primly on her thighs. She was very blond, very pretty, very much something that made every hair on the back of my neck rise. My skin wanted to crawl down between the mattress and its frame. It was her eyes, I decided, that had so thoroughly upset me. They were wide and green where they weren't dilated pupil, a noxious and effulgent shade of absinthe. Paired with the docile smile she wore, her eyes made her look like a wolf serving time in the brain of a fawn, a wolf so starved it would eat through its own belly if only it could reach.

"I'm Johanna," she said meekly. Healing sores dappled the cream of her throat, like bite marks.

"I think you're my roommate, which is *not* what I was expecting."

She ended the sentence with a frazzled laugh, both an accusation and an apology in her expression. There was something in her tone I did not like, a thoughtless possessiveness over our current environment that said to me this wasn't someone who had ever been told *no*. Johanna wound a hank of golden hair around a finger until the skin of the digit turned white.

"Did you wake up here too?" I said, in lieu of asking, *What were you expecting?*

"I came here the normal way," she said. Cathedral windows sprawled over the wall opposite my bed, showing mountain peaks crowned with snow. "Me and my best friend, we applied to be students in Hellebore and were approved."

"Good for you."

When I said nothing further, Johanna added: "Her name is Stefania."

"I didn't ask."

To Johanna's credit, she hardly reacted to my vitriol. If I hadn't been eagerly looking, I'd have missed the sudden flutter in her mouth and at the corners of her eyes, as if a current had been very briefly run through her, but I was, and it made me grin to see. She was human enough to upset, then. *Good.*

"So," she said, too well-bred to be kept on the back foot for long. Her expression cleared and it was like the sun coming out after a thousand years of dark. Her smile should have reduced me to worshipful cinders; it should have made me want to beg forgiveness for being such a hateful little gremlin. Under different circumstances, it even might have. However, I'd been recently kidnapped in my sleep by educators and I was *pissed.* "What's your name?"

"Alessa," I said absently, looking over the room again. A

distant bell tolled what I assumed to be the hour. Softer still was a murmur of voices seeping through the pearl-colored walls. "Alessa Li."

Johanna nodded and freed a small leather-bound notebook from a pocket in her dress, licked the tip of a finger, and began leafing through the water-warped, much-highlighted pages until she arrived at a blank space. She wrote my name down, underlining it twice.

"Is that your full name?" she asked conscientiously.

I stared at her in blunt amazement.

"What?"

My new roommate colored. "East Asian people tend to have more than one name, don't they? Alessa would be your Christian name—"

"I'm not Christian."

"Okay, that wasn't the best choice of word, but you know what I mean."

I did, but I glared balefully at her instead, happy in my meanness.

"I was wondering," she said, clearing her throat, "if you had an Asian name too."

It took me entirely too long to parse her question, so appalled was I at her presumptuousness, and when I did, all I could do was bray with laughter.

"What's so funny?" she demanded.

"Listen, just listen for a second," I said when I had the wherewithal to speak coherently again, swabbing the tears from my eyes with a sleeve. "It's very clear to me that I am the last person you wanted in this room with you—"

"That is *unfair.*"

"—and you are trying so very hard to be polite," I continued, inexorable, remorseless as the heat death of the universe.

"But with all respect, I don't want to be here. I don't want to be your friend. And I damn well don't want to play twenty questions. Also, *really*? Do you not think it's maybe a little bit gauche to ask for someone's whole and truest name? I have absolutely read up on what people do with such things. Haven't you?"

The flimsy edifice of her self-esteem broke at last, her smile vanishing like kerosene-soaked paper touched to a flame. She bleated something that might have included the word *sorry* as she rose, stiff-limbed and sobbing, to totter out of the room.

In her hurry to leave, Johanna left the door ajar, and I watched in silence as the corridor filled with people. A great majority were in their late teens, early twenties; a few anomalies drifted through the throng: sorcerous-looking geriatrics in jewel-hued robes and prepubescents who all but sloshed in their school attire, hems dragging. Most strode past without acknowledging the exposed entryway. Those few who did met my eyes with a mix of disapproval and uncertainty, their expressions ranging from furtive to frightened. It wasn't until much later that I would understand why that open door was such an egregious sight in Hellebore.

More bells began to sound, deep and mournful. The students increased their pace, all funneling in the same direction. I wonder sometimes what might have happened if I had been kinder to Johanna, or quicker to move, if I had been savvy enough to close the door, hide myself, scale down from a window, do anything other than gawk moronically at the crowd while in plain view of the hall. If nothing else, I think I'd at least have kept my dignity.

"Assembly," slurred a custardy, rotted voice, a voice that could only have come from lungs that had ballooned with decay and a throat so rimed with bacterial overgrowth it was borderline useless. Yet despite this, the word was spoken with no little volume. It boomed loudly enough to echo through my bones.

My mother used to tell me that in the seventies, there had been a preoccupation with anthropomorphizing food—likely to disguise the fact none of it was very good. The massive figure leering through the doorway might have been a Christmas centerpiece from back then. Its head resembled a child's papier-mâché masterstroke in all but one way. Whoever had created the thing hadn't had any paper on hand and so had resorted to sheets of raw muscle instead. It had eyes but no eyelids, a lipless grin of a mouth. It wept lymph as it stared at me, never breaking eye contact, not even as it ducked to enter the room, upsettingly graceful for what was essentially a giant Lego figure crafted of uncooked meat. I screamed. I screamed like a little girl handed a frog for the first time.

"Assembly," it said again, shambling forward, and that was very much it for my escape fantasies.

The meat man waited until I dressed before herding me into a vaulted corridor, the ceiling frescoed with dead men swaying from nooses of their own intestines, all hung on the branches of fig trees so heavy with fruit their boughs sagged almost to the ground; with black-haired, blank-faced women who had the eyes and wings of wasps, hovering above labyrinths of books; sweet-faced knights too young and too lithe for their pitted ancient armor; and carnivorous deer. The last was an especially prominent motif. The artist was obsessed with those deer. They had them in every scene. Sometimes, the deer were prey, supine before triumphant hunters, a glory of entrails bared to the eye. Most times, though, the deer were the predators, stalking frightened men through black woods, their muzzles steaming, a red glare in their eyes, which were only pupil.

"The painter was a woman named Bella Khoury," came a conspiratorial voice in my ear, its timbre low, amused. "Legend has it that she used her own blood to create those."

I looked over. Beside me, falling in graceful lockstep, was an older girl in an ensemble—she had on at least three layers of finely made, carefully layered tweed—that should have had her basting in sweat but somehow did not. "That so?"

"Oh yes. That part was true. The part that was a lie was that she did it because a man had broken her heart," said the girl drolly. "Can you imagine? A *man* inspiring such art?"

I laughed. She laughed. I guessed my companion to be about twenty-five from the soft lines beginning to fan from the corners of her eyes and the edges of her mouth; she carried herself like someone much older, though. The horn-rimmed glasses and slightly myopic stare didn't help that impression at all.

"Was she the one who came up with the school's heraldic crest? Seems like her style."

"I think it was the other way around, actually. She spent the entirety of her time in Hellebore painting the ceilings like she was possessed. After graduation, she purportedly vanished, and the school decided to honor her by incorporating her favorite design elements into the armorials," said the girl, shedding her glasses to raise them up to a slat of pale light. No dust traveled the beam, which seemed impossible given the walls were drenched in gold-shot, ancient-looking tapestries. There should have been dust everywhere, no matter how vigorous the janitorial staff. There should have been at least *some*, but against all logic the air remained clean and unpleasantly equatorial.

"Did all this work get her extra credit?" I asked.

"It got her immortalized."

"Good enough, I guess. What can any of us ask?"

The girl buffed her eyewear on a sleeve, then replaced them on her nose, smiling thinly at me when she was done. She was unreasonably beautiful even with her eye bags, which were the density of neutron stars: she had a face for magazine covers, a profile someone with more smarm might have described as editorial, with its high cheekbones and amused mouth.

"Portia," she said.

"Is that what they ask for?" I couldn't help myself, a hint of a flirt in my voice. "Your name? I don't blame them."

Her answering melancholic smile had my heart misplacing a beat. "They usually start with your name. Then it gets much worse from there."

I didn't have an adequate response for that. Everything I thought of felt too glib, too naïve. Her voice carried a burden of history and it felt then like if I wasn't careful, the weight of it would crush whatever might be growing between us. The fact I worried about the early death of this small and uncertain thing would surprise me later when I had time to sleep and ruminate on the events of that first day. I couldn't remember the last time I cared to nurse a conversation like that, couldn't remember *wanting* tenderness or ever having any knowledge of its shape. Right then, though, all I wanted was for her to stay.

"I'm Alessa, by the way. Alessa Li. Now that you have my name, we're even. I can't do anything to you that you can't do to me."

Her smile dimpled along her right cheek. "Shame."

In lieu of acknowledging that, I cleared my throat and asked, "Are you a teacher?"

"Do I look old enough to be one of the teachers?"

"Recent kidnappee, I'm afraid. I don't know much except for whatever is in the marketing pamphlets," I said, making note of our surroundings: the archways feeding into smaller corridors; the many doors and their matching brass plaques; the occasional stairwell, glinting bronze as they spiraled through ceiling and inlaid-tile floor. Hellebore stretched like memory and, like memory, it was imperfect, made of smudged angles and movement at the corners of the eyes. "The teachers could be hot."

"You think I'm hot?" Her left cheek didn't quite indent, but it made an earnest attempt.

"I plead the fifth, as the Americans say."

"I'm afraid American law doesn't extend here. Hellebore's a land of its own."

"Like a country?"

"Like a prison run by secret police."

"That isn't worrying information at all. I absolutely wasn't already concerned about their disinterest in bodily autonomy," I said as we turned a corner into a new corridor, the walls of which were a deep burgundy where they weren't polished wainscoting; the trimmings oxidized gold instead of wood, and paneled with yet more paintings. They were everywhere. Whatever else Bella had been, she was certainly prolific.

"It's not *ideal*," said Portia, her smile receding to a thoughtful frown, even as she slowed beside one piece of artwork, this one older, starker than the rest. Students gusted past. "But I like to tell myself that the benefits outweigh the costs."

"The costs," I repeated, my regard for her cooling.

Portia seemed to take no notice, her eyes softening as she

took in the painting beside us. Gone, the nightmare deer and their soft-faced prey. Gone, the women with their wasp wings and iridescent eyes. Gone, the expansive detailing, the sumptuous foliation of the background, the weird medieval animals in the margins. In lieu of all that, a textured black background, roughly swatched onto the canvas, and the equally rough sketch of a woman, sloe-eyed, furious-looking, standing alone before a canvas, palette and brush in hand

"Only known portrait of the artist," said Portia conspiratorially.

"I expected someone less . . ." I considered the second part of that sentence as it formed on my tongue, strangled it so I had space instead to say, "I take that back. She looks the correct amount of angry."

"And why is that?"

The first months after I left home, caked in my stepdaddy's remains, were made up of a formless spread of days, the hours seeping together, like blood when it is still fresh from a vein. I'd spent most of them in one library or another, careful never to drowse: An alleged student, shabbily dressed as she was, they wouldn't throw out, but an unhoused *derelict,* on the other hand? No city in the Americas is truly good to its unwanted, at least in my experience, and I'd been young enough then to be at risk of being returned to my mother, something I promise you neither of us wanted: she'd not taken well to the death of her husband. I could still recall how I looked in those first difficult weeks, could still remember my expressions in the mirror. I'd been angry. Angry at myself. Angry at the world. Angry most of all at the fact I had to *behave,* to play by their rules prescribed or else.

The girl in the painting held the same sullen, smoldering, clenched-jaw rage I'd carried, and more.

"Well, I'm assuming Bella was never paid for her work."

Portia erupted into laughter. "No, not according to the stories. Like I said, she apparently worked like a thing possessed. And we have to imagine Sisyphus happy. Otherwise. it'd all be a bit depressing."

"Which confirms what I suspected, unfortunately," I said, patting the portrait like it was a stag's flank. It hadn't been obvious at first but when I moved, the light shimmered on patterns in the background: lines scratched onto the black, like tally marks, like wounds gouged into the wood by someone's desperate clawing. "She was made to work for exposure—"

"Please! Recognition amid her peers and her betters."

"A corpse by any other name. You can't fill your stomach with praise. I'd bet you money she asked for compensation and then they said no, but you can have the privilege of doing the work. And this portrait was her protest. Gods, I'd be pissed. Wouldn't you?"

"For a little while. In my experience, though, that kind of anger is unsustainable. After a while, it simply burns itself out and you're left instead with"—Portia cocked her head one way and then the other, two distinctly staccato motions, insect-like in their abruptness—"the hope it'll end soon, and if not soon then at least as painlessly as possible."

I glanced at the painting again and then at Portia, smiling calmly, her expression abstract, the slight curious glint in her eyes at odds with her words. Her tone too, which while it wasn't blasé seemed preternaturally mild. Scholarly, almost. Like everything she said was someone else's nightmare, alien to her own experience. A case study, an old story to peel open and dissect in case a way to avoid a similar fate was engraved in the entrails.

"Might as well go down biting if it comes to that," I said.

"Easier said than done."

"Do I want to ask?"

Some trick of the light and the paint on the walls sheened her eyes with a bruised-plum purple with an oil-slick iridescence like a crystal had shattered there in her pupils. Her smile was calm, dreamy almost. "Oh, mostly definitely not."

A chill snaked down my back. There was a road I could take the conversation down. I could see it and the dark, lonely place where it ended, but as mesmerizing as Portia was, I didn't like anyone enough to visit them there. I already had too much baggage of my own.

"Anyway," I said, wedging a smile between my lips. "Why are you here? If you're not a teacher, what did they get you for?"

"I'm a teaching assistant," said Portia, her response jarring in its sudden cheer. All traces of her earlier despondence evaporated as she spoke, her expression and tone sunny as a summer afternoon. "Hellebore doesn't believe in scholarships, unfortunately. So I provide the faculty with help and they give me room and board as I labor to finish my PhD."

"You do a lot of kidnapping for them?"

"I help the faculty," said Portia without apology, winking, the little gesture so charming I almost forgave her complicity in the system. Almost but not quite. "Student enrollment is someone else's business."

I was back to distrusting her and everything around me, the nascent rapport gone—things for which I was grateful. Easier this than that bone-deep, marrow-level need to impress her, to want her near, to want her to smile at me and to count her freckles like I was a poet and she a muse. Easier this suspicion than *want*. Safer too. I learned that early on.

If she took any notice of my suspicion, Portia said nothing. Instead, she began to walk again, chattering in a very ambassadorial manner. I listened and nodded and exclaimed at the appropriate intervals, my responses as sincere as her confidential smiles, which is to say not at all. Everything she said sounded like paper-thin fiction: Portia allegedly had spent three years in Hellebore, graduating before going abroad (she wouldn't elaborate on what *abroad* meant, but that was hardly a surprise) to spend three more years in training with her sisters of the Raw Grail (the name caught like a splinter; I filed it away for future contemplation) before coming back to the school to pursue her post-graduate work.

"I thought it was an institute," I said. "Not a university."

"I'm using the terms loosely. Don't mind me. We can dissect that another time," Portia said, winking, wafting a hand through the bright antiseptic air as we pulled up to an overcrowded vestibule. The walls were the same deoxygenated red as Portia's hair, softly embossed with the school's heraldry, a repeating pattern of antlered skull and wasps. Stairs rose on either side, leading to an elaborately stuccoed mezzanine, its floor cradled by plaster gods. Overhead, a chandelier rocked impotently, unneeded with the pitiless white sun gouting from the skylight. Everyone under its glow looked terrible.

"Oh, I have to go help with getting everyone inside the atrium." Portia sighed, rubbernecking at the crowd.

The older girl peeled away then, vanishing into the throng. It wasn't so much an assembly as it was a crush of bodies, like cattle herded into an abattoir. The flesh mannequins were doing their part in teasing the knots of gathered students into proper queues, an endeavor that was only partially successful: no one wanted to be within ten feet of the stinking, towering automatons and each time one moved too close, the crowd melted back in disgust. Sometimes, this meant a line against the wall would form. Other times, students simply fled the hamburger-faced caretakers, pelting up and down the steps, creating even more chaos.

I felt a light touch on the small of my back as I was staring at the tableau.

"Assembly," gurgled a meat man, nudging me forward.

"Yeah, yeah, yeah," I mumbled.

It was less of an ordeal than I thought it would be, even with the pheromonal stink of about a hundred very sweaty twentysomethings in close quarters. We were bullied up the stairs and into an enormous atrium, operatic in size, with balcony windows and an orchestra pit that was being aggressively mopped by a trio of masked individuals. All three shared an androgynous litheness, their crimson-wrappered bodies lean but wide-shouldered. I stared at them, unnerved for reasons that wouldn't explain themselves, until my attention was taken by one of the meat men as it lumbered up to me.

"Phones," it said.

"You want my phone?" I shook my head. "No, what the fuck?"

"Phone," it said again gently, and with an urgency I hadn't expected from a talking stack of uncooked burger patties. Its tone was conciliatory, as if it knew how terrible a demand it was making of me, but also what would happen if I refused to comply. It stooped so we were at eye level, and clots of meat wept from its subsequent attempt to contort its face into a smile.

"Jesus." I withdrew a step, producing the aforementioned item. The truth was I didn't care; it was a burner, like every phone I'd ever possessed. The Internet was a mistake, as they say: being traceable is never good, especially not here, not now, not in a world where something might come stalking down the road to ask for your soul. Never mind the fact I probably had a few warrants out for me. "Take it."

It accepted the device with a slow, sage nod before turning to a Korean girl, who produced a rose-gold iPhone without comment but with a roll of her eyes. The meat man continued trundling down the queue of students and the air smelled faintly rotten in its wake. The girl and I exchanged looks as it vanished into the press of bodies.

"All this power in the school and what they're afraid of is a few telecommunication devices," she said. She had on a spectacular *hanbok,* red upon reds, the colors of muscle. White peonies were embroidered on the fabric; they looked like scars trellissing her thighs, the curve of her torso. "It makes you wonder, doesn't it?"

"Maybe they don't want us to post anything incriminating."

Her smile was venomous. "Who'd believe us?"

We shuffled into the auditorium, drifting down two different aisles only to find ourselves seated in the same row. I sighed in relief at the chilliness of the room, sinking into a velveted copper chair. The Korean girl sat on the opposite side of a gorgeous tawny-skinned boy, his ruby-buttoned dress uniform as beautiful as his face, its elegance only slightly marred by the pattern of symbols monogrammed over the fabric. Everyone looked immaculate. Hellebore loved youth and worshiped beauty. The girl paid me no attention despite our earlier interaction, keeping her unblinking stare on the stage. The boy however looked sympathetically over to me. I glared at him. Anyone wearing the Ministry's heraldry was immediately suspect.

"Your luggage hasn't arrived then, I assume? It can take some time, I'm told. Something to do with the school's helpers being so new to the role," he said, nodding at the three in the orchestral pit. "The reanimated rarely make for good workers."

"You should listen to Sullivan," said a familiar voice. "He's Ministry-born. They know all about corpses. Well, the making of them, anyway."

That explained the branding.

I strung an arm over the back of my chair, looking over as Portia seated herself, her smile languid and slightly animal. A challenge lounged in her expression, one that the boy didn't take, only met with a cool stare: her charms washed over him like rainwater. Instead of gawking like me, he twirled a finger in the air and half bowed at the waist.

"Miss Portia du Lac," said Sullivan in a voice coached to resonate through ballrooms and trading floors. His accent made me think of New Orleans, except with the vowels tidied and trimmed by years of finishing school. "It's always a *pleasure*."

"What about my luggage, anyway?" I said.

"Your outfit," he said, eyes sliding over to me again. With a little thrust of his chin he continued, "You don't look like someone who'd *choose* to wear that. The uniforms aren't mandatory, you know."

Sullivan smiled with earnest compassion, like this was a favor he'd extended, a kindness of unimaginable scale. When I didn't answer, he bobbed his head graciously, and looked back to the stage. A second passed and then another before he said, less graciously, "We don't *try* to make them."

The Korean girl looked over, a perfect eyebrow creeping upward. "Lying doesn't become you."

"I'm not lying, Minji," he said. "The entire point of Ministry families is to minimize the risk of unnecessary casualties.

I'd prefer there be no corpses. But sometimes, one does what is needed to survive."

Sullivan spoke with, if not the arrogance, then the self-possession of someone whose family was paid handsomely to submit to routine inspections, to being surveilled from cradle to cremation. I didn't want to throw in too early with any one party, not before I had a better understanding of the ecosystem of personalities, but I suspected he was being truthful. That was the whole point, after all. Ostensibly all that surveillance was for the safety of the families and the security of the world at large: if they could predict when a god might come to drive them to destructive impulses, countermeasures could be devised. Suicides could be arranged. It made sense that he didn't want for there to be more death.

Then again, the Ministry wasn't *actually* a governmental body with the best interests of the world at heart. (Although how many governments care, honestly?) They were a conglomeration of corporations who'd purportedly sworn to serve and protect in the legislative sense of the phrase, but there were the rumors of the Ministry contracting out the services of those families under their care. Only when it was strictly necessary, of course.

"Sullivan Rivers," he introduced himself politely to me.

"He's a bit of a whiner, I'm afraid," said Portia. "He complained so very loudly when they said he couldn't share a dorm room with his girlfriend, Delilah. Kicked up an *actual* tantrum. I thought Professor Hammer was going to have a kitten."

"I wouldn't be surprised if he did," said Minji. "The faculty here is . . . strange."

"Strange? Try fucking weird? Like, everything's off about them. Don't you think it's kinda suspicious how all their names are nouns?" hissed a pompadoured boy to her right. "Hammer, Crystal, Rock, Cartilage."

Sullivan stared at Portia, his calm facade still uncracked. "We were *told* we could share quarters. I merely pointed that out to the administration."

"Total tantrum," said Portia.

"Don't you think that's a bit judgy?" Minji asked her seatmate. "Maybe it's school policy."

"How the hell would that make for good school policy?" demanded Pompadour.

"A complaint is not a tantrum, Miss du Lac," said Sullivan.

"I'll stop here," said Portia. "Wouldn't want him throwing another one of those."

"Miss du Lac—"

A tremor of music ended our chattering. Unseen cellos were joined by a low bellowing of trombones, with trumpets rushing after like they'd arrived too late to the performance. The sound of them drove the masked workers in the orchestra pit into comical panic: they flung their arms up, sprinted in pointless circles, colliding with one another, before at last surrendering to whatever fate they had briefly thought of eluding and prostrating themselves, bowing and scraping, quivering like gelatin. The lights dimmed until only the raised dais was illuminated and, as if on cue, the restive crowd began to quiet, silence rippling outward from the stage. Soon, there was no sound at all, not a cough or a chuckle, barely a hiss of respiration, only two hundred eyes warily evaluating the stage with the care of rats being proffered a poisoned cheese roulette.

The air flinched; the light winked out for a papercut's width of a second, barely long enough to be registered save as the tiniest of haptic jolts. Between one blink and the next, a figure made itself known: tall, straight-backed, imperious, and narrow as a rapier. Like the servitors in the pit, who were now emitting agonized noises, it was masked and impossible to gender, its silhouette such that it could be male, female, some fantastical conjugation of the two, or neither. Unlike the miserable figures in the opera pit, it was dressed beautifully, the folds of its opaline robes seizing and refracting the light. The overall effect was mesmerizing, a carefully plotted performance. The figure looked as if it were enameled in church glass, ethereal yet formidable.

"Students," it said in an old woman's voice, cracked but still impossibly resonant. "Beloved class."

Portia: "That's the headmaster. Headmistress. Interchangeable, really. Depending on how much you like the patriarchy."

"Very little," I whispered.

"Oh, we *can* be friends then," said Portia with a dazzling smile, and despite earlier, I felt myself warming again.

"It is my honor to welcome you to Hellebore. My great joy to say yes, this is where you begin your journey to redemption, to wholesomeness—"

"Wholesomeness, my god," grumbled Sullivan. "You'd think they could have hired a speechwriter."

"Not everyone has Ministry money."

"The sins of the father shall be inherited by the son, I see."

"The sins of capitalism, more like it," Portia bit back.

"—to a future where you are loved, *accepted*," continued the headmistress, walking up to a pulpit that origami-ed up from the floor, lacquered panes of pale wood collapsing upward into place, gaining elaborate cartouches, growing foliated, "where your potential is fulfilled. Where you can be of proper use to the world and to the people around you because yes, it is important that we are of service to our communities."

"Communities that abandoned us," said Portia. "My parents sent me to boarding school and never came back for me. Ended up living in an attic for years. Miss Minchin was a godawful substitute."

"Minchin?" I said. "Like in the book?"

Portia opened her mouth, halfway to an answer, face lighting with delight, when the headmaster drowned out whatever reply she was assembling.

"For the next year, you will be trained, you will be taught how to comport yourself, to function as people instead of monsters."

"I thought you said you did three years here, Miss du Lac," muttered Sullivan. "When did they change the policies?"

"I've no clue. Maybe they found a more efficient way of dealing with us miscreants."

"All of you, shut up," hissed the Korean girl. "I'm trying to listen."

The headmistress went on and on and on. Her speech was an ouroborosian affair: a tide of promises feeding into denouncements of our characters and then assurances that we could be better than we are, that we could be refined, improved upon, *cleansed.* Over and over, she tore us apart and stitched us up with hope, dragging us under until we were drowning in the sweetness of her voice. Wouldn't it be lovely, she said to the enraptured crowd, her words boring deeper into us, to be wanted by the world, welcomed by it? All our sins forgotten, the error of our conception forgiven. With great vehemence, she read out a list of names: alumni, she said, who'd gone on to be taxonomized as heroes, ministers, leaders, people who could come and go as desired, be allowed mortgages and mistakes, picket-fenced dreams of families and legacies that wouldn't upset the world.

"You could be like that too," she said. "You could be loved. You could be *useful*."

Here's what they don't tell you about little boy lucifers and girls who won't stay dead: being needed is all any of us really wanted.

So, yeah. Fuck that bitch for knowing the right words.

Because if she hadn't, well, maybe Sullivan would be alive right now.

BEFORE

Spoiler: *they ate him.*

We were all there, in fact, when the faculty ate Sullivan Rivers alive. And by *ate him alive,* I mean, *ate* ate. This isn't at all the colloquial use of the word. They digested him. You ever watch that old movie *Society*? The one with rich people who could turn themselves into flesh taffy for the purpose of absorbing nutrients from the unsuspecting proletariat?

It went exactly like that.

The professors writhed out of their clothing as they swarmed Sullivan on the podium, their bodies losing cohesion as they did. Ear lobes, bellies, wattled joints, prolapsed vulvas, dicks long past their use-by date, they all clotted together first into something like a mealy stew before smoothing into blousy, billowing sheets of finger-bone-scaffolded skin. Gristle unspooled from groping hands, macrame-ing with the fat runneling from our faculty's grinning faces. Offal tasseled the gory lump of their conjoined bodies, slicked the floorboards with pancreatic fluid and synovia. What I remember most though was their shoulder blades carving through that sea of meat, the fins of suddenly naked bone—impossibly clean despite all that effluvium—making me think of sharks. Sullivan didn't stand a fucking chance.

I wonder if he knew he was one of the lucky ones.

But we're getting ahead of ourselves.

Let's walk that back a little. Bring it back to the moment we barricaded the library, pressed our backs and our shoulders to the carved rosewood doors, adding our meager weights to the ancient barrier, hoping to the hells and back that it'd hold under the tsunami of carnivorous flesh outside. The faculty tried everything: they gouged at the hinges, pulled at the screws, peeled the bracing from the ancient timber, shoved, pressed, gnawed at the wood until it splintered. Unfortunately, and I do mean unfortunately, as it'd have been easier for all of us if they'd just eaten us whole, ending the story there and bloody then, the library at Hellebore was older than their appetite. Their vandalism wouldn't take, no matter how enthusiastic. The door repaired itself, over and again, regrowing whatever the faculty had destroyed, reassembling whatever they had dismembered with impossibly violent speed.

After several futile hours, the faculty retreated, and we listened as they oiled away, the wet, sticky squelching of their myriad appendages becoming quieter and quieter, until there wasn't anything to listen to except our own thundering hearts.

We'll start here.

DAY ONE

The first one to speak was Adam, who was, to give credit where credit is due, a work of technical perfection: six feet three, a body that could have been—and was, *actually,* repeatedly and with considerable enthusiasm—used in anatomy studies. Radioactive blue eyes, Ken-doll features, a singular dimple indenting his right cheek, a soft cleft bisecting his chin, and so much blond hair it looked like he was wearing a gold-plated sheep rug for a hat. He was gorgeous in a very airbrushed way, which would have been fine if not for the fact this was real life and no one in real life should look *literally* airbrushed.

Adam ran a hand through that ridiculous overgrowth of golden curls, and sank down onto the floor with a jangle of iron chains.

"Well," he said, the beginning of a laugh collecting in his rich, French-inflected voice. "That was exciting."

Portia impaled him with a withering stare.

"People get cavalier in life-or-death situations," he said before jauntily adding, in a way that suggested he was not only amenable to being wrong but rather hoped he was, "It's not a crime."

"A hundred and seventeen dead," came the phlegmatic rejoinder. Portia's voice, in contrast, was more muffled, less mellifluous. It warbled. It sounded *mealy*. Like she was trying to talk through a mouth crammed with sharp hairs. "Wasted."

"But not us."

"No," said Portia. "Thank the Mother."

Adam shrugged. "Thank *me*, you mean."

Portia bared her teeth at him. The damp, grayish dark made the threat display look almost like a human expression. Almost but not quite as from between her teeth protruded the furred and dichroic points of a jumping spider's chelicerae grown overly large. Her eyes went from his face to mine, and I mouthed a tired *What do you want me to do about it?*, earning me a not insignificant rolling of the eyes, which unnerved me more than I cared to admit, the conspiratorial playfulness at odds with her physical circumstance.

"Nah, I don't wanna."

I looked over to the owner of the voice. I nodded at him; Rowan nodded back. There was a lot we'd probably have to talk about when there was an opening. We hadn't exactly resolved the whole bit where I'd been standing above his dead maybe-but-not-official girlfriend, Johanna, utterly sodden from the kill.

"Rowan," I said.

"You'll be relieved to know that Stefania didn't make it out," he said, patting himself down for a cigarette. "Or maybe mad? I don't know. You seem like a likes-to-get-her-hands-dirty kind of girl. I used to like to think that you two were getting it on while me and Johanna were doing the deed."

"Nice to see you're still alive," said Adam with sincere cheer, raking his eyes over Rowan. "Ironic, though, isn't it? A death-worker still kicking it while everyone else is dead."

The temperature in the already frigid library dropped several more points.

"I'd argue it's fucking perfect, actually," said Rowan, lighting a cigarette, sucking hard on it before blowing smoke into Adam's face. "When all of you die, I'll have an undead army."

"You won't." It was a pale, soft-faced, utterly terrified-looking Scottish boy who spoke the words. He had a doleful voice and a dense brogue and beautiful, long-fingered hands. Eyes a washed-out, indeterminable shade of something maritime. "This lot doesn't leave anythin' behind when they're done. Bones, skin, sinew, everything. They just absorb the lot. Can't raise an army out of nothing."

"How do *you* know so much?" I said.

"I accept your challenge, Eoan." Rowan stabbed his cigarette in his direction, interrupting whatever response he might have had for me. "But first, Alessa—"

"Half live if Rowan dies," said a deep male voice, one that made us all turn.

Ford, who had kept from the door throughout the faculty's onslaught, was sitting with his legs splayed and his back to a bookshelf. He lifted a loop of his own intestine and waggled it at us. His other hand held a bloody athame. The act of clutching his own viscera was clearly soporific for him: he looked drowsy, content, utterly at peace with how his guts pooled between his thighs.

"Half live if Rowan dies."

There was a drawn-out, uncertain silence.

"Are you sure?" said Adam.

"The entrails cannot lie." He fished out and weighed his liver in the hand his intestines had previously occupied, the latter tossed onto the marble tiles with a greasy *schlorp*. Once satisfied with its poundage, he lifted the organ to the blade of ashen light knifing from one of the library's many narrow windows and frowned at its underside. "Half live if Rowan dies."

The word *hirsute* didn't begin to describe Ford's abundance of beard and curls and overgrown brow, dark and sleek; he was a bear of a man, a figure cut straight from the annals of Viking history, a fact he recognized and celebrated, I think. No one else on campus swanned through the winters swaddled in a bearskin coat with the poor animal's head for a matching, still-attached-to-the-body-by-a-strip-of-neck-fur toque, and if Ford wasn't quite so massive, so oppressively jacked, he'd have looked like any white trust-fund kid with a costume budget.

Mostly, what he looked like was a particularly unsavory kind of dangerous.

"Well, in that case," said Adam brightly, "*come here,* Rowan."

"Fuck. You."

"Everyone *stop,*" sobbed a quiet voice, and we did.

A short, wide-set, very doll-like person stood huddled against the library doors, their brow still pressed to the wood. They'd been crying. The knuckles of their clenched hands were crusted with blood.

"Gracelynn, I can't believe it. You used the *voice* on me," said Adam, with unsettling pleasure.

"Eight of us," said Gracelynn brokenly. "There are only eight of us left. Kevin, they, they—" They let out a tea-kettle shriek of despair, unable to help themselves, hands balled, a fist shoved into their teeth. They screamed until they were wrung of breath and it was just an airless keening, almost too high-pitched to hear, their expression so mangled by their agony, they were made into a stranger in the ruin. When Gracelynn had exhausted their capacity for that, they said, pantingly, "We can't fucking fight with each other. *We're all that's left.*"

"Eight?" floated in Rowan's voice. "Who's—oh, there's Minji. What are you doing *on* the bookshelf?"

"So?" said Portia quietly to Gracelynn, her mouth working like she was trying to exorcise a lump of taffy from between her teeth. I knew better though. We all did. "What does that matter?"

"We need to take care of each other," wept Gracelynn. "People sacrificed themselves for us."

"Sacrificed?" said Adam. "I don't know about that. I'm pretty sure Kevin would prefer to be alive right now in your stead. They probably were just coy about it."

"Jesus Christ," I snarled. "Lay off."

Countless poets and philosophers have made a career out of asserting that love is the strongest force in the universe. Before that moment, I'd have disagreed. Entropy seemed a better contender for the title. But I found myself revising that opinion at the sight of Gracelynn staring up at Adam with a naked pity.

"They're a better person than you ever were," said Gracelynn like that was enough, like that was all the answer needed. And I thought, *Yes, Kevin was that.* There'd been no pause. Kevin had not faltered when the faculty washed from the podium, they only stood to shove Gracelynn into my arms, resolve in their expression. *Don't let Gracelynn look back,* they told me.

"They're also *dead.*" Adam laughed, sounding like Christmas had come early for him. He practically sang the next words. I didn't know someone could make an accusation sound so frolicsome. His attention pinballed through the room before it set itself on me. "You know, I'd heard rumors about you but I'd thought they were all lies. Then you got that one kill just under the wire. Although killing your roommate seems rather cliched, doesn't it? Was it jealousy? Was it because she was prettier than you?"

"It's more complicated than that," I said.

It was.

"I know I'd love to hear all about it," said Rowan.

"Wait, wait, Alessa did what now?" Eoan turned his doleful gaze on me, some of that habitual misery leaching away so horror could overtake his face instead. "Johanna—no, she was a joy. She was the brightest thing in the school. She can't be dead, no."

"As a doorknob," said Rowan with suicidal affability.

"But *why*?" demanded Eoan.

"She might be dead, but I don't believe Alessa did it," said Gracelynn, raising their head again. "That's not who she is. She wouldn't."

"Actually, I would," I said. Unlike Adam, I didn't believe in taking credit where it wasn't due. "But like I said, it was complicated—"

"It's Hellebore, after all," said Minji from her perch. "We're all monsters here."

Gracelynn's face lost its color, went as pale as their brown skin would permit. They shook their head, lavender bangs clinging to their forehead. Like the rest of us, they were soaked in other people's insides, a nice shared souvenir from our recent troubles. "No, no. That's not . . . Alessa, tell them—"

"Makes you question everything, doesn't it?" said Adam ecstatically.

"Shut up," rose Portia's voice. "And look."

It was then we all saw that a note, written in our headmaster's very officious hand, had been slid under the door and was being waved at us. When we fell silent, whoever was on the other end gave the paper a little push, and it fluttered fully into the room.

"What the fuck?" said Rowan.

Adam squatted down, picking up the note. He read through it several times before crumpling it in a hand and tossing it on the floor.

"What the hell does it say?" I asked.

"That only one of us can survive this," said Adam, with no expression at all. "And the winner gets to leave Hellebore."

We all scrambled for the crumpled paper, in case Adam was fucking with us, liar that he was. Rowan managed to grab it first, plunging onto his belly to seize the paper, and we relented—none of us wanting to risk bumping up against him. Bad enough we were trapped here. No one wanted to add dying of accelerated sepsis on top of it all.

Beaming triumphantly, Rowan rose and unfolded the note, holding it out for us to read. There it was, in the headmaster's unmistakable scrawl:

Finish the job. Last one alive will be allowed to leave Hellebore. Be quick. You have three days.

DAY ONE

Let no one tell you it doesn't suck to be in close (*former*, I suppose) acquaintance with everyone's favorite people pleaser. Johanna had fans, many of whom I suspect were really just nostalgic for her prescience, her eagerness to do whatever they wanted at any given time: codependence absolutely could work if both parties had an interest in feeding the other's appetites.

Eoan and Gracelynn mostly just wept for answers for beloved Johanna. Rowan snarked. Portia stared at a point in the rafters, rocking slowly in place. Minji ignored us, more preoccupied with watching Ford attempt a recreational bout of self-enucleation. (Eyeballs weren't traditionally used in haruspicy; they were too prone to just disintegrating into a slather of aqueous humor. It's possible Ford was trying to scoop one out for legitimate reasons, but I maintain he was doing it for fun.) As for Adam, he was having the time of his life, goading the rest to ostracize me, distrust me, *kill* me first. His joy in watching us fracture was ironically one of the purest things I'd witnessed. It made sense, though. He was one of Satan's countless sons, after all.

My patience, never generous to begin with, gave out when Gracelynn and Eoan began bickering for the umpteenth time about whether I had misremembered the events leading up to Johanna's death and whether maybe, just maybe, I was a victim of implanted memories. Maybe there was a conspiracy worse than the one that had penned us in here. Maybe it was more chicanery on the faculty's part. We had no idea they were going to reveal themselves to be a horde of ravenous aberrations. The notion of them fucking with my mind didn't seem far-fetched, not after that first climatic reveal. And god, it didn't help that Adam was laughing like a coyote and Rowan's chain-smoking was filling the stagnant air with smoke. Had things gone slightly differently, there might have been a few early casualties—only the gods know whether it'd have been me or them, but I wanted blood to drown out the noise. Then a sound, a moist one, like a stubborn Band-Aid being slowly peeled from skin, broke through the tableau.

I turned to see Portia gnawing on her wrist. No, no, not gnawing *on*. Memory softens the truth too much. That wasn't right, wasn't what I witnessed. No, Portia was gnawing a flap *through* the skin around her wrist, tugging at the flesh with her fingers even as she chewed more of it free. I saw the wet shine of bone as it came undone like a ribbon. Portia then delicately wadded up her work and laid it on the red tip of her tongue, sighing, eyelids fluttering. I watched as she swallowed it whole, shuddering with a voluptuous, almost masturbatory relish, and it felt almost voyeuristic to witness this act of autophagy.

Rowan cleared his throat. "What," he said, "the actual fuck?"

"I was hungry," said Portia, as if that was all the explanation anyone could need. It was perhaps a mercy that whatever transformation Portia was undergoing had also clotted her blood, leaving it jammy and curdled and dark, too viscous to spray over us. "I'm so damned hungry. Isn't anyone else hungry? Must be all that adrenaline."

"Must be," said Rowan, backing up.

Eoan made a frightened noise somewhere behind me.

"You know, she has a point," I said before anyone else could interject. "We should probably start thinking about food, water. A plan for escape."

"The faculty said *to finish the job*," said Eoan, slumping partway into view. "What's the fuckin' point? We're all going to be dead in a day or two, anyway."

"Or later tonight. I bet we could all die tonight too," said Rowan, who could always be trusted to know the worst thing to say.

"Look, I'm the furthest thing from an optimist you're going to find, but murder doesn't have to be our first option," I countered.

"I guess we could kill ourselves in protest. Make it stop and they don't get what they want," said Eoan morosely.

Gracelynn mopped at their eyes with the heel of a hand. Their mascara was ruined with all the recent hysterics; their cheeks were just faded tributaries of ink. Gingerly, they held out a hand to me. When I refused to take it, Gracelynn closed their fingers into a fist and rested them against their heart. Their expression was one of defeat and I was sorry to have been the cause of it, sorrier still that we'd ended up here. They'd been kind to me. They and their spouse, Kevin, had saved me over and over again. If there was justice in the world, Kevin wouldn't be dead and the two would have a house with a dog and a good-natured cat. They'd live long, boring suburban lives, dying in their sleep at ninety with their hands entwined.

If there was justice in the world, anyway.

"Tell me why you lied about killing Johanna. Please. It's okay. We'll make it okay. You don't have to hide," said Gracelynn haltingly.

"I didn't lie," I said. "I killed her."

"But I don't *understand*. I can see you're kind. This conversation alone proves it. Why would you—"

"Sometimes, you do terrible things to survive," I said and before they could answer, before any of this circus could interject, I left the foyer. The Librarian was likely still in the building somewhere but if I had to choose between a confrontation with that creature and this endless wailing melodrama, it'd be the former every time.

Rowan called: "Alessa, *wait*."

I didn't.

∿◎∿

The library of Hellebore was a rank and unrepentant replica of the one in Dublin's Trinity College, at least in terms of aesthetics. It shared much of the same dimensions: it was over two hundred feet in length, barrel-ceilinged with towering windows, oaken partitions and recessed shelves, gorgeous pilasters and the obligatory marble busts (which looked decorative enough if you weren't paying attention). They were very beautifully carved. From one angle, they were hyperrealistic monuments to past geniuses: philosophers, poets, the odd politician, anyone who had contributed to the edification of society. But from another, the lines warped, peeling away to an extraneous dimension. Faces swam, becoming something neither brain nor eye could agree upon, but instinct recognized enough to scream at. Their shadows moved if you regarded them too long, and other things threatened to come to focus. Fortunately, we were all cautioned early to avoid such mistakes. Hellebore's statuary wasn't for observing, not unless you wanted to be observed in return, something that could have fatal consequences.

Half live if Rowan dies. I turned the prophecy around in my head as I walked, wishing there'd been more to it. What did half even *mean* when losing Rowan would leave seven of us? Was one of us fated to become a ghoul? Like seriously, what the fuck? Would Rowan's death catalyze an irreversible transition to undeadness? Worse, what kind of undead were we talking about? The thought of deliquescing into one of Hellebore's meat men was worse than the idea of being eaten alive. My mouth filled with an old-penny taste; I paused, realizing I had chewed straight through my lower lip.

The problem with prophecies really was how fucking oblique they were. What I wouldn't have given for clarity. Still, I wasn't completely without options. The last time I was here, I discovered the library was honeycombed with secret passages. Of course, access to them was through someone the faculty had just digested. Nonetheless, there had to be an entrance somewhere. If I could find one, I might be able to wait out the inevitable slaughter.

Maybe. So many goddamned maybes.

Despite everything that happened in the school, there was a stillness to the library. The air smelled of old books, rust, old wood, and dust, all intermingled with an herbaceous *something,* a medicinal scent that wasn't unpleasant but was nonetheless unsettling. Above, the ceiling was bronze and glass. It felt like I was walking through a jewel box, an art installation, someone's over-ornamented fantasy of their favorite place. It was almost peaceful. My drifting gaze snagged on signage riveted to the wall: a simple brass plaque on which was engraved the word ARCHIVES.

I followed the arrows until I found a small room stuffed with traditional card catalogs. Serried rows of wooden cabinetry filled what was left. Everything in the space was cabriole-legged, rococo-souled: over-decorated behemoths with giltwork on the drawers and embossed metal rings.

Something *bleated* as I walked deeper inside. I jumped, startled. The noise was horrible: a meaty, wet-lunged honking that reminded me terrifyingly of the school's own skinless attendants. What I saw was actually worse: it was the very squashed remains of a rat, largely limbless, seeping maggots from now-dried wounds. It lolled its head so I could see each of its eye sockets before it brayed moistly again.

I began to back away.

"He won't hurt you, promise," came a familiar voice from behind me. "He's just trying to say hi."

I turned to see Rowan standing in silhouette, a scarecrow figure with an even thinner shadow. The low light cragged his face unnaturally, made him look older than he was.

"Did you follow me?"

"What answer would make you happier?" said Rowan, splaying fingers over the hollow of his throat, an absolutely scandalized expression on his face, the feathery stubs of his eyebrows raised as high as they'd go. "It's okay to admit you've always had the hots for me."

Against my will, I recalled how he'd looked that night in the dark: how his upper lip crooked at its rightmost edge, the corner fletched with the ghost of a scar. "Fuck off into the sun."

He dropped his hand, a thumb hooking into a pocket. "I think I'm going to name this little guy Tim," Without apparent revulsion for the worms spilling from every wound, Rowan stroked the back of a finger along the rat's swollen throat. It leaned into his touch. "There was a kid who tried to be friends with me in the hospital. I had to tell him to go away, of course. But he was cool."

"Not here to walk down Memory Lane with you, Rowan."

"Kind of wish I could have given Tim a hug," Rowan nodded at the rodent, who was still actively decomposing and whose effluvium was beginning to stain the shelf on which it was perched, and was somehow now on its back, writhing like a happy cat in a puddle of its secretions. "But I guess they will do."

It took everything I could to avoid making a face. "Were you following me or were you not? Answer the damn question."

"I didn't set out to follow you. But as it happened, I ended up in the same place. So, I suppose that's following you," he said very nonchalantly. "I think we're both looking for the same thing."

"Please don't say it's answers. I've had enough of that from Eoan and Gracelynn."

For as long as I'd known him, Rowan had been—except once, just once, as we stood over Johanna's sad, folded-up corpse—pathologically incapable of treating anything with even an iota of seriousness. He was an indefatigable peanut gallery, the kind of person who'd make his last words a wisecrack. But there was none of his usual irreverence at that moment. Rowan stared at me with a pensive, thin-lipped expression. Black was beginning to bleed from the confines of his pupils, tendrilling into those hoarfrost irises.

"You don't have to tell me why you did it. It'd be nice if you did but you're not obliged. And just in case you needed someone to say it, you don't need absolution from me."

"I wasn't looking for that, but thanks for telling me."

"Sure." His eyes were black from pupil to sclera. I tensed, not knowing what to expect. But I could sense his rabbiting pulse, feel the structures of his muscles, his bones, the yards of nerves stitched under his skin. One tug and I'd have him unspooled on the floor like so much yarn. Nonetheless, I still took a wary step backward. "I'm just saying that if you find yourself seeking forgiveness, you probably want to do something more productive with your time. Everyone knows these are weird days."

"Okay. Can we move on?"

"And you were wrong, by the way." A muscle in his right jaw seemed to flinch from the words queued up in his mouth. "When we were in the dorms? When you were yelling at me about how I didn't know she loved me? I did, actually. She deserved better than we gave her."

"Excuse me. What the hell do you mean *we*? I—"

"Johanna was a lot of things and she had a hell of a savior complex, but all of it was coming from a good place. She wanted to make the world better. She was kind—"

No, I thought, remembering what Johanna had said in those strange minutes before I unbuttoned her vertebrae. *She'd been angry.*

"—and she really liked you. We talked a lot about how sorry she was that you were stuck at Hellebore. She tried to come up with ways to get you out. She knew how much that mattered to you. And how much you mattered to me."

With reverential tenderness, Rowan took one of my hands in his own gloved ones, stunning me into a nerveless silence. I was at a loss for an appropriate reaction, couldn't do more than stare as he raised my knuckles to his mouth, almost—almost!—grazing them with his lips. I couldn't think of a quip, a retort, could just gawk like an idiot.

"I wish it'd been different. That we could have all met in a different life," said Rowan gently. The nearness of his lips, his breath, it all stung like salt water dripped on a raw lesion.

"So you could have a harem?" I managed, my voice huskier than I'd have liked.

"No? So we could have had the option of being normal. Haven't you ever wondered what that'd be like? To be without all this baggage? To have the freedom to fuck up and not worry if it'd destroy the world or turn a person into sludge? When I was a kid, I used to dream about meeting someone who could tell me what that'd be like: being normal. It's why I enrolled, you know? I couldn't figure out a way to talk to Hellebore's graduates, so I thought—"

I would think about his face and his words every night to come, rotating the memory in my mind, studying it like a wasp preserved in amber, how his eyes had looked, the earnestness in his expression, and wonder what would have followed and what I might have said if a deep, amused voice hadn't intoned: "Am I interrupting something?"

Rowan and I leapt apart. I turned to see Adam leaning against the doorframe, half in light, eerily lovely as he always was: less a man than an idea, a fantasy loosely distilled into meat and sinew, bone and bored disdain.

"What do you want?" I asked.

Rowan slipped his smirk back on and for once, I was glad to see it in its usual place. "He's had a crush on me since he saw me. Sorry, Adam. You're very pretty, but I just don't see you that way."

I would have paid with my soul to have Adam's ensuing look of disgust bottled up and preserved for my future pleasure. He let out a matching noise, a sound like a man offered piss when he had asked for wine.

"I should have let you die."

Rowan cocked his head. "But that'd have required you being good enough to keep me alive, which I don't think you are."

We were united then, he and I, all previous awkwardness and resentments shed in the company of a mutual foe. I didn't like Adam. Never did. Long before everything imploded, he had already established himself as a fucker. He had made no secret of the fact he was septic with envy for the respect Sullivan commanded. As far as he was concerned, he was better than Sullivan: more handsome, more facile with his abilities, more in command of his identity. Our dearly deceased valedictorian had struggled with nightmares. Adam had none, dreamt of nothing but ownership of the world. Why *indeed* did his peers look to his rival instead of him? Such was his narcissism that it never occurred to him that even here in Hellebore, no one liked a killer who made off with their smiles, their mannerisms, the little idiosyncrasies that made them individuals. Every beautiful thing about Adam was stolen; he was a mimic, empty of actual personality. The only thing he had of his own was his sense of envy.

"What do you want?" I repeated.

"What do *you* want? What *are* you two doing here?" said Adam with a dazzling smile, all glint and no warmth at all. "Are you perhaps looking to see if there is a way to survive? Let me tell you there isn't. Not unless I decide it."

"What we're doing is still none of your business," I said.

"Actually, I think it's very much my business," he said, taking several purposeful steps forward so he wasn't just encroaching on my personal space but dominating it. We were practically chest to chest. I could feel the heat radiate from him, the inferno of his parentage barely held back by his skin.

Adam grinned down at me, eyes half-lidded, pretty despite his brazenness or maybe because of it. It irritated me to no end that I noticed the fact.

"Back the fuck up."

"Or *what*?"

"This," I said.

My response, I'll admit, was disproportionate to the situation. I raised a finger-gun at Adam, lifting my hand so the tip of my index finger bumped against his perfect nose. As his smile widened, I traced a path across his chest, down the long path to his wrist. I tapped it thrice, bent my thumb, and mouthed the word *bang*.

His right wrist exploded into a bloom of red sinew and bone shrapnel, little gore-stained chips of scaphoid going everywhere. His hand, bereft of support save for one rapidly fraying tatter of skin, plopped onto the ground a second later. Where most people might have screamed, Adam only addressed me with a pissy little stare. Not with any subtlety, Rowan crowded in to attempt a fist-bump.

"Nice," he said, pronouncing the word as an exaggerated *noice*.

"You're kidding me," said Adam, his voice thinning with rage. "You're fucking kidding me."

I adjusted my stance. You could call the thing on Adam's face a smile if you wanted to: it had the right curvature, an appropriate number of teeth on display. It even reached his eyes. But I wouldn't. It had that certain je ne sais quoi I'd come to associate with people about to lose their fucking shit. If I had any reserves of self-preservation, I'd have tried to diffuse the situation, but I was still mottled with gore from the deaths of the graduating class, and to be honest, at that point, I was just sick of marinating in other people's company. I didn't care that Adam was mad. I didn't *want* to care. I wanted a fight down to the wet bones of me. I bared him a grin as I backed up to curtsy dramatically at him.

Adam wagged his still-suppurating stump at me, something like joy in his expression, jets of arterial blood fountaining through the air. He began to incandesce, the nuclear brilliance growing until he was an effigy of himself, a column of eye-watering light, fatal as a star in its death throes. The air smelled of broiling keratin and charred polyester, and it took me a second longer than Rowan—his arm touched my clavicles, nudging me back—to understand we were beginning to burn from proximity to Adam.

"I know you think that was incredibly brave," said Adam. What gore I had spilled was gone, immolated, a sacrifice to himself. It was with the cadences of my voice that he spoke, his tone playful, even eager, "But you're going to regret it."

"I don't know what you think you are, but I know you're still meat under that fire," I said, reckless with trauma, feral with grief. I wasn't mourning our eaten peers per se but my god, was I done with being so afraid. I resented the tension. I resented his smug manners and the future waiting for us. I could not stand the idea of Sullivan's slow death, of dying under a blanket of geriatric horrors. The fucking ignominy of it all. To die like that, to have the capstone of my life be feeding our former professors.

Or worse, to die so Adam could be the last one standing.

They say burning alive was one of the worst ways to go but the metaphorical *they* weren't trapped in this library.

I ducked under Rowan's arm before he could object, jolting forward and unflinchingly toward Adam. Like I said, even under that cocoon of white fire, there was still meat, a chorus of synaptic instructions propelling him onward, keeping him upright. I could feel the ladder of his spine; I could sense every contraction of his ventricular chambers. It'd have been a question of who was quicker on the draw, of course, but I'd never gone wrong betting for myself.

"All this for a boy who can't even fuck you?" asked Adam.

"Sex," said Rowan from behind me, "isn't just about penis in—"

"No, all this because I'm tired of your face. I can end what I started. Don't fucking try me."

To my surprise, Adam laughed.

A single luminous finger rose—the line from his shoulder to elbow as exquisite as the one from elbow to wrist—and drew a circle in the air. Almost instantly, I felt a matching pressure tighten around my right wrist: a truth spell. The physics of it was simple. Upon submission to one, the afflicted had to tell the truth and nothing but the truth, or the spell would shear clean through bone and muscle. I tipped my chin up, defiant, refusing Adam any show of emotion outside of boredom.

"Tell me this," said Adam, still a human flare. "If it came down to it, if you had to choose between Rowan and getting out, if the condition of your escape from the awful vaulted halls of Hellebore was that you had to feed Rowan to the faculty, would you?"

I didn't hesitate.

"In a heartbeat."

The light wicked from Adam's frame, taking with it any vestige of modesty he might have possessed, the cinderous remains of his clothes staining him with ash: he stood naked as his namesake, grinning like the devil, hand restored because the Great Adversary doesn't shortchange his brood apparently. Ignore them, sure, but not leave them destitute of limbs; I stared at that fresh limb, filled with a sudden furious despair even as he waggled fingers at me, nails growing over their beds.

"You're *fun*, Alessa. Let me know if you ever want to partner up with someone who isn't a walking corpse."

And before either of us could fire off a retort, he began strolling away, the light especially kind to the shape of his ass. "By the way, the Librarian's awake. Might want to move quietly."

BEFORE

The rest of the Hellebore welcome assembly was rather standard compared to its hypnotic beginning. Once the headmaster had us deep in our feels, she then turned to administrative banalities: her expectations in regards to our behavior (*Yes, your frontal lobes are still in development, but for all that is holy and otherwise, don't embarrass the school, please and* thank you); Hellebore's code of conduct (be exemplary in all matters always; understand that if you are not of use, you are of no value); an introduction to the faculty (mostly geriatrics or those on the verge of being such). Tittering, she suggested that we might be sorted into *houses,* a prospect so repellent the crowd spontaneously lost all fear of her and began groaning objections.

"I am just kidding," she simpered amid the thunderous murmurs. "Although the way you're all complaining, I might have to make it happen."

Though she retained her mask throughout, what mystique she possessed was lost in the wake of that awful joke. Now, she was indistinguishable from any elderly relative: an inescapable embarrassment to be tolerated until we could emancipate ourselves. In hindsight, I wonder if that had been strategic, a wolf putting on its lambskin and capering for effect.

After the last professor (Fleur, Botany, recognizable by the fungal-shaped bouffant that was her hair) finished with her own tedious version of a welcome, we were permitted to leave, ushered out by Hellebore's meat stewards. Some of them had begun to ooze, and they smelled overpoweringly of rich fat.

"I'd have hoped some of them would be *hot*," I told Portia halfheartedly, less because I cared and more out of courtesy: I had an allergy to authority figures who didn't practice good boundaries.

"When I was a freshman, there was one attractive lecturer. It was the year the Raw Mother came to Hellebore. She Who Eats and the Ministry had come to an agreement. The school was filled with young women who could commit to her without worrying about their virtue, and she could have her worship without destroying families and ending marriages."

"That's some patriarchal bullshit."

"It was," said Portia, face soft with remembrance. "But it worked out. Those of us who were drawn to her went to her, and it was *good*, Alessa. She took care of us. The one thing in the school that didn't want us dead."

"The one thing in the school that didn't want you dead, huh?" I repeated gingerly. "I sure hope things have improved since then."

"Anyway, there was one very hot lecturer back then," continued Portia like I hadn't spoken, roping an arm around my shoulders. She smelled delicious, like honey and vanilla. "But we—"

"We who?"

"Oh, the Raw Mother's girls, of course. We all started arguing over him and he ended up torn apart. It was a whole thing," she said. "They've only just found his right earlobe."

The crowd swam past us, led this way and that mostly by the skinless automatons although occasionally, I'd catch sight of a masked servitor, tugging a student down a narrow hallway. Sunlight poured through the windows in beveled spears and Portia was run through by one as she paused. She glowed like a saint.

"How long ago was this?"

"How long ago was what?" said Portia, smile empty and bright as glass. "Twenty years."

"*Twenty—*"

"I thought it'd all been destroyed but apparently not. Although by the time the janitors found the ear, it was a mummified, rat-gnawed morsel. They almost made the mistake of throwing it out." Her eyes twinkled. I still couldn't tell the color of her irises: they seemed an impossible purplish red, like wine, almost dark enough to be black.

"You said twenty years, Portia." I asked. "What the hell did you mean by that? And, more importantly, what the hell did you mean by *the only thing in the school that didn't want you dead?*"

"It's in a reliquary somewhere now. I could show you," said Portia, answering a question I definitely did not ask. Her smile was bright, innocent, dazed: the smile of a woman waking from a dream. Before I could interrogate her further, a commotion stole everyone's attention.

Portia grabbed my upper arm without a word, yanking me forward. We threaded through the rubbernecking throng of students until we reached the front. A circle had formed around Sullivan, a black-eyed girl with the most magnificent trove of dark curls with whom he was holding hands, making her Delilah, and an absolutely gargantuan boy.

The other boy dwarfed Sullivan by an impressive seven inches or so; impressive, as Sullivan cleared six feet himself. He was wider too, built like the archetypal lumberjack. He had a despondent, miserable face and a mealy complexion, the face of someone who had never heard of skin care. Delilah held on to Sullivan's arm, her face buried against his sleeve, mostly occluded by his bulk.

"I know you," the unhappy boy said to Sullivan, his tone dull. "I would know you in my dreams."

"If it's any reprieve, it's why I'm here. I want to redeem that bloody history of mine." Sullivan stared at the taller boy, his lips pinched together so hard, they were a bloodless gray. His voice nonetheless was calm, the same exquisite and unbothered tenor that he had used to critique my wardrobe. "We don't have to fight. Please."

"You've taken so much."

"For what it's worth, I am sorry."

"You took *everything*." The boy's voice broke under the weight of the word *everything*, turning shrill. "You and your family. You fed on us."

"Not willingly," said Sullivan. Had I been standing at any other angle, I would have thought him utterly bored by the other student's blandishments, so neutral his tone, but I could see how he held one hand clenched in a white-knuckled fist, how it shuddered at his hip. "Not by choice."

"I can't let you live," said Sullivan's opposite. He shook his head and then once again, harder the second time, eyes widening until they were mostly whites. "No, no, I can't let *her* live. She's the source of your power, isn't she?"

"Leave Delilah out of this."

"They're all dead. My family—you *owe* me."

"Me, perhaps, but not her."

"I can't let any of you live," said the other boy hopelessly. "I can't."

The threat in the other boy's voice was unmistakable. A

prematurely excised fetus would have been able to say, *Yes, that man very definitely wants to cause harm.* Sullivan did not withdraw nor did he posture or jeer at his adversary. Instead, he ran a hand along his hair. He laughed tremblingly, as though his amusement were a living thing, squirming in his grip.

"You don't know how many times I've heard that already. The first person to want me dead was my mother. Poor girl. They carved out her memories, you know? Told her she was going to get a white-picket future. Might have gotten it too if I'd the decency to be born a daughter. When they found out I was going to be a boy, the cicada-lords filled her lungs and her thoughts and her womb. Everyone was so happy. She, though, wanted to smother me in my own placenta. Tried to, I'm told. They didn't allow her, of course," said Sullivan and his voice smoldered with warning although he was painstakingly gentle as he unhooked the girl's arms from his waist. "And the last person to tell me that Delilah needed to die, well. I didn't allow them to do that either."

"Sullivan, no, don't, it'll be okay. He can't hurt me. Please, let me—"

"It'll be all right, my love," he said, lips touched to each of her fingertips in turn. The love enshrined in his gaze was a holy thing and that holiness was what made it dangerous: worse wars had been waged by men with less faith than this one, who stood there looking like he'd bring the world down for this girl.

"Sully," Delilah whispered.

"It'll be all right," he said again and I saw her shoulders drop. Later on, I'd find out how many times she'd died, how over the years Sullivan would find her broken-doll corpse on an altar over and over again: throat cut, ribs split, just raw meat sometimes. Delilah, I would learn, was what they call a Lamb—an immortal sacrifice—and that the first time Sullivan had sat waiting for her to come back, he'd been thirteen years old.

Sullivan rested his forehead against Delilah's before he pressed her into the embrace of the crowd, turning to regard his adversary. He said: "It took them eight generations of careful pollination and meticulously applied eugenics to create me. Do you really think you have a shot? I hold all my gods in me. Turn around and leave. We don't have to do this. I don't want you to die."

He said all this as the other boy mimed hefting a weapon, his hands locking around thin air. No, not thin air. Not ultimately. A labrys *coalesced* into reality as the boy made the motion to swing. The creation of the ax left grease smears in the air.

"If it helps at all, I do wish sometimes that *I* was never born," said Sullivan, still with that strange hungry earnestness. "If I hadn't come into this world, none of this would have happened. You wouldn't have suffered whatever you did. Lila wouldn't always be at risk. It'd be fine. All of it. If I knew all this could have been stopped, I'd have let my mother asphyxiate me. And I wouldn't have to listen to the cicada-lords screaming in my head. Every night, every day, every hour of my existence. Buzzing away. I never sleep." His voice again slipped into an abstracted softness, the words spoken for him and no one else. "Do you know what it's like to never sleep? To only dream of wings?"

I saw it a second before the other boy did, the wet orange membrane closing over Sullivan's eyes; saw it flutter against the corneal surface, saw mucus come away; saw the cicadas emerge, boiling from his tear ducts, distending his face.

Sullivan opened his mouth and gods poured out of his throat and Delilah's answering scream was a knife, cutting through the air. There was just enough time for Sullivan's opponent to jolt backward, horror filling his expression.

"They're so hungry," said Sullivan, and his voice was plaintive—audible, somehow, clear as despair in spite of the bugs wriggling out of his mouth, slick from his saliva—as he sank his fingers into his would-be killer's shirt, pulling him lover-close, a hand moving to cup the nape of the other boy's throat. All the while, cicadas continued to pour, and pour, and the crowd, seized by an idiot animal terror, pulled back as the cicadas began to eat.

We watched the boy die.

If the universe had any mercy in it, the swarm would have blanketed him, obscured his death from view, but it didn't. His death was a spectacle. We saw him denuded of skin, saw them burrow through the spongy tissue of his bones, and gnaw through heart and lung, liver and stomach. In seconds, he went from boy to Swiss cheese monument, a juddering colander trellised by strings of crawling, jewel-shelled insects.

I inhaled, sharp, as oily clots of organ patterned the floor. Beside me, I felt Portia do the same: a brisk gasp, although there was something sexual in its release, a panting want.

Out of nowhere, an unfamiliar voice, nasally, quintessentially New York: "Is this *turning you on*?"

Portia responded with bared teeth, "What the fuck?"

I looked over to see a boy standing about five inches behind us and to the right of me. Something about his shit-eating smile said he couldn't be much older than me, but his skin was precociously weathered and there was something equally ancient about his eyes, which were almost the white-blue of a flame save for a drip of hazel like spilled petroleum. Upon noticing my scrutiny, he winked.

The boy went on, clownishly good-tempered. "You're from the Raw Beef—"

"*Excuse* me?"

"—sorority, aren't—"

"We're not a sorority and that's not what *she* is called."

I didn't know whether to laugh or shriek, or to try to pinch myself awake, the juxtaposition of this argument and the slaughter unfolding so absurd, so truly bombastically weird, nothing seemed real any longer.

"Makes more sense than the name you're using," said the boy.

"*Sense,*" Portia repeated with a laugh that had as much to do with humor as a gut wound with comfort. "You're the one—"

"I have so many questions for you, but give me a second," said the boy, who clearly thought of himself as the funniest person in the room. He turned his attention to me. "Name's Rowan. Heard about you from Johanna. She said you're prickly. Didn't tell me you were cute, though."

I recoiled from his once-over. "How do you know my roommate?"

He waggled eyebrows in answer and said instead, turning back to Portia, "So what's this about the Raw Grail offering immortal life? I hear that you girls have a partnership with Hellebore. Something about making soldiers for the Ministry? Because if so, I'd love to know more. I don't personally want to live forever, but I have this *condition*—"

"Someone is being eaten alive here." Portia pinched the bridge of her nose between two fingers. "I'd rather focus on that."

"What's death but going into another room?" said Rowan,

peering over the carnage, utterly flip despite the fact that what was left of Sullivan's victim was a porridgy smear on the floor. "Many other different rooms, in his case. Possibly hundreds. Oh, that's *impressive.*"

"Thank you."

Sullivan's thoroughbred voice with its impeccable diction, its singer's lilt, gently cut through the air. He was staring at us, his outfit wrecked, cicadas promenading over his shoulders, rappelling down his trouser legs, the light greasy and gold-red on their amber shells. I realized with a slight lurch in my stomach that they were *cleaning* him, eating particulates of organ matter, tugging at the rucked seams: there was no helping the bloodstains but he could at least be unrumpled. That more than the gore, more than Sullivan's languid expression, disturbed me.

He smoothed the last wrinkles from his collar, a cicada crawling up to rest on the first joint of his right index finger. Sullivan's mouth bled in rivers still. Very informed gossip had it that the Ministry paid for more than the right to keep their pet families under scrutiny. Some said they were breeding new lines, developing living weapons. I had to wonder what Sullivan's home life was like. Delilah kept her distance, her expression desperate, even lost. When Sullivan held out a longing look, she turned away, melting into the crowd.

"You might want to get that," said Rowan, touching the knuckle of his thumb to his own lips.

Sullivan, sighing, looked back to us and daubed at his mouth with his fingertips, then looked down at the jammy mess. "Well, that happens sometimes, I'm afraid."

He ran his tongue over pink-tinged teeth. Cicadas gathered in his dark hair like a crown, like they were comforting him in his abandonment. They buzzed softly. "They try so hard, but my throat tears each time. They'll fix it eventually, however."

"Does it hurt?"

"Which part of the process?"

"All of it."

"Always," said Sullivan in a hiss, beautiful and terrible and holy, and I forgot to breathe until Rowan spoke.

"Did you have to kill him *that* way?" he said.

"Worse ways to die in Hellebore." Sullivan's smile was pitying. You could describe it as kind if you wanted to, but only if you were willing to ignore how practiced it was. His attention swiveled and his eyes weren't black as the cicadas burrowed back into him, but gold. "Did they tell you that when you enrolled? That you've come to a place of monsters?"

"Right where I belong then."

"Do you remember being so confident, Miss du Lac? So full of joie de vivre?" His attention flicked to Portia and then back to me. A patina of honest amusement coated his smile. "Keep your innocence as long as you can."

"I'm afraid that was lost a long time ago," I said. He was agonizingly condescending.

He smiled thinly. "Then make sure you're ruthless enough to survive the next few months. I'm sure you've heard the stories. The few rumors that have escaped Hellebore's publicists. It's supposed to be hellish in here."

"Oh, leave her alone, *Sully*," said Portia, and she wore no expression at all despite his jovial tone, her face no more than a death mask. She did not blink. She barely breathed. "She's not yours."

"Is she yours then?"

My heart lost a few beats in Portia's answering silence.

Chuckling, Sullivan said after a moment, "You and your

sisters think you're so different but we come from the same kind of gods. Mine are just more honest."

"More cruel too," said Portia with that same insect stillness.

"Perhaps." Sullivan's attention drifted to me again. "Sometimes, we do terrible things to survive, don't we?"

I tensed. It was hard to tell who was the worst person to have my back to. Sullivan, in his awful glory. Portia, in her quiet. Rowan, in whatever the fuck you would call it, smiling broadly with his fingers steepled, a kid let loose in his favorite toy store.

"Fuck or fight. Who wants to start a betting pool?" Rowan chirped, breaking the tension like glass.

"Do you *ever* shut up?" Portia hissed, reverting to animated humanity.

"No," came the unrepentant answer.

Sullivan looked over to Rowan then, a certain wonder in his gaze. Surprise too, as if the two hadn't already exchanged words, as if Rowan were a dead rat he had discovered in a shoe. His smile collapsed into an expression of pure incredulity.

"And who," he said, "are you?"

"Rowan," He bounced from one foot to another, gleefully clapping. "But I *also* have questions. First off, do you or do you not think that Miss du Lac is very much goth mommy material and—"

"We should leave." Portia's voice in my ear, low and urgent, and it wasn't five minutes ago when I might have let her tow me away to safety, but Sullivan's words were branded into the marrow of my skull: *We come from the same kind of gods.*

"We could," I murmured back. "But I don't know if I can trust you."

"Do you want to, though?" said Portia.

"I'm sure you have a million questions," Sullivan said. "Unfortunately, I don't want to answer them."

"Fair."

Sullivan nodded, the matter concluded as far as he was concerned, his attention beginning to swing away. Except Rowan then reached over *to grab his shoulder* with a gloved hand.

"But I really, really," said Rowan, his grin continuing to extend, a caricature of itself at this point, "*really* want those answers, though. Pretty please?"

Rowan's impropriety shocked all the languor from Sullivan's expression. For the second time that day, that look of dreamy resignation closed over his face. His eyes unfocused, softening. I heard the buzz of cicada wings, their droning song; saw again the boy and his despairing gaze as they bit down and broke skin. Looking back, I wonder if I might have intervened had I not been standing so close to ground zero. There wasn't anything about Rowan I liked except how he'd winked at me.

Whatever the truth was, I justified it then as not wanting to leave it to chance. No telling just how much fine control Sullivan had over his gods and if they had an indiscriminate appetite. I'd just seen what they could do. I wasn't going to let that happen to me. And there was Portia too, staring at me, a smile spreading her mouth like a fang, waiting for an answer I wasn't sure I wanted to give.

"Let's not turn more people into a slushy," I said.

"*He's* the one insisting on overstepping my boundaries." Sullivan let out an aggrieved sigh. "I'm tired. All I want is to be done with the day and to spend the evening reading with Delilah—"

"Reading! Is that what the kids call it these days?" said Rowan.

"—if that's all the same to you," said Sullivan. "Just let me kill him and we can all go our separate ways."

"No," I said.

"The Raw Grail stands with Alessa," said Portia very softly.

"This doesn't have to escalate," said Sullivan, sounding truly appalled.

"It doesn't," I said. "So back down."

"Are you serious?"

"Serious as cancer," I said. I kept my eyes on him, on his impassive face, his cheekbones like cornices: he had an architectural quality to his good looks, like someone had plotted even the shadow under the overhang of his lower lip, the faint panes of stubble across a jaw so cut, you could have used it as a measuring tool. "What's it going to be? Fight or fuck off?"

Predictable as a clock, Rowan began to say: "You know—"

Sullivan mashed his face with a hand.

"Fine. You lot win," he said with great finality, swearing up a bilingual storm, the word *fuck* and its variations delivered with unsavory gusto, interspaced with some rather liberal use of *merde* and *putain*. "Let's just fucking go to lunch."

And that was that.

BEFORE

We went to lunch.

That's not a euphemism for violence. We did actually go off to find ourselves food. With his casual pomposity, Sullivan—after shrugging loose of Rowan's grip—led our mismatched group to the dining hall, lightly stepping over the spongy remnants of his opponent. The crowd withered from him like flesh from a flame. If he cared at all about the impression he made, if he noticed their terror and their nervous appraisal, Sullivan evidenced no indication of it, his face as expressive as the mostly eaten one spread over the floor.

Portia stepped daintily around the mess without comment, remote again, almost secretarial in her poise. Rowan was the only one of us to pay any mind to the sad heap of remains: he went down to a squat beside a white curve of rib, and touched conciliatory fingers to the damp bone. His usual effrontery was nowhere to be seen. In its place, an intense thoughtfulness that vanished when he realized he was being watched.

"Why the gloves?" I said in lieu of what I wanted to say instead, which was, *What are you hiding under all that vulgarity?*

Rowan looked down at his hands, turning them slowly in the light. He was, for the most part, dressed in the uniform of every emo-grunge kid I'd ever met: washed-out flannel, graphic tee, skinny jeans, black Converse. The gloves, however, were straight out of a falconer's or welder's tool cabinet: they were thick and utilitarian, meant to protect the wearer. The fingers were hachured with creases, wrinkled in every angle and direction. Rowan had gone out of his way to force some dexterity into them. *No,* I adjusted the initial thought. *He wasn't wearing those gloves to protect* himself.

On cue, with perfect and practiced dickishness, he said, "Gloves are a kink of mine."

I left it at that.

As with everything else in Hellebore, the dining hall was unnecessarily grand with its frescoed ceiling—another clever trompe l'oeil (the school was lousy with them), this one depicting a blue sky fleecy with clouds and wasps the size of airplanes, false sunlight coruscating through their massive wings—and overdecorated windows, the latter briared with flowing traceries and inlaid with lead-light. Every student in the hall, and there were surprisingly many, was sheened with the rainbow light streaming through the stained glass.

Even the hot food station was a vision of excess. Instead of being set on steel steam tables, the troughs of entrees— these were ordinary enough, comprising of sausages, orange chicken, steamed broccoli, and all the other victuals familiar to anyone in college—were set in carved camphor structures, and the salad bar rose above a sculpture of a forest in which skinless deer hunted frightened knights.

"Gross," said Rowan, sidling up beside me as I ladled a generous portion of kung pao chicken onto my plate. My mother was *generically Asian,* as she liked to put it. Whenever someone prescribed an ethnicity to her, she acknowledged it as what she was, though whenever I'd seen her do so, it was with the same bored expression. My stepfather had joked about her being inscrutable and exactly how he liked his women: difficult enough to read that he could justify not giving a shit. After all, it wasn't his fault she hadn't tried harder. She never laughed. When we were alone, she'd tell me our work in the world was to endure.

Fuck that.

Anyway, as a result of this disinterest in her heritage, our home never saw home-cooked meals, only an abundance of the nominally Asian takeouts that my stepfather had loved; it was an improvement, however, over when my actual father was alive, the latter disdaining anything but the blandest, beigest of meals. For the most part, I haven't regretted leaving, but a part of me would always be sorry I never got to become the kind of middle-aged woman who could berate their mother for her choices in men.

"Don't knock it until you try it," I told him absently.

"The kung pao?" he said. "No, that I like. Talking about the weird carvings. They could at least make them sexy."

I pretended I hadn't taken any notice of the wooden friezes, the stark and frightened faces of the knights mouthing an exaggerated *oh,* which earned me a throaty chuckle; Rowan was buying none of it. He winked.

"Gruesome stuff, huh?"

"More of Bella Khoury's work, I imagine."

"You know, I've always wondered why she was so *obsessed* with carnivorous deer."

"Probably a metaphor for how the poor dream of eating the rich," I said, adding a token amount of broccoli. I thought of her portrait again, her sullen eyes. "Or something to that tune."

"I think it could be for shock value," said Rowan loftily, the eternal contrarian, heaping a bloody mass of chopped-up steak onto his plate, the white ceramic pinking with the run-off. "Art exists because the artist doesn't want to be forgotten. Because the *artiste*"—he stretched the word into its French counterpart, taking clear pleasure in the act—"wants to live forever in the minds of their audience."

"Do you really think that?" I was amused despite myself. Rowan grinned at me from the other side of the steaming trays, ladling gravy and fries atop a throne of red meat to create what looked like an American's idea of poutine. "Given everything I've heard, I somehow doubt it."

Toward the north end of the hot food station, right under the tray holding the massive serving of badly stirred risotto, was a bas-relief of six fawns, identifiable by the speckled pelts and the softly drawn ears, with their muzzles buried in the unspooled mess of a hunter's entrails, the man still alive despite being unraveled, his face a rictus of agony. There was a filmic quality to the whole hideous affair. I had to wonder if Khoury had carved this from imagination or if she'd used references, and if references had been used, had it been a collage of images or had she a specific muse?

"No," said Rowan.

"What do you think then?"

Rowan waited until I met his eyes again to say: "I think she needed to do something with her rage at the world or she'd burn it all down."

A shiver wormed through me. Before I could reply, he added, diffusing the moment, "Pity I was born too late to meet such a goth mommy. I bet she was a freak in the sack."

I laughed. I was beginning to like him. It was hard not to. Rowan was caddish and crass but he was funny and self-deprecating about it which made all the difference. Here was a man who didn't just disbelieve his own hype but took an active pleasure in making himself a fool for the world's entertainment.

"Maybe the curriculum will include necromancy," I said. "That way you'll be able to find out."

"If I should be so lucky," said Rowan, his shit-eating grin at odds with those eyes of his, blue like the bottom of a lake. They held a dangerous sincerity, an interest I couldn't help but be flattered by: it felt like an invitation to share in a conspiracy, like a heart carved out and held up to me on a plate. Like I said: dangerous. In another life, I might have bitten down on that bloody bait but I wasn't looking to stay at Hellebore and even if I was, it wouldn't be for him.

I snuck a glance over Rowan's shoulder, and saw Portia sitting beside Sullivan, reanimated, jovial, laughing. Any animosity that the two had possessed toward each other seemed to have since dissipated. As I stared at them, it occurred to me that Portia's inconsistencies hadn't killed my interest: they had deepened it, something I resented. Relationships were nooses and people deadweight: the romantics always ended up hanging from their hearts.

And I hadn't survived this long to die for a pretty face.

"So, your name is Alice, huh?"

"Alessa."

"Huh," said Rowan. "Short for Alexandra?"

"Nope."

"Alessandra?" said Rowan, overemphasizing the middle syllable.

"Nope," I said, filling the last crescent of empty space on my plate with pickled radish, less because I had any craving for it and more because of the incongruence of their presence. An entire array of Americanized food and then for some reason, authentic *danmuji*. "It's *just* Alessa."

"Weird name but okay."

"Glad you approve, I guess," I said sourly. This was the second time today someone'd taken an unwholesome interest in my name, both of whom were white as cocaine. I was ready then to find a different table to nurse my lunch when a short, skinny boy rushed up to us, his heavily freckled face a rictus of badly suppressed terror.

"You don't want that," said the boy to Rowan. His Scottish accent was thick enough to slather on a piece of toast.

"Don't want what?"

As a collective, we weren't old enough yet to have accumulated even fine lines, but there was something about how the skin hung on the boy's bones that made me wonder if he'd ever had a day's worth of joy in his life: it was around his mouth, the basset hound tilt of his eyes. His pale green gaze twitched between Rowan's plate and the door to the kitchen. The boy cleared his throat and pointed a bony finger at the bastardized poutine.

"*That.* The meat's, well"—he swallowed, blatantly nervous— "it's not good, you see?"

"It's rotten?" I said, squinting at my own plate and what little I could see of Rowan's under its armor of gravy. I hadn't taken any of the steak but if one entree had been allowed to spoil, the state of everything else was now in question.

"I heard that in haute circles, rotten steak's kinda like a delicacy," said Rowan with far too much glee. "Well, they don't say it's rotten. It's dry-aged. But technically, it's the same—"

"No, n-no, it's not rotten." Panic had usurped terror's place in the boy's expression. I realized then that while he had on one of Hellebore's uniforms, his waist was aproned and his shirt was splotched with rust-colored patches of what I hoped was grease but suspected was not. The humiliating pièce de résistance: a name tag identifying him as Eoan. He fumbled for Rowan's plate. "Please. Just pass it over here. I'll make you something else—"

"If it's not rotten, why can't I eat it?" demanded Rowan in a bright, happy voice, swooping his plate out of reach: he had five inches on Eoan but even if he hadn't, Rowan had pendulously long arms and a reach that might have had the NBA knocking had he seemed remotely predisposed toward athleticism.

"Because it's *not for you.*"

We all turned as a fourth voice boomed. We turned to see a man of considerable age, thin white hair slicked back over a skull conspicuously absent of liver spotting. His eyebrows were of identical color as was his neatly trimmed goatee, his flocked jacket, his pants (these were textured by gray pinstripes), and his shoes. He was an obnoxious sight: no one wore this much white unless they were convinced the world would turn itself inside out to avoid dirtying his ensemble. I'd have been more disdainful if not for the fact I couldn't help but shudder each time his eyes grazed my skin.

"Professor Stone," said the boy, nearly prostrating himself onto the floor. "I-I—"

Stone sucked his teeth at him, ignoring Rowan and I. "You put one of our meals in the wrong tray, didn't you, Eoan?"

"No, no, it wasn't—"

"Then who else could it be? Certainly, the servitors know better."

"*Servitors?*" trilled Rowan, lowering his plate. "Tell me more."

"There's nothing to tell. They're just automata that the school uses," said Professor Stone, reaching over so he could harpoon a piece of meat with the tip of an extraordinarily long fingernail. Gravy and other fluids dripped down a hand so bare of collagen, it was practically leather over bone. He fed it almost sensually between his teeth, chewing open-mouthed as he spoke. "I'm afraid the educational department's budget is incredibly sparse."

"Isn't Hellebore a private institute?" I asked.

I had to repress the urge to run as Professor Stone's attention reverted to me. His eyes weren't white, per se, but they were close enough: not the pleasant milkiness of cataracts but something more artificial, almost like paint. His pupils swam in those eggshell pools, and I couldn't tell if he was looking at me or through me. Next to him, Eoan was making hushing motions.

"You have me there. We're semiprivate, does that help?"

I would have said no if not for the fact there was Eoan, looking like he was about to collapse into tears, and the sight of his abject misery had every alarm bell in my limbic system clanging in panic. Rowan was backing toward a trove of cutlery, indifferent to the standoff. I met Eoan's eyes again, saw him mouth, *please, please.*

"That does indeed," I said, sweetening my voice. "Funny things, those presumptions, huh?"

"You could say that," said Professor Stone as he took Rowan's plate in both hands, just as the latter was preparing to dig in. "Like I said, though, I'm afraid this isn't for you." His tone raised in pitch, becoming fussy: it was the voice you'd use on an infant or a misbehaving puppy, nauseatingly saccharine. "Faculty only, I'm afraid."

"I call this rank discrimination," said Rowan, grinning, but there was something in his eyes now, a wary light cousin to Eoan's terror. "But solving that is probably above your pay grade."

Professor Stone only smiled, lowering his head over the plate and then, like a dog, began lapping chunks of meat and potato into his mouth, his tongue an ungodly red as it dragged over the mess.

"You know what? I'm not hungry anymore." Rowan backed up, hands flung up in objection. "I'll grab an espresso or something. What do you say, Alessa?"

"Way ahead of you."

DAY ONE

Rowan looked at me as Adam's laughter faded down the hallway. "Really?"

I shrugged. "I don't think he has any cause to lie about the Librarian."

"I meant the other thing," said Rowan. "*Feeding* me to the faculty?"

His words would have elicited guilt in most people. All it got from me was exasperation. Rowan's kicked-puppy expression offended me. It was sincere. He was *hurt*. Deeply, truly, monstrously hurt; it said something about the magnitude of that pain that it cracked through his habitual smirk and something about who I was as a person that all his agony solicited was a faint worry it'd slow us down. With the Librarian up and moving, we couldn't afford dramatics.

"I'm sorry," I said.

"I can *tell* you don't mean it."

"No, I don't," I said, eyes going to the door. "But can I grovel later? We should be trying to get out of here."

Rowan hesitated, but self-preservation won over self-pity. He straightened his smile and touched two fingers to the edge of his right brow bone, where a pale white scar feathered the skin. I had to wonder if he'd done it to himself on purpose.

"What's your plan then?"

I ran my tongue over chapped lips. The thought of the Librarian undulating through the stacks unnerved me in a way I wasn't prepared to address; not then, not in the near future, not ever. I was fully prepared to shelve every memory of the creature away in the *repressed* folder, damn the consequences of having more unresolved trauma. As a result, *out* didn't feel like an option. I scanned the room hopefully and, to my relief, spotted a narrow passage with stairs leading into a grayish murk.

"Up?" said Rowan, following my gaze.

We heard a *thunk* outside the room as though an enormous weight was setting itself onto the mosaiced floor, the scratching of nails against wood, fingers tapping tunelessly along the walls; it could have been anything, a trick of the space, our exhausted imaginations. Nonetheless, Rowan and I both exchanged looks and without saying much more, slunk single-file up the steps, our breath held tight in case something was listening to see if we were there.

One set of stairs became a dozen more, a spiraling assortment: some were wood and others wrought iron, the former sleekly oiled and the latter so rusted, ochre flaked away at the touch of our hands.

"I didn't know the library even went this high," whispered Rowan.

I glanced over the rails. The world below flickered, fractalizing: it lost depth, gained it the next breath, seemingly adjusting to whatever (I realized as nausea welled) I thought it should be.

"It doesn't," I said. "Don't look down."

Eventually, there were no more stairs to climb, ending at a single windowless corridor that led us to a cul-de-sac.

The wall before us showed a canopied autumnal glade, the shadowed ground soaked in the gory light of a dying day. Through the trees, I could see antlered shapes that seemed to shift position each time my attention drifted, advancing closer until I could almost see leering bone. I ignored them as best as I could.

"I did not do all that cardio for a dead end," sighed Rowan, both hands on his thighs as he bent over, dry-heaving from exertion.

"That's because this probably isn't a dead end." I trailed my fingers over the carved stone, feeling my way through the bas-reliefs, the bronze and blood foliage. Whoever had made them had taken care to engrave the veins of the leaves too. "This thing's way too obvious. It can't *just* be a wall—"

"Well, Occam's razor—"

One of the branches let out a click as I pulled on it.

"Point made. Carry on," said Rowan, straightening.

Stone warped and wood shuddered as unseen mechanisms woke behind the wall. Dust fountained through the stale, varnish-smelling air and a door appeared where there was none before, swinging inward, allowing access to a flight of stone stairs.

"More stairs?" groaned Rowan, looking behind us. "Maybe I'll just go and let the Librarian eat—"

Wordless, I grabbed a fistful of his shirt and dragged him along. We went up the stairs, the narrowest we'd had to navigate yet. There was no light source, just whatever seeped through the door we'd entered and that didn't last, thinning to near nonexistence by the time we reached the final step, thready and gray and unnatural.

"Wouldn't it be funny if we walk straight into the Librarian's mouth?" said Rowan as we reached the top.

I ignored him. The room we eventually found ourselves in was barely larger than a broom closet. Its walls and floor were scratched with so many tally marks, they gave the room a lenticular effect, undulating whenever I moved. I wondered who'd carved them onto the bare stone and how long they had spent time here, trapped. I could have counted the tally marks, I suppose, but that seemed churlish somehow, cruel even. There was something peculiarly vulnerable about the gloomy confined space; it had the air of a forgotten child, one hidden away out of shame. A single slit window let in almost no light from the world outside and standing there, breathing that dust, I felt a jolt of recognition—like I'd put weight on a bone I had not realized I'd broken. Somehow, I knew this place. I had no idea how or why, but I knew it the way a child knows to be scared of the dark.

In the center of this barren claustrophobic space was a familiar pulpit: the headmistress had given her speech during orientation from here, I was sure of that. I recognized the belled roof and its excess of gothic ornamentation. At the time, I'd sat too far away to see what else it was decorated with and, of course, there were wasps, split-open figs, the carnivorous deer that seemed common to Hellebore's aesthetic but instead of the knights, there were slender, lissome youth of varying genders, like what you might see in the paintings of the old masters. They laid prone under the insects and stags, eyes closed, faces calm: a pyre of bodies, an offering.

"Pretty on the nose," I said.

"Well, to be on the nose, they'd need to be eating . . ."

I ignored Rowan. The carved rosewood of the pulpit held a sheen of fresh lacquer, its panels scratched in places by claw marks. As I strode closer, I realized something unexpected: inside the pulpit, curled up fetally, was a person.

"Eoan?"

The Scottish boy raised a bleak frightened stare.

"No more," he whimpered. "I know you're hungry but no more, not right now."

"Eoan, what are you talking about?" I asked, gingerly approaching him. His eyes were a perfect smoldering white, smoke wisping from under their lids. I touched a hand to his shoulder only to flinch away: he was hot, scalding hot. Steam boiled from his collar and his rolled-up sleeves, his miserable mouth: he smelled of blood and a tang of something bitter.

"Something's wrong with him," Rowan said urgently, shifting his weight from one foot to another. "You might want to give him some space."

"No more," moaned Eoan again, shuddering. The front of his shirt was very red and so damp it plastered over the ladders of his ribs.

"You're okay," I said, wishing I had some way to protect my hands. Luckily, Rowan had his gloves. With care, he lowered himself to a knee, gathering Eoan from the floor.

"What's going on here, Eoan?" said Rowan.

Eoan laughed shakily, eyelids trembling.

"I had to—I had to make sure she—"

"It. They tell us to use *it*."

"—the Librarian's not a thing, is she? She's a person," moaned Eoan as Rowan carefully draped an arm under the former's own, holding him upright. Despite the boy's delicacy, Rowan still staggered a little from his weight. "Should treat her like this one."

"What happened, Eoan?" I asked, registering too late he'd mentioned the Librarian.

"Fed her. Fed her until she was stuffed. Only thing I could do. If she's full, she won't eat us. Maybe that way, she

wouldn't—" Whatever else he might have said went lost in
the paroxysm that followed, Eoan seizing first at the fingers,
the wrists, the arms, back arching until he lifted out of the
cradle of Rowan's embrace, toppling onto the ground again,
convulsing.

"What the hell is going on?" I backed up as did Rowan.
"Did you let him touch your skin?"

"No, no. Fuck, no. I was *careful*."

Whimpering in agony, Eoan began to creep toward a machine embedded in the pulpit. The contraption was a bizarre
monstrosity of glass tubes and metal filaments, unidentifi-
able blocks of metal through which tendrilled a million small
wires, weaving it to the inside wall of the pulpit. A funnel
constructed of matte black plastic protruded from the stand
where a scripture might have rested. Eoan, groaning, crawled
up to his knees and bent his head over the funnel.

Then he started to retch.

What came out wasn't vomit but slick white meat, meat
that writhed and wailed and laughed sometimes like a child
as it was fed down into whatever pipes circulated through the
pulpit because there had to be some; where else would it all
be going? Thank fuck I couldn't see its face, couldn't tell if
there was a mouth or eyes. In my life, I'd witnessed some
truly profane things—the consumption of Sullivan Rivers being a prime example—but this still was a firm contender for
the cake.

Rowan went pale. "The fuuuuck."

"The goddamned steak," I said suddenly as Eoan continued
to groan; he was practically bellowing, the sounds crawling
out of him scarcely human, more tortured bull than anything
identifiably person-like.

"What are you talking about?"

I shook my head as Eoan lolled bonelessly back onto the floor, drenched by a spray of pale tendrils, like intestinal worms or maybe veins leached of all color. "That's why their food was separate from ours in the dining hall. The faculty's."

"I thought it was because it was fancy shit."

"If only."

Gently, Eoan removed a shimmery blue pocket square from his coat—the color was surreally bright, lurid even like a piece of the open sky cut out and placed in his palm—and cupped it over his mouth, gagging as he began to pull at those colorless threads. Clumps loosened and came free.

"You kept the school fed," I said with a brittle tenderness even as Eoan wadded up the bloodied pocket square, storing it away. "The faculty, the Librarian. You kept them from digging into us."

"They told me it'd only be a year," the Scottish boy panted, lacquered with sweat, his eyes no longer white but their soft pastel green again. "Serve for a year and they'd close up the portal inside me. But they lied, I suppose. I don't know why I thought they wouldn't."

He broke into a sobbing humorless laugh, cackling until there wasn't any air left in him and he was wheezing like an animal with its throat cut.

"I should have known better," said Eoan when he had recovered enough. "We all should have."

"You knew?" Rowan was hollow-eyed. His hands crooked into claws, face blazing with a fatal grief. "You fucking knew. You knew this was waiting for us. How could you let this happen? Why didn't you tell us?"

"*I* didn't know anything about this," whimpered Eoan, crawling backward from us or at least trying, his hands skidding frictionless through the gore he'd left on the base of pulpit. "They didn't tell me. They said to feed them. That's all. I didn't know. I thought, it's not actually human flesh, is it? Whatever comes out of the portal. I'm sorry, I'm so sorry. If I'd known I'd have said something. I swear it. It's my fault for not asking the right questions, but I did not know this was how it'd end. I—I only did this to make the pain stop. Please, you have to believe me."

"Give me one good reason," Rowan said.

"You'd have done the same too."

All the color fled Rowan's face: he was white as chalk, as clean dead bone. He withdrew a single step, his face closing like a door, his expression banging shut. It was so hard to ascribe any malice to Eoan, with his soft eyes and softer brogue, the congenital melancholy that seemed to permeate his elfin features, but not for the first time I wondered if it was an act. I scanned his face as he spoke but from where I stood, it remained sinless as marble. "None of us are good people. We aren't. We deserve this."

"Just because you're a sell-out," hissed Rowan.

"I am. Never said I wasn't. But I fed her, the Librarian," said Eoan after a moment, curling into a ball. "So she won't hurt anybody. I did it for all of us. That has to mean something, doesn't it? Don't hate me. I didn't want to hurt anyone."

"Too little too late on all those fronts, don't you think?" I asked. "We're still fucked."

"But we're not dead. Not yet."

I couldn't help the sneer from crawling onto my face.

"Ain't that a pity."

BEFORE

Silently, we made our way back to where Sullivan and Portia sat. More students were pouring into the dining hall, their voices echoing strangely in the cavernous space. A queue was forming through the doors and was being kept honest by a trio of those meat stewards. The presence of the latter only helped to confirm Professor Stone's comments, an attempt by Hellebore's administration to keep costs down because already, the air was spoiling with the reek of decay. I risked a backward glance at where Stone had stood but if he was still there, he'd been swallowed by the crowd.

"Is it something related to epic fantasy?" said Rowan as we came within inches of the table, startling me.

"What?"

"Your name," said Rowan. "Is it like a *Lord of the Rings* reference or something?"

"Nope."

"Is it a science fiction thing?"

Sullivan smiled courteously up at us both as I sat down beside him, Rowan settling beside a less than enthused Portia.

"No," I said to Rowan, grateful despite myself for the irreverence, this break from being so thoroughly unsettled.

"Did you make it up yourself?" said Rowan, ignoring Sullivan.

"No."

Then as Portia was about to speak, Rowan bellowed with unabashed delight.

"Noooo. No way," he said, pointing at me.

I froze.

"Are you named for the *Silent Hill* chick?"

"Silent *what*?" said Sullivan, too well-bred to know his schlocky franchises.

Thinking back, that was perhaps my best memory of Hellebore: Rowan barraging Sullivan with lore and theories about the lore surrounding the inescapable cursed town, Portia adding non sequiturs where she could, winking at me where she couldn't, her earlier aloofness somehow eradicated by our camaraderie. It was good and if I'd known what would come later, I might have savored those hours with them, the last vestiges of safety I'd possess, tenuous as they were given the company I was keeping. I learned both Sullivan and Rowan had enrolled voluntarily: Sullivan out of obligation, Rowan because he, in his own words, wanted pussy.

"There are easier ways to get laid," said Sullivan.

"But not hotter," countered Rowan, waggling his eyebrows at Portia who'd left and returned with a glass of iced coffee, which she poured over his head without a second word.

"Why are *you* here?" Portia asked me, after Rowan had staggered, cursing, away to the bathrooms and she had come back with a cup of *hot* coffee, settling back into her seat.

"They kidnapped me."

She and Sullivan exchanged looks.

"It happens," said the boy gently, something ineradicably different about how he looked at me: his face was gentler, his eyes softer, so much softer. Someone else might have melted like butter but I knew that expression. He was looking at me like the corpse of a dove he'd found on the roadside, beyond saving but not above pity.

"Like Sully said," drawled Portia.

"I'd prefer you not call me that."

"—it is something that happens. Student Affairs reportedly has a comprehensive Intelligence division, and they go out of their way to find those most at risk of becoming a danger to both themselves and the world."

"Well, keeping me here," I said, trying to keep the poison from my voice, "will *definitely* turn me into a danger to myself and the world. So I fucking hope there's a way out."

"Afraid not," said Sullivan.

"Kidnapping is a felony," I said, stabbing at the last curd of kung pao chicken, the crispness long ruined by its bed of sauce.

"I'm afraid it isn't," said Sullivan, collecting our trays into a neat stack after I'd set my fork back down. "Hellebore has an agreement with the world governments. It has carte blanche to do as it will to preserve the safety of the general population."

I ground my teeth. "Doesn't make it right."

"Doesn't make it wrong either," Sullivan said.

"I don't care." I shook my head. "One way or another, I'm getting out of this place. I didn't consent to rehabilitation or whatever you call this. You might have but *I* didn't."

Portia said: "There are only two ways out of the school: in a body bag or graduation. You'll find Hellebore's locked tighter than Alcatraz ever was. You aren't getting out of here before the year is done." Her voice dropped to a whisper. "And you shouldn't publicly state you're intending an escape plan. That's stupid."

"Stupid or not," I said, mouth warm with a tang of rust.

I'd done more than ground my teeth, it seemed: I'd chewed straight into the side of my tongue. The pain felt good, stabilizing, like an old friend setting their hand on my arm, reminding me I was here, that I was alive. "I'm getting out of here."

"You really are not," said Portia. "Trust me on this. More desperate people have tried and failed."

"*Watch me.*"

Our initial weeks in Hellebore passed quickly, each day indistinguishable from the last. Our schedules were rigorous if nonsensical: we were assigned classes seemingly at random, without thought toward affinity or even cohesion in our learning experiences. Each week yielded new restrictions, new expectations. Our *rooms* migrated through the wings of the dormitory, complicating our routes to our classes: getting anywhere early became a problem if you couldn't figure out where you were going to wake up. The only consolation was that Hellebore was more horizontal than vertical, meaning while there was a panoply of wings to sprint through, there were only a few stories of stairs to navigate.

Not that it actually mattered. The lecturers themselves seemed perennially disinterested in us at best and openly contemptuous at worst, ignoring all attempts at questions and worse, homework assignments. We were given plenty to do but nothing was ever graded and no feedback was ever provided.

At least, not in my case.

Johanna insisted I was just lucky: she purportedly was the center of an unwanted amount of attention, something I'd have been more sympathetic about if not for her clear pleasure in this. Some of us were masochists, it seemed. Likewise, Portia, on those rare occasions I saw her outside of our classes, seemed to be getting worked to the marrow. When not otherwise discharging her duties to Hellebore, she was carrying out tasks for the Raw Grail. All of them had to be performed in absolute secrecy, Porta insisted, although I had the feeling she wanted me to prod her, that she might even relish the thought of being provoked into revealing whatever she was up to.

"She's flirting with you," said Johanna one night after Portia had cut short an unexpected visit to our room. Apparently, there'd been a party that had ended with an excess of leftovers, which had to be distributed before they went bad. I pointed out refrigeration existed as a technology, and she had smiled and said nothing to that, instead going on to explain who had made what. The fact the student body was not allowed independent access to the kitchens went uncommented on. "I bet she wants to convince you to join her sorority."

"I really hope not. I have no urge to be part of one."

"They're really not that bad," drawled Johanna, patient. She told me she was of Eastern European origin, a promiscuous mix of nationalities, but her accent was pure Jersey with its overly pronounced vocal fry. "When I was in college, I was in—"

"College? You went to college and then you came here?"

Johanna's expression flickered.

"I didn't want to," she said in a voice like lead, all her airiness used up in that confession. "But there was . . . well, he wasn't a man, but he might as well have been one. I thought he was a friend. He wasn't. And I had to get away. So, I came here."

It didn't surprise me. There were only so many species of

girl once you got down to it. Some breeds ran and some breeds fought and then some took to gutting themselves for their wolves, because if you were going to get eaten, you might as well choose how. I could see it in Johanna's overbright cheer, that sickly need to cultivate everyone's approval.

"Okay," I said, hoping she could hear the concession in my voice.

Thankfully, she did.

"Anyway," said Johanna, brightening. "I was in one. Well, sort of. We were all cheerleaders—"

"Too much information," I said. In the last few weeks, we'd done a fair job at dividing our shared space, jury-rigging a curtain wall to permit a nominal amount of privacy. I'd been rigorous about keeping our corners distinct but then Johanna convinced me otherwise by setting up an alcove with a little hot plate (contraband, to my surprise, raising her several notches in my esteem), snacks smuggled from god knows where, and more tea than I'd seen outside a grocery store. I wouldn't say I warmed but my territoriality lessened.

"Anyway, I don't know. It might be, like, good for you. The Raw Grail's got their own sorority house. You can go somewhere that isn't constantly under surveillance."

"They do? Where the hell is it?"

"It's that burnt-up-looking building next to the green house," said Johanna, sliding forward to the frilled edge of her bed, nail polish brush waggled for emphasis, the bristles slicked with a bright electric blue.

I knew what she was talking about. I'd walked past it several times, bewildered by its condition: it had the look of a barn taken by an inferno and allowed to burn down to the bones. As far as I recalled, the windows and doors were boarded up, admitting neither entry nor exit.

"People *live* in there?"

Johanna shrugged. "That's what they say."

Under different circumstances, I might have gone to Sullivan for answers, but he'd gone the way of the popular kid. He drifted through those first strange days on a cloud of lackeys, a king with his wandering court, perpetually hand in hand with that pretty, coal-eyed girlfriend of his who looked far too kind to belong in Hellebore, although really, who the fuck knew. I was the last person who could pass judgment. At twenty-one, I still looked about fourteen in bad lighting, which had been the delight of several men's days and unequivocally the reason they were dead.

I could have asked Portia herself, I suppose, but I did not. Mostly for fear Johanna was right and I would be subjected to a full-frontal attempt at recruitment but partially because some animal part of me was afraid I'd find out what was inside the alleged sorority house. After my conversation with Johanna, I found myself dreaming of girls with smoke for hair walking noiselessly through an unbroken darkness, up and down, up and down along the ceiling of an empty house. It didn't help that once Portia shyly handed me an invitation to a soiree they were holding, but no one else I knew had received similar invites. It'd been handwritten, overly eager in tone, and to this day, I believe the signatures emblazoned across the card were all hers. I'd declined. Portia never brought it up again. But the damage was done. She was no longer even my last port of call.

There was the library, of course. Unfortunately, while a reservoir of information both eldritch and mundane, it too wasn't an option, much as I might have liked it to be. Which might sound strange, given the very function of such institutions, but we'll get to that.

The one bright spot of those first few weeks was finding out I would share four classes with Minji, who was becoming the closest thing to a friend I had at Hellebore. She was slyly funny in private: prone to dad jokes, puns, long spiraling critiques of capitalism and Western interpersonal dynamics, but only if first lubricated with vast amounts of *makgeolli*. The rest of the time, she was the archetypal example of the model minority: quiet, obedient, academic. Once, I'd asked her if she ever worried that she was reinforcing racist beliefs and in answer, Minji had only shrugged.

"It's better when they underestimate me."

We became friends after that, though Minji continued to keep her own counsel on most things, which I might have taken offense to if I wasn't so relieved to be in the company of someone as incurious as I was. Sure, a part of me wished we had more of a rapport at times or at least enough of one for us to discuss the matter of her stalker.

Not that she called him such or even acknowledged his existence. It was Ford, of course, one of the few haruspices to walk the halls of Hellebore. We saw him rarely enough. The school made regular and rough use of his abilities. But when he wasn't otherwise being gutted to tell the future, Ford spent his time in dogged pursuit of Minji, begging for her love, her time, whatever else she'd give. And miraculously, Minji never spoke an unkind word to him. Then again, she did not speak to him at all, only ever stared at him in silence as he told her of the life he foresaw for them, one where she birthed daughter after daughter for him, each more beautiful than the last.

"I see you inside me," he said once, trailing us between classes. "I see you beneath my skin. I see you standing in the church of my lungs and you are there, holding my bones like a wedding bouquet."

"That is the weirdest way to say you want to get pegged," I shouted over my shoulder, eliciting nervous glances from passersby. Ford had no aptitude for violence but his power meant he was beloved by more than Hellebore's administration. In particular, one Adam Kingsley, who was alleged to be the forerunner in the race to become the definitive Antichrist.

"And you," Ford said, eyes like the light radiating from a crematorium, "you will get what you want. But it won't be what they deserve."

It was the first time he'd acknowledged my existence. His gaze flayed me, stripped me down to the muscle and my tired heart, and if I was anyone else, I might have been unnerved at being so disrobed, but I was angry instead. I whirled around and stalked up to him. He wasn't the only one who could see under the surface, who could look and find the library of one's tendons, the archive of soft organs and softer veins: I reached both my hands outward, fingers splayed, spreading my arms. In answer, his flesh did the same, unseaming gladly for me as all flesh did when I asked, and I would have had him in two halves a second later if not for the small hand settling on my left wrist.

"No," said Minji, her expression incomprehensible.

I resisted for a moment. "But—"

"He's mine," said Minji. There was such a concussive possessiveness in her voice, such warning in her face, that there was nothing to be done but relent. I stopped what I was doing and Ford fell onto the corridor in a soup of exposed viscera. Minji went to him, blotting his blood-gummed lips with a lavender handkerchief, coiffed and beautiful next to the mess I'd made of Ford. She was so tender in her ministrations I found myself stunned. Maybe his attention was welcomed and this was a love affair—just one alien to my world view. Who was I to judge?

Regardless, of the things I saw in Hellebore, even considering what came after, Sullivan's death and ours and all those that took place in between, little came close to unnerving me as much as that moment and the memory of Minji's eyes, the light such that I couldn't tell if she was looking at him with love or something worse.

Which, again, is saying a whole damn lot.

DAY ONE

With the Librarian allegedly fed by Eoan, we had time to re-convene, to think. It took a while, of course, to gather the scattered eight. Were it not for Minji, we probably shouldn't have been able to but somehow, she found us, corralled us into one of the reading rooms. This one was muraled with pastel depictions of happy children engrossed in picture books, the dusty shelves filled with content for that demographic; it'd have been cute if not for the fact that there weren't any kids on the grounds. I wondered if those books were meant for the masked servitors or if they brought comfort to the meat men: neither of those possibilities sat particularly well with me.

Rowan wanted us to come clean; I wanted Eoan to owe us. And Eoan, who became numbly docile once he stopped puking meat down a funnel, regarded us with hollow eyes as we bickered about how much we would say, the light seeming to melt the flesh from his skull so when I looked over to him, all I saw was a corpse. In the end, we agreed there was no need to tell the others about what Eoan had done.

Not yet, at least.

When we were all assembled, Eoan said, in a trembling voice, he could make us some hors d'oeuvres, having allegedly found a cache of ingredients. I don't know what surprised me more: that Eoan offered or that the group accepted, knowing what we did about the library, the school, and everything beside. But I said nothing and Rowan averted his eyes as Eoan kindled a small fire. Neither of us acknowledged him emptying a small gunny of its bloody contents, nor did we have anything to say when he impaled its oily white contents to roast them slowly.

"It's *meat*, I suppose," said Gracelynn with a tremulous smile.

"It's not *not* meat," said Rowan diplomatically.

I elbowed him in the side.

The floor-to-ceiling paintings of little kids were obscured at intervals by framed portraits of men and women who had been captured mostly in shadow, almost entirely silhouette save for where light gilded a nose, a cheekbone, a too-long finger crooked at the artist. Above us, a fat chandelier pouted from the ceiling, its wooden frame crowned with melted candles.

Adam ripped more pages from an encyclopedia, feeding the blaze until it burned almost blue. I'd put up a halfhearted argument against using books as fuel but even Portia agreed the furniture was a worse gamble, treated and varnished as it was: there was no telling if we'd end up poisoned by the fumes or worse. (I pointed out that worse was, given the circumstances, the superior option, and Adam extended an offer to end my misery for me.) That became moot when Ford brought in a dying fig sapling, whose branches Eoan used to skewer oily clumps of pale meat. I'd have argued more but there was Portia, gnawing on her exposed wrist bone like a rabid coyote. Her face had begun to petal, spreading into quarters: you could almost see the mandibles now, lacquered with blood and phlegm.

So I left it there. Partly because if the Librarian found us and took umbrage, it'd be Adam who would have to, euphemistically speaking, field the complaints. Partly because Portia looked hungry enough to be a problem shortly and would have been, I suspected, if not for Eoan grilling his alleged find. She watched the meat brown with a dazed expression. Minji alone seemed enchanted by the whole situation.

"Is it chicken then?" she said. "Beef? Pig? How many legs did this thing possess beforehand?"

"It looks like it might be shellfish," said Gracelynn with care. "I wonder if it's scallop."

Minji turned to them, radiant with mischief. "And where does one find *scallop* in a library?"

"It's a magical library. Maybe they magicked some up?" said Gracelynn, hope shining from their round face. I couldn't meet their eyes.

I focused instead on Eoan's work. A charred rind was beginning to form over the cubed meat; it'd been a noxious white at first until the fire had time to warm its color. Now, it made me think of good, expensive beef. I stared into the fire until my vision blurred with tears. Adam crumpled up another page and tossed it between his hands.

"Forget the food. Rowan, how do you want it to happen?"

"I'm sorry, what?" said Rowan.

"Ford said it already," said Adam lightly, like he was proposing brunch options. "Half of us live if you die. So, how do you want to go?"

"Half still die," said Minji. "We should probably figure out how that happens."

"The normal ways, I suspect," said Adam.

"They said we have *three days,*" wailed Gracelynn. "This doesn't have to happen now."

Adam's answering smile was serene, his accent and his diction become theirs, high and sweet and trembling. "Time flies when we're having fun, though. Best we figure it out now rather than later, don't you think?"

"Let's start with Ford," I said, blinking away the glare. I glanced sidelong at Ford, who was staring at Minji like a forlorn dog. Something in his expression made my skin want to scuttle off my bones to garrote the fucker right there and then. It wasn't his clear hunger for her, although that was nauseating to see. It was the willing patience: it said it'd bide its time, wait until she was alone or vulnerable, until *yes* was a simpler story than *no.* "He's done his job. We don't need him anymore."

I thought of Johanna and her wolf and his appetites.

"I'd argue that we do," said Adam.

"For what? He's already told us if Rowan dies, half survive," I said. "That's enough prophecy for me. In fact, let's send Ford out there. He's been feeding the faculty prophecies for months. Might as well go all the way."

Snap. Portia had chewed her arm and her hand hung now from a ribbon of frayed tendon, useless. I could see something protrude from the gray marrow, something like a sliver of black glass.

Or chitin.

"I want him," hissed Portia. "Give him to me."

Ford turned in such a way that nothing of his face could be seen except for one blue eye, his head engulfed entirely by shadow. It was dramatic, I'd give him that. His shirt, having been bled on for hours, had dried to something with the texture of jerky. He smelled of bile, and of rust, and a little bit of shit.

"You're not my death," he told Portia.

Then Ford moved his attention to me, announcing in sepulchral tones, "You will get what you want. But you will wish for a different fate, you will wish for death to take you in its arms. Your destiny will be terrible. You will beg for the mercy of their mouths. You will . . ."

I rolled my eyes. Here at the end, posturing did little to move me.

"If we're going to go down that route, we should start with the weakest of us," said Adam, like Ford and I hadn't spoken, his attention roving through the group. "The most expendable."

"I feel like we should be addressing the fact Portia *just ate through her wrist,*" said Rowan.

Adam boomed with laughter. I hated the noise. On its face, it was pretty enough, a sound plundered from a politician's toolbox: rich, warm, reassuring. But like everything from a politician's toolbox, it was entirely performative and like everything about Adam, it was probably stolen.

"If Kevin was still around, why they'd be the first one to die," said Adam in faultless mimicry of Gracelynn's own lilt, accurate to the smallest nuances of their twang. His eyes settled on them. "Bet they'd love knowing their spouse was a coward who hid so someone else could die in their place."

"There's no guarantee you're going to be one of the ones who live, you know?" I said. "Maybe it's time to stop pretending you're the one in charge here."

"I know it's not going to be me, at least," said Minji primly. "We've got plans."

"But I am. You all know it," said Adam, attention veering

to Rowan. "This doesn't have to be difficult. This can be a beautiful death for half of us."

"Fuck you, man." I said.

"Maybe later," said Adam.

"*I'm hungry,*" keened Portia.

Right then, I found myself thinking: this was it. Soon, we'd be picking bits of one another from the wall. If violence broke loose, hell would come stampeding after. I looked over the gathered survivors, trying to assess who'd fall into what camp, who'd throw in with Rowan and who'd cozy up to one of the Devil's own spawn. It was only a question of time. Though at least I could still buy that. Eoan, who'd said nothing throughout, shuddered as our eyes met.

"*Stop,*" said Gracelynn.

"We should just start with you," Adam practically purred, swaggering up to Rowan, who was on his feet again, chest puffed impotently. "Get the ball rolling on that prophecy."

"I said *stop!*" cried out Gracelynn this time in their *voice* and Adam, to his naked surprise, stopped.

His eyes widened infinitesimally, attention now wholly on Gracelynn. Adam was unaccustomed to challenge. Especially from someone so innocuous-looking and pastel. Gracelynn was the shortest of the three in that tableau, barely chest-height to Adam. Their dress was a confection of creamy fabric and lace, the panes of the skirt embroidered with occult symbols and, inexplicably, very round cats. (When I met them, it had been moons spangling their skirts, moons and soft-eyed lambs.) They barreled up to Adam, planting themselves between him and Rowan. To glare at him, they had to crane their head back and tip their chin up: they resembled a child who'd waded into an argument between adults.

But there was no apprehension in their demeanor, no doubt,

nothing that could even be described as fearful, the meekness burned away by need. Gracelynn was either suicidally bold or just plain suicidal. Either way, they didn't flinch where bigger men would have run.

"You don't get to decide this."

"We can decide together then," said Adam, raising an arm. "All in favor, say—"

"*No.*"

"This really is about Kevin, ain't it?" said Adam, smiling like a dog, his accent shifting fractionally, so the twang was a little longer than Gracelynn's, the vowels thicker. *Kevin,* I remember thinking. He was using Kevin's voice on their widow. "You couldn't save your blackbird so you're going to save this crow? Poor Gracelynn. Must have just about killed you when you watched your best beloved die. The way they screamed. I'm going to hear the sound every night for the rest of my damn life. What about you?"

"Quit it." I stood up. There were certain lines you didn't cross.

"I'd be careful on that high horse, Alessa," said Adam now in Gracelynn's breathy tones and their molasses-sweet accent, a move that had me nauseous. "Fall and something might stomp your spine to dust. Didn't you *just* murder a certain girl?"

"*Adam Kingsley, stop talking right now.*"

If they lived long enough to wrinkle into a little old person, that voice of theirs would mature into a power that could speak the universe to a stop and a new start: theirs was a voice to end worlds, to begin new ones. Sometimes, I wonder if the Christians had been right. Maybe there really was a god who jump-started creation with the phrase, *Let there be light,* and the Bible's only error was thinking anything happens in linear chronology. Gracelynn wasn't *quite* there yet but they weren't far. Adam rocked backward from the force of that command, his eyes rolling up to the whites. It took a good thirty seconds before he could speak again.

"That was good," he said, mopping his mouth with the back of his hand. "Almost good enough to make me *think* about never saying a damn word again for the rest of my life. Do you ever wish you were more than *almost* good enough?" The mask dropped enough that we could see the solipsistic contempt he held toward them, toward us, toward everything that wasn't him. His grin wide and cruel, his eyes as expressive as plastic. "Do you ever wish *you* were good enough? Good enough to keep the one thing that ever loved you alive."

"The Librarian," I blurted, a new idea forming as the words left my mouth.

An expectant silence laid itself over the group.

"Let's deal with the fucking Librarian before we start offing each other. Eight people have a better shot of doing that than four."

To my surprise, Eoan came to bolster my ludicrous proposal. He passed each of us a skewer and Rowan and I handed ours immediately to Portia, who ate it all, branch and meat, cooing with animal pleasure; Minji turned hers over round and round and round, contemplating the meat; Ford ate his with a groaning pleasure. Adam turned his down, expression impish, so a fourth stick went to Portia.

"Alessa's right," said Eoan. "The Librarian's probably still full and tired. If there was ever a time she could be defeated, it's now."

"Or we could just feed Rowan to the faculty," persisted Adam.

"Half live," said Ford unhelpfully. "If Rowan dies."

"Sullivan would have taken down the Librarian himself," said Gracelynn.

"Sullivan," said Adam, "is fucking dead. If he was worth anything, he wouldn't have just stood there as they devoured him."

He hadn't just stood there. Sullivan had fought. Not immediately, but he'd fought. He'd called his cicada-gods and they'd come loyally to his aid. But it hadn't amounted to anything. I remember how he'd struggled even as he began deliquescing under all that concentrated stomach acid, how he had bobbed again and again to the surface of that mass, only to be dragged under. Each time Sullivan emerged, there was less of him: less meat, less organ. Until he was only growingly porous bone—and eyes, rolling in panicked circles—through which I could see spongy marrow and brain. It took him forever to die.

But he had fought.

If I lived to be a hundred, which seemed unlikely then given my circumstances, I would remember that Sullivan Rivers had fought.

Minji, perched on the armrest of the battered couch, swung her legs as she said, "You know, we've only seen Ford read one organ. Perhaps we need him to take a proper look at the rest of them. That way we can be sure of who is making the right decision."

"You know what?" said Adam with a dazzling smile, striding over to Ford. "Let's do it."

With that, Adam drove his fist straight into the other man's belly. His knuckles sank through fabric and flesh like so much butter warming on a counter, his arm igniting when he was elbow-deep in Ford's abdominal captivity, and Ford screamed like a pig halfway in the slaughter.

With excruciating care, Adam removed loop after loop of blackened intestine.

"Tell me what happens, oracle," said Adam in his normal voice, smiling throughout, smiling like it was nothing, like it couldn't possibly hurt.

Ford squealed in idiot torment, a black stain leaching across the front of his jeans. The air filled with the smell of piss, of bowels dispensing what little they'd collected.

"You're *killing* him," Gracelynn, snarling, desperate, half rising. "Stop it!"

"Haruspices don't die that easily," said Adam, holding on for a moment longer before he released his grip on Ford, flinging him away, viscera suppurating out of the cauterized hole in the other man's belly. Ford tumbled forward, facedown on the mosaiced floor. I thought I heard Minji giggle.

"Happy?" said Adam, looking at me, ash sleeting from his fingers. "Don't tell me I never do anything for you."

"I won't," said Minji. "We promise."

"You're a fucking bastard, Adam. You're a monster," came Gracelynn's bellowing rejoinder, and I could chart in the inflection of Adam's smile, her transmutation in his mind, how she went from risible novelty to an insult that required addressing.

But before he could do anything more, the room filled with the sound of Eoan screaming.

BEFORE

To my absolute dismay, I shared more classes with Johanna than anyone else I had come to know, which was to say we were in five together. Three of which we lacked any aptitude for, as they either involved some talent with fire (Adam lorded over the rest of us there) or economics (banal, everyday economics, entirely unmagical, taught inexplicably by the snow-haired counselor whose general advice involved variations of the word *endure*). I excelled at Abdominal Infrastructure, along with Rowan, of course, though none of us had any love for the professor, a starched and formal horror of a man named Professor Cartilage, who droned on and on and on while the corpses we were meant to autopsy and process rotted before our eyes.

One day, Cartilage made us descend into the bowels of Hellebore for class. From the roof to its grandiose main hall, the school was three stories in height. It'd been intimated that there was a basement and though we weren't expressly forbidden from exploring the subterranean levels, those few who'd ventured bathyal-ward in the first few months of our enrollment did not come back. So we left it alone. We were already learning there were too many ways to die in Hellebore. Thus, when Professor Cartilage gave his instructions several days ahead of our next class, we all railed against them, suspicious of his intent.

"Could be a test," said a pale, fox-featured Russian girl, wringing the ends of her hair, which fell long and straight, a shade of blond only fractionally deeper than her skin. "Back home, one of the rehabilitation centers would do it too."

"Do what?" asked Johanna, all naïveté and wide eyes.

The girl rolled her eyes in answer. All twenty of us were sprawled in our usual classroom, a carbon copy of every other: glossy dark wood, an omnipresent scent of pine resin, uncomfortable chairs. Twin oak-skinned boys, taller than the rest of us, exchanged looks.

"See who complies. See who doesn't," said one of them.

"The ones who don't," said the other, tone as clipped as their companion's, "die."

"We could just ask the professor, you know," said a beautiful older woman who looked for all the world like she'd survived a bad marriage and single parenthood and now was pursuing second chances through an education in something new. Except, of course, this was *Hellebore,* and I had to wonder why she was here.

It was a reasonable enough proposition and we went en masse to his office, an ordeal that took nearly all day to complete due to Hellebore's spatial inconsistencies. Hellebore kept changing: slowly, illogically, expanding in places, narrowing in others. Facilities moved, the professors' wing especially. We'd nearly given up when a door presented itself, a brass placard announcing the name of its occupant: CARTILAGE. Entering, unfortunately, we found nothing but a note that stated in his swooping calligraphic writing, *Latecomers will be punished.*

We took the warning to heart.

Getting to the basement proved as difficult as locating Professor Cartilage's office. On the ground floor, we discovered more doors than were reasonable. One yielded a path to the gardens, although it was placed on the opposite end of the building to them; one opened to darkness and the sound of a girl sobbing rhythmically; one to a pool in which a thing with no face swam; one to a rock face. We tried eight doors next. Two hid a masked, shrieking thing that leapt out and dragged a student inside. The first time it happened, Johanna wailed until an older student slapped her with military efficacy: teeth clattered out of her mouth as she slumped on the gray concrete, clutching at her jaw.

"I heard stories about Cartilage," said the woman heartlessly. The weak light grayed her face, made her look older still, and tinged her eye sockets green. "If we're late, we're going to wish it'd been us instead."

The second time a student was taken, no one even looked back.

The ninth door we opened spilled into a stairwell that helixed down into a deep apricot-tinged darkness. Someone sang softly at the bottom.

It was Ford.

"If this is another of his weird-ass performances, I'm going to stab myself in the eye," said Johanna, uncharacteristically mean, as she walked past me to go down the steps, vanguard for our now spooked group.

For the first three floors down, there were nothing but half-rotted steps, landings that went nowhere, and wrought iron rails so old they'd completely oxidized. Naked bulbs coughed from the walls, their presence a surprise given Hellebore's animosity toward technology. Then again, this was probably less taxing to maintain than an armada of oil lamps. The light was pus-colored and gave a jaundiced shine to the flooring. It was also useless, only really pooling where it was unneeded. I tripped twice within the first ten minutes of our excursion.

"I wouldn't hurry to my death like that," said a short, leonine-looking girl with a mass of black braids, even as I caught myself. "Being dead isn't that fun."

"How do you know?"

She smiled thinly and kept walking.

There was debris throughout the landing and while I could have tried to identify it, something in how it crunched—chalklike, brittle, familiar—under our shoes made me decide against it. The air was still and soundless save for our footsteps. Ford's singing continued on, amateurish but not unpleasant: it was a dirge he was singing in a language none of us recognized, though we seemed to represent every continent and country.

Doors began appearing by the fourth floor: twelve at first, each too slim for even the boniest waif to inch through, and they rattled hopefully when we neared; on the fifth floor, there were eleven; on the sixth, ten. And it continued like that for a time, the air growing clotted with humidity, the doors increasing in size and lessening in number. Once in a while, I thought I heard footsteps that weren't ours.

By the twelfth, the doors were large enough to use comfortably if we so wanted but we sorely did not. For one, we'd seen what lived behind some of them. For another, someone seemed to be sobbing from behind all four of the doors at once. The crying had an artificial quality, a wrongness, a crackling that made it seem like it might have come from a recording, which begged the unfortunate question of *why*.

What was even more unfortunate was how quickly my brain answered:

Lure, it told me. *This is a lure.*

The fifteenth floor held a single French door: enormous, gothic, beautifully ornamented with the school's symbols, the fig trees and the wasps. The handles were a bisected deer skull, with its antlers shorn to a usable length. Unlike the landing, the doors looked clean, even glossy. As I neared, I heard the low hum of machinery behind it, like a hundred air conditioners operating in concert. More inconsistencies, more weirdness; it'd be more disarming if the school as a rule wasn't so unwholesomely eldritch.

Johanna marched straight up to the doors, hypnotized somehow by the sight.

"There's something," she told me, urgent, a child warning of the thing hiding under the bed.

"It used to be there were so many more of us," said Professor Cartilage from a plain door—a door I was sure hadn't been there before—behind us. He was equally plain, with thinning hair and deeply recessed eyes, skin softly yellowed in a way that suggested extensive damage. "We'd come and go as we pleased, but the Ministry sealed the doors. No matter, every door opens in the end."

"Professor?" I ventured.

His mouth cracked into a curve. "Come along."

There wasn't anything inside save for a basalt altar, a black plastic bucket, a single bulb dangling from the ceiling. And Ford, of course, laid out on the polished black surface like a corpse, still humming. He'd been opened up, skin delicately pinned back at aesthetic intervals. We were all acquainted with the sight of his insides. When he wasn't being consulted by the faculty, Ford would host readings in the gymnasium. With the help of a pretty assistant, he would vivisect himself as the audience barraged him with questions. It was always the same routine too. She (always a girl, always with the same straight-cut bangs that Minji wore) would dramatically pass him an assortment of instruments: bone saw, scalpel, rib shears, sternal saw, and more varieties of scissors than I knew existed. Then he'd extract one organ after another, studying them in turn, dispensing koans instead of real answers. But none of us were there for guidance, not really. We just wanted to see if this would be the day he slumped over dead.

"Each of you should select an organ," said Professor Cartilage, gesturing for us to arrange ourselves in a uniform circle. "No fighting over the good bits. No pushing. The intestines earn you additional credit."

I looked down at the pulsating tableau, barely resisting the impulse to ask if there *were* any good bits. Instead, I noted, "What are the extra credits good for?"

Professor Cartilage extended a ghastly smile. "Painkillers."

Before I could press him on that frankly disturbing clarification, he raised his voice over the murmur of us deciding between organs, some gravitating toward the more vigorous specimens, others to their quieter peers. Johanna and I ended up sharing a lung, both of us marking our claim with a single finger touched to the fluttering pink tissue.

"Now," said Professor Cartilage once we'd quieted. "There is a field of human science—"

I glanced at Johanna, who nodded obliquely. She'd heard it too. *Human.*

"—called forensic entomology, which is the study of arthropods in association with violent crime, among other things. Specialists within the field can tell you many things about a cadaver based on what insects are present: its age, its

time of death, any post-mortem movement. But Ford is alive."
He chuckled, palming the haruspex's cheek. "So we are unfortunately unable to do that."

"Why bring it up then?" said the older woman, cagey.

Professor Cartilage stared at her until she dropped her eyes
before he chuckled again, a sound like dust blowing through
an abandoned room. "Because I enjoy the knowledge that
such a thing exists. And because occasionally, forensic entomology will review the consequences of myiasis, which is
what we will study today."

"Myia," began one of the oak-skinned boys.

"Fancy word for maggots colonizing living tissue," I said.

Ford stopped his singing.

"Wh-what? *Wait*," he whimpered.

"Correct," said our teacher monotonously, hands swimming down to Ford's neck. "There's a bucket with live dipteran
larvae just behind you. The scoop is inside. Be generous with
your application of the larvae. Today's research involves understanding what occurs when undying tissue is subjected to
myiasis. Will the rate of consumption be outpaced by the rate
of healing? How much oxygenation do the dipteran larvae require in order to continue growth?"

"Please," said Ford. "I don't want this."

"Why?" I said. "This is—"

Someone retched. This felt like unmerited grotesquerie,
even for Hellebore. I stared down at Ford, repulsed by our
mandate, sick to my bowels at the idea of us systematically
introducing maggots into a man's living tissue, all for irrelevant hypotheticals.

"Science," said Professor Cartilage.

"Bullshit," I snapped.

"In the same way pig carcasses are used in lieu of human

cadavers," he said, unmoved, "we must use alternatives where necessary in order to continue our studies. If it helps, Miss Li, this is important work you will be doing. You'll be ensuring the survival of species outside our own."

There it was again. He'd called it *human* science.

"What species?"

Ford was trying to eel free of the altar, kicking at the air for leverage. Skin tore as Ford writhed, begging, and if not for the professor's hands around the haruspex's throat, the man might have escaped. But for all Professor Cartilage's featherlight appearance, his grip on Ford was steel. When Ford opened his mouth to scream again, our professor, with the expression of someone waiting his turn at the post office, broke his neck.

"Begin," said Professor Cartilage.

DAY ONE

At Hellebore, it was monsters all the way down.

Bad enough we had to worry about the faculty outside and the Librarian sleeping in the walls. Now there was a new concern right in our midst. We turned as a group to see Eoan backpedaling from the stop-motion nightmare Portia was becoming, the latter twitching forward on her hands and knees. She was *molting*. A sheath of muscle tissue and crumbling bone trailed from her, like a dress half-shed, clinging wetly to her waist.

Gone, her skin and her very red hair. Gone, the leanly muscled slope of her back and her lithe legs, her expressive hands. Gone, those velvet-soft eyes of hers—no, I amended the thought as I took in her new face, the cracked skull with chitin blooming through a maze of fractures, like she was a piece of *kintsugi* inverted. No, her eyes were still there, only multiplied: a shining constellation of sable gazing benevolently down on us. I'd thought her gorgeous before in her humanity, but she seemed a miracle now, with the near translucence of her frame. Portia shuddered. Through the mess of her transformation, I could see organs shifting inside, undergoing mitosis and metamorphosis still: intestine fractalizing into tubules; a heart becoming seven then unfurling into a single red organ like a crooked finger set over her still human spine, which was reassessing just how many vertebrae she really needed.

She chirruped at Eoan, a dissonantly kittenish noise, almost cute (a word no one should associate with an overgrown arachnid). She'd been human a second ago. I was sure of that. Had we missed something? Did something catalyze this? Those thoughts came after, long after the fact, and the blood was pooling black and thick. The only thing resounding in my mind then was:

Oh shit.

Portia exploded forward.

I started in her direction and slammed into Adam's outstretched arm.

"Wait," he said, calmer than anyone had the right to be, his expression one of academic interest. "Just listen to what she's saying—"

"She's going to kill him," panted Gracelynn, feral with worry. "We have to—"

"No, she's not. Just *watch.*"

"She's hungry," said Minji from somewhere behind me, unbothered.

Not everyone who came to Hellebore was a murderer. Accidentally guilty of manslaughter, sure, that part was inevitable. Powers like what burned through us have an elemental voracity, the carnivorousness of a natural disaster: they can't help but cause hurt. But most of us never started out wanting to commit homicide, for all that the school made it so easy to forget such aspirations.

By graduation, though, there wasn't a student in our class with clean hands, and anyone who might have objected to this was dead. The eight of us were not what anyone would call good. Even Gracelynn, for all their softness. Someone with more of a heart would have told Adam to fuck himself, would have hesitated less, would have leapt to help Eoan because that was what you did when you were a good person.

But we hadn't survived this long by putting too many others first. We'd been taught too well.

So we did nothing.

Surprisingly, Adam was right. Chelicerae scythed out from the ruins of Portia's face as pedipalps reached from her throat, all said appendages coming to close gently over Eoan's cheeks. And while spiders had no tongues, Portia seemed to have no knowledge of that: a red stem of muscle wormed out of her mouth and between the boy's lips.

"Is it weird I find this kinda hot?" said Rowan.

"No one asked you anything," said Minji.

"What is she doing?" I hissed. Adam had his arm lowered by then so I advanced on the unfortunate sight, less out of compassion, more out of an abject fascination.

Foam bubbled from the corners of Eoan's mouth, his eyes like a frightened animal's; they were framed by white as they rolled to stare at me. His throat was distended from its invasion: it throbbed as Portia crept up onto his torso, his own body flat and prone on the beautiful floor. Rowan wasn't wrong. There was a terrible intimacy to this, to Portia straddling him, her legs coming to cup his head, press him to her chest: she looked like a bride ready to slough her innocence. He gagged, spasming under Portia's body.

"The meat," said Adam, understanding dawning in his cruel eyes. "You two didn't want any of it. *You knew.*"

"I wasn't hungry," I said.

Rowan let out a hoarse chuckle. "I am a vegetarian except when it comes to, you know—"

"Eoan's a portal, isn't he? I've heard of them. They'd win wars for people if they could get that shit under control. Poor lad," He sighed then, shaking his head. "Probably had such a bad life. I heard it hurts like a bitch."

As though on cue, Eoan bucked in Portia's embrace.

"So now what?" said Rowan.

I ran my tongue over my incisors.

"Well," Minji said, coming to crouch down beside the pair. She stroked a hand through his thin claret hair, ignoring Portia's chitter of warning. "If he's what you claim he is, he's probably incredibly used to being parasitized. His kind—"

"His kind?" demanded Gracelynn. "He's a person. *Like us.* What are you talking about?"

"Like you," corrected Minji smoothly, teasing the wrinkles from a fold in her dress. "Eoan's kind is meant to be fed on. We should do what we can to keep him alive for as long as possible. He can keep the Librarian and Portia occupied while we figure this out."

Gracelynn shook their head. Their attention shot to Rowan and I.

"Say something," they demanded. "One of you. You can't be okay with this! This isn't right." Their dark eyes found mine. "Look, I—I know you've done some terrible things. But I know you. You're better than this. We can't let Eoan—"

"Why not have it both ways?" interrupted Adam, smiling, encroaching so deeply on Minji's personal space that she had to withdraw a step. He lifted Portia from Eoan while we were processing the utter cognitive dissonance of him using a meme. As he hoisted her upward, a single arm clasped around her belly, Portia's tongue came unstoppered from Eoan's throat, revealing that it was, really, more of a second mouth:

there were jaws there at the tip, with its teeth locked around a curd of squirming meat.

"I'm going to be sick," moaned Rowan but no one paid him any mind.

"Adam," I began. "Whatever you're thinking, *don't.*"

"Softness isn't a good look on you, Alessa," he chided, and with a writhing Portia draped over his shoulder, he touched a single luminous finger to Eoan's navel.

"*Stop,*" Gracelynn howled, faster on the uptake than the rest of us.

Blood erupted from Adam's ears as the command burrowed into us, forcing all the rest of us to seize in place: lungs and hearts and nervous systems suddenly torn between their genetic prerogative to keep us alive and to listen to the word. But it wasn't enough. Adam smiled at Gracelynn, and it was a testament to their power that his expression seemed strained. I went to my knees, gasping, then fell onto one shoulder. A blue-white light ignited along Adam's palm, spreading over his fingers, climbing to his wrist. As it did, he pressed down, sawing through Eoan's belly like he was a pat of warm butter.

The smell of roasted meat boiled up through the air. My mouth watered instinctively, guiltily, even as Eoan screamed, unable to do more than lay there as Gracelynn slumped to the ground in horror, legs splayed outward.

"Stop, please, stop, Adam Kingsley, stop." They repeated until the words lost their meaning and it was just them weeping softly.

I think sometimes it'd have been kinder if Adam had used a cleaver. Easier certainly for Eoan. Blood loss would have resolved his torment speedily enough. But that would have compromised Adam's scheming. No, he wanted Eoan to live. The rest of us emerged from the fugue of Gracelynn's command,

retching, as Adam completed his brutal work. With the con-
tented sigh of a man pleased at a good day of labor, he set
Portia on the ground and then both hands on the halves of a
now-bisected Eoan, pushing them apart for our review.

"There," he said, patting Eoan on the cheek as the boy
panted the hummingbird breaths of someone going into shock.
"I have a confession. I was actually concerned when Ford made
his prophecy originally. Without Rowan, there's only seven
of us. It made no sense. Half live? How would that work? But
now we can fling Eoan out of the door, prove our first kill.
If anyone needs a more guaranteed chance of survival, well,
I can happily"—he made a *whoosh*ing motion with a hand—
"amputate them."

Rowan, wiping at his mouth with the back of his hand,
spat black onto the ground. He stared at Adam without any
of his usual irreverence, a chill I'd never seen on him crossing
his long, knobby features. "You're sick."

"And you're a corpse who doesn't know he's dead."

"Hungry," whined whatever had crawled out of Portia's
body. I couldn't bear calling it by her name anymore, though
it retained enough of her features to be mistaken for something that could be saved.

"Hun. *Gry*," it said again, snapping chelicerae.

"Take it," said Adam magnanimously. To give credit where
credit was due, he'd done an excellent job bisecting Eoan:
both sections had their arteries cauterized, their veins seared
shut. His work was so clean, the halves almost looked like
artifacts from some medical college: props some lecturer
might use to illustrate the parts of the human alimentary system. No, that's a lie. The top half looked that way. As for the
bottom . . .

I will always recall how the thing that had been Portia

flung itself at the latter, burying its face in the bowl of Eoan's belly, a sight that would have been unnerving enough ordinarily, but there was neither stomach nor liver, gallbladder nor kidneys, just—exactly like Adam had said—a portal through which foamed up shivering curds of pale wrinkled meat. Portia, the spider-creature, ate it all down like it'd walk us back to when we thought we'd get to leave Hellebore.

"I want you to stop breathing," said Gracelynn, mascara bleeding across their cheeks. "I want your heart to stop. I want your—"

Adam winced at the volley but stood nonetheless, dusting himself off before he took Eoan by a limp arm. "You doing that isn't going to change the fact that he's dead already. We can fight, if you like, but I'm going to win and Kevin's sacrifice is going to go to waste. Wouldn't that suck?"

That shut Gracelynn up so hard, I heard their teeth clack together.

"And besides, this way no one has to die so Portia can feed her appetites. Isn't that nice?" said Adam to his stunned audience, his gaze lingering on me. "Sometimes, we do terrible things to survive, don't we?"

I bared my teeth at him. He was right. It was over for now. More violence would be imprudent. At least for now. So we watched as he lugged what remained of Eoan to the doors, tossing him out. And though I'd thought him catatonic from the trauma he had endured in Adam's hands, Eoan still screamed when the faculty found him.

And he kept screaming until morning broke over us like an emptying skull.

BEFORE

The rare times I will unfold him from my memories, like a map to somewhere I can no longer go, I think of my father in the context of mountains. He loved them passionately. According to my mother, he was an arid person: dry in wit, dry of anything resembling emotion. She sometimes blamed it on his tenure in the military, although there were no records to prove he ever served. Sometimes, when she had been drinking too much, she said it was because there was a half-life to being human, and my father had simply run out of time.

Mostly, I agree with her assessment of him. Except when it came to mountains. He loved them with a fervency most parents reserved for children or gods. The few good memories I possess of him involve us hiking along the Laurentians, drinking coffee together on a ridge of stone as he stared out at the gore of a new morning, an oracular yearning in his mild face. He was rarely as animated as he was when we were trekking through such boreal landscapes, fervid with information about every geologic eccentricity we encountered. I wonder sometimes if that was him introducing me to the other half of my genealogical history: neither him nor my mother ever admitted to him having living relatives, after all. Hell, they'd never admitted to him having relatives at all.

The worst thing in the world is dying because someone else said so.

I wasn't a mountaineer. At best, I was an acceptable hiker. But he'd indoctrinated a certain fearlessness when it came to heights, a quirk I planned to capitalize on, given our environment. There was no walking backward out of Hellebore's gates, middle fingers brandished. Those wrought iron horrors were patrolled day and night by the meat stewards, which I'd have happily thrown down with if not for the fact any attempt to even touch the foliated metal was stymied by an advanced example of spatial magic. Once, I spent an hour angrily stalking toward the gates, only for them to remain perpetually ten feet away, the road beyond becoming painted black by rain I could smell but not be anointed by. As a rule, it never rained in Hellebore. Only God knew why.

While there was no official route out, Hellebore wasn't inescapable. At least not if you were inventive. There was a canopied bend of road that curled behind the school's greenhouse, a monstrosity of plated glass and cast iron painted white. A behemoth disrobed of its meat, green where its lungs should have been, green along the carved ribs of its roof. Condensation slicked the glass like sweat: it seemed to pant some nights, heaving with life. Most of the time, Professor Fleur marched us past its front door when leading us to class. But on this day, we had to make use of the more circuitous route—a failed ritual had left a thin lamina of living godbrain over the usual path. If I hadn't already been looking, if I wasn't so desperate to get out of Hellebore, I might have missed it.

But I *was* looking.

In lieu of masonry, the dappled path was corseted by rose bushes grown into barricades, red blooms crowned with thorns as wide as my thumb, the briars themselves so dense only a faint lattice of light gleamed through. Dim and dilute as it was, that light suggested there was an exit there. Professor Fleur led us to a vast copse of fig trees, which seemed to overrun the grounds behind Hellebore. It was under their shade that Fleur had established what could tentatively be called an herb garden and what really should be named a health risk: the plot of land she had cultivated so replete with poisonous flora, it was a wonder we didn't all die breathing the air. Oleander and nightshade grew in pastel eruptions. Rosary peas sprawled everywhere, ladybug-patterned in their gray husks, vivid as a fresh heart. No small amount of the school's namesake bloomed there too: dusky pink and slate, maroon and apricot, the hellebore petals lustrous as fine metal. There were other things too, plants I hadn't names for, vegetation I suspected did not exist in the natural world and were instead immigrants from weirder places.

Because of this and because Professor Fleur had a way of smiling—a very reptilian expression forbidden from ever reaching her eyes—when a student leaned too close to one luminous flower or another, we sat in defensive clusters on linen picnic blankets, careful to always keep an eye on the plant life.

"Here," said Professor Fleur, waddling between each student. On top of being in charge of Botany, she was Hellebore's solitary gardener or so it seemed. "Take this fig and hold it in your hands. I do not want you to eat it yet. I want you to look at it. Smell it."

I held the fruit up to the gray light and turned it one way and then another, recalling some apocrypha about wasps and their role in the pollination of the plant: I'd avoided figs for that reason. There was a hole at the very base of the fruit, wide enough to admit an insect, something Rowan discovered seemingly at the same time, much to the horror of everyone in his immediate vicinity.

"Do you think some wasps have death cult suicide *orgies*—"

"When you see the fig," began Professor Fleur in her quavering voice. "When you taste it, when you crack it in half in your hands and lick the sweet florets, you do not think of the wasp. Although you should. Without it, we wouldn't have this bounty."

She gestured at us to halve our figs, splitting hers with just her hands. Juice ran down her fingers like plasma, dripping onto the grass.

The air stank of a heady sweetness. "It is important we honor the wasp."

From across the garden, Minji asked, "Is it true that there are dead wasps inside every fruit?"

"Dead?" gurgled Professor Fleur. It'd take me another eight weeks before understanding that was how she laughed. "No. Made holy. Sainted."

"Holy," Minji repeated after a moment. "What a choice of words."

The inside of my fig was vulvic red, soft and flushed, whorled with yellow seeds that at certain angles almost looked like eyes but at others resembled the walls of a lamprey's mouth, but instead of teeth there was only flesh. Fascinated, I tried to see if I could pick out a wasp leg or black chitin among the rich pink.

I felt a certain nostalgic affection toward Fleur. Her accent was pure provincial French, slow and languid, every syllable turned into a concatenation of musical notes, so even when she was berating us, it was oddly nice. "The impregnated female wasp drags herself into the fig, anointing the florets with pollen she gathered from the womb in which she was hatched. Then she lays her eggs and in doing so, gives herself to the cycle of death and life, and to the fig to survive. And so, she becomes one of the many unnamed saints."

"I thought this was Botany," said Rowan with considerable glee, patting himself down. "Not Vore 101. Don't hate it, though. Keep going. It's kinda hot."

"Professor Fleur," said Minji again, raising her hand. "I don't understand why this makes the wasp holy."

"Because what is holier than giving yourself up to something better than you?"

Mountains, I thought but did not say. *Clean air. Nights jeweled by frost. First snow. The last light of summer. Being free.* I could think of a hundred things holier than being sacrificed to something that doesn't even love you back. Judging from the guarded looks on the faces of the students around me, I wasn't the only one.

I raised my hand. "Professor Fleur?"

"What."

"Are we the fig or the wasps?"

"Eat," said Professor Fleur, tone unctuous. She threaded through the clots of seated students to where I hid under the roots of one of the school's rare strangler figs. My mother called them banyans, though no else I knew did. I'd only seen them once myself in person on a trip to Cambodia and I'd loved them on sight. Banyans were the opportunistic carnivores of the plant world. Their life cycle wasn't dependent on parasitism: some banyans could go from epiphyte to deadwood without ever hurting another tree. Every now and then, however, their roots would grow in such a way that they'd choke their hosts to death and when those unfortunates had rotted to fertilizer, the local fauna would come to inhabit the bones, thereafter proving that sometimes, things had to die for the greater good.

"There are dead wasps in this fig," I stalled.

"Everything you eat was alive once," said Professor Fleur. She was so exultantly ugly, there was something mesmeric about her: you couldn't be this odious without putting real effort into it. "Anyway, it's not like you will find an actual wasp in your fig. The plant releases an enzyme that breaks down the little insects. Nothing is wasted and sadly, nothing can be tasted. I've always been of the opinion figs could use a more interesting mouthfeel. Don't you agree, class?"

No one said a word.

"Eat," said Professor Fleur again. I could smell her. An oiliness that every old person seemed to possess. Talcum powder. Good dirt, which surprised me. Healthy loam like the sort in which nothing cruel could grow, like what farmers might dream of. Wholesome; a word I'd never think to associate with the school.

"I'm allergic," I lied.

She leaned closer. Her teeth were too numerous and too small for her doll-like jaw, the only delicate feature in a face better suited for a snapping turtle. Skin tags laddered down her jowls; there was a frothing of them at her throat. Fleur was practically cancerous with these gleaming waxlike growths. "Eat."

Trammeled, I did as told. The jamminess of that first bite surprised me as did my pleasure at crunching down on the seeds, the honeyed flavor saturating my tongue, so heady and sweet I was reeling from the taste. I was intoxicated. I wanted to gorge myself. I wanted to eat until I was full and aching with figs, until I could do nothing but wait for the wasps and the other small creatures of the garden to make me something new.

When I was done with that first fig, someone placed a second into the cup of my palms, and I ate that one with as much gusto as the last, lapping at the pith like an animal. I'd have done the same to a third except none came into my possession. Lovelorn, I gazed miserably up for more, every pretense of dignity forsworn for my gluttony. I saw Professor Fleur gazing fondly down at me, with the expression of a doting shepherd looking upon her flock. *Eat,* her expression seemed to urge. *Eat and grow sleek, grow soft.*

In my amber-tinged stupor, I barely noticed Rowan raising a hand.

"Professor Fleur?" he said. When she did not answer the first time, Rowan followed it with a train of "Professor Fleur? Oh, Professor Fleur. Professor Fleur!" in different intonations and with varying degrees of nasality until at last the beleaguered woman turned and snapped, exactly like a reptile, "What do you want?"

"You didn't answer Alessa," he said with complete innocence. "Are we the wasps or the figs?"

Before the woman could answer, Rowan added with a daggered smile, a softening in his voice that did nothing to corrode the cold lapis of his eyes, one corner of his mouth crooked into something dangerous, something like an invitation, a gauntlet thrown at her feet.

"Or am I thinking too small? Should I be asking if we're the non-union farmhands who have no choice but to work for minimum pay, or the fat-cat consumers gleefully piling prosciutto and figs in their mouths as they get ready for that day's orgy?"

"Mr. Rowan Gravesend, I could look forever and I would not find a subtle bone in your body, would I?"

"You're making this too easy, Professor Fleur. You can't tell me you weren't asking me to make the joke."

The fig-induced delirium was beginning to ebb and the void it created soon became tenanted by a migrainous sensation. It wasn't quite the same as the real thing. My vision fractured into zigzag lines, half of it becoming nauseatingly kaleidoscopic, the other like an inverted film negative. But where pain should have followed, there was instead a pressure in my belly, like I'd swallowed gallons of concrete and it was beginning to set. When I licked my teeth, I tasted salt, rust, rot.

Rowan, digging through his pockets, made a small *ah* of pleasure as he found what he was looking for: a beat-up, jaundiced carton of cigarettes. Without so much as a polite check-in to see if everyone else was all right with his habits, he lit up a cigarette, eliciting a tiny yowl of dismay from Fleur, the moment blessedly ruined.

An imperative, shrilled out without interest in decorum: "You will put that out."

"You know, it's hard to have sex when you have to avoid any skin contact. Like, unbelievably hard. No pun intended." He jogged the elbow of the freckled, knob-jointed, red-headed boy to his immediate left. Poor Eoan. He probably didn't expect to be forced to continue associating with Rowan. "But there are ways. Johanna—"

Oh. That was how the two knew each other. *Biblically,* as they say.

At that point, I was coherent enough to muscle past the discomfort of those ocular distortions. The edges of things still bled a liquid white flame and I continued to have to squint in order to focus, but that seemed meager enough a price to pay for the opportunity that presented. With Professor Fleur distracted and the rest of the class mesmerized by

Rowan's antics, no one was watching me. I staggered onto my feet. Sure enough, she ignored me, taking a few steps instead in Rowan's direction.

"—is quite acrobatic, so that helps. You need someone who can come kissing-close to your short and curlies, and preferably, doesn't mind actually kissing the short and curlies—"

"You can stop now," said Eoan tremblingly. His watercolor eyes flicked in my direction. I shook my head, index finger raised to my lips. He dropped his gaze. "We don't need to hear all of it."

"Look, Professor Fleur asked."

"She most certainly did not."

"You will put that cigarette out," repeated Professor Fleur, her voice wobbling with each effortful word, arrowing toward him. Other students were beginning to notice my meanderings to the garden's very edge, their expressions that of cats surveilling an interloper in their territory. Lucky for me, they were still in the process of evaluating if my movements could be construed as misdeeds and whether, in an environment fickle as this, there was more value in tattling or ransoming my secret. We weren't yet elbows-deep in each other's guts yet, you understand. Outside of a few earnest killings, most of us were still hopeful for absolution, for atonement. Murder tended to complicate receiving either. "You will take off your gloves. You will put your hands to the grass, and you will tell my garden you are sorry."

Rowan sucked on his cigarette until he rendered it to a stub. When he spoke, it was through a gargle of smoke. "You don't know. You really don't know."

"I will not say it again: put out the cigarette."

"*N*," said Rowan. "*O*."

As casually as I could, I strolled in the direction of the roses.

The other students were melting from where Fleur and Rowan were having their confrontation. Though the murdering in the school was still unenthused, the atmosphere in Hellebore was such that everyone understood an increasing body count was inevitable. Sullivan's actions the first day had been illustrative. Absolutely fuck-all happened after he murdered the boy, whoever the hell he was. Not a single member of the faculty remarked on what he'd done. The masked janitors—the servitors—simply mopped away the slaughter and that was the extent of it. No investigation, no ostracization. Nothing. So as Rowan continued mouthing off, our classmates provided him an increasingly wider berth.

"Put your hands on the grass."

Rowan considered this. His eyes trailed over the garden until they reached mine, at which point he winked, a stage magician about to perform his favorite trick.

"You know what? Since you asked so nicely, I'll do as you say," he declared, cigarette hanging from the pout of his thin mouth. "I'll put my hands on the grass."

He shucked his gloves, making a big show of liberating his fingers, wiggling them at first as if to say, *Look, I have nothing hidden.* Theatrics concluded, his face shuttered, Rowan then set both very ordinary-seeming palms on the grass outside the borders of his picnic blanket.

And I *felt* it. I felt the innumerable microbial bodies, the vascular systems of the greenery, the tiny, half-awake saplings still in the soil, the beetles, the worms, the nameless worlds in the dark beneath the earth begin to die. Softly, at first. Stutteringly, then in progressively more violent fits: death rolling across the patch of land. The other students shrieked, clutching at one another, trying to avoid the brown rippling outward, the grass crisping, turning black, disintegrating.

"You're a deathworker," said Professor Fleur, withdrawing a step.

"Mmm."

"How is he doing that?" A girl's voice from somewhere behind me.

"Law of Contagion, I'm told," said Rowan with far too much cheer. "If two things have been in contact with each other, a link forms. Saints make shit holy and, well, deathworkers make things dead."

Fleur, her face entirely blanched of color, said, "Stop it."

"I thought you told me to touch grass and apologize to the garden." He bent his face to the dying green. "Sorry, garden."

"Yes," said Professor Fleur, her teeth gritted. "But now I need you to stop."

"But I'm *enjoying* myself."

I didn't hear what Professor Fleur said in return because I saw my opportunity, and had slipped away as the fig trees were shriveling, and the students were beginning to realize those thin barriers of fabric would do little to shield them from Rowan's power. It was a gamble, but what wasn't? I was still calculating my options when I saw Rowan look up to me and mouth the word *run*.

So I did.

DAY TWO

A pall of tension hung over that following morning, suffocating any attempt at conversation. The seven of us separated quietly. I thought about hunting Ford down to demand a more complete picture of what was to come but that felt too much like submitting to one of those tests where they diagnose your potential for developing any variety of deadly ailments. Knowing what hereditary cancers were advancing in your direction always seems like a strategic move until you realize there's no actual stopping them.

So instead, I found an alcove in which to hide, somewhere that felt halfway defensible, removed from the main corridor. The light that wept through the stained-glass windows of the library was blistering, molten. I was exhausted. Enough to pour myself into a piebald armchair the color of tanning vellum and stay there. I think I dozed. I must have. But between the temperature and the grime crusting my skin, the knowledge the Librarian was somewhere in here with us, I did not sleep. But I dreamt nonetheless of its faces, its laughter—or hallucinated such things, at least. I'm not sure if it mattered.

"You look like shit," came Minji's voice at some point, waking me from those half dreams.

As the story went, Hellebore found Minji in the basement of a concert hall, the building staved in, beaten into rubble by a series of freak automobile accidents: like a skull, masonry could only take so much trauma before it broke. Depending on who you asked, the school wasn't even looking for Minji in the beginning. They were there investigating the crashes, and what might have possessed stockbrokers and suburban *ajummas* to run their vehicles into the concert hall in a mass suicide event of unparalleled scale. The answer was Minji, of course. In each of the drivers, they found an overgrowth of papillae in the meningeal stratum, foreign cells livid with what looked like villi. The doctors said it was symptomatic of parasitic worms, but our experts in Hellebore knew better.

It was Minji's hair.

No one knew why her hair did what it allegedly did or how those people came to be infested by it. What was known was that it took Hellebore eighteen days to extract Minji from under the floorboards, and another week to pry open the teratoma in which she was encysted. When she woke, she'd asked the medical team about her twin, except there was no trace of anyone else, nothing save for a swathe of corpses she admitted to having no knowledge of making.

"I feel like shit," I said, blinking, trying and failing to augur the hour from the slant of the light. "Could be worse, though."

"How so?"

"I could have been the one to encourage Adam to cut Eoan in half."

"We're alive, aren't we?"

We. I recalled then that she had said *we* several times last night, had not thought about it then but was certainly thinking about in that moment: we, not as in us survivors, but as a pronoun for herself. I was sure of that. Minji cocked a look at me before she stared out at the wall behind us, its surface papered with a reflective teal material. Deep in the verdancy, gold-eyed foxes prowled through shrubbery and undergrowth, hunting the rabbits cowering in the stylized foliage.

Unable to help myself, I asked, "Has Ford—"

"Has Ford what?" said Minji.

I swallowed. "Has he tried anything?"

She considered this. Her smock was blotched with blooms of rust and flaking gore, but it only somehow added to the tenderness of her appearance. Bathed in the light, with her wide face and ascetic features, she was a lithograph of a fairytale princess: a child bride awaiting her hero, simultaneously very young and terribly ancient. Her eyes however belonged to something older and hungrier than royalty itself. When she spoke, it was without emotion.

"Does it matter if he has?"

Minji cocked her head in one direction and then the next, an animalic gesture exacerbated by her unblinking regard.

"Honestly? Yes," I said, tapping at my cracked lower lip. None of us had thought to bring lip balm to graduation, which feels like a collective oversight when I think about it. Perhaps there is a divergent timeline where our success was recorded for posterity and our pictures were distributed to all the major newspapers. Wouldn't it have been terrible if we were inducted into adulthood looking less than groomed? "Yes, it has always mattered. Even if you don't seem to think it matters."

"It doesn't. Men have been terrible for as long as your kind have existed," said Minji with clinical plainness, the *your* in that sentence given no special inflection, spoken in the same deadened tone as the rest of her statement.

"*My* kind?" I repeated. There it was.

Minji shrugged. There wasn't any challenge in her expression, nothing that suggested she thought this revelation significant or even an epiphany at all. As the line goes, for her, this was a normal Wednesday. "Mine too, I suppose. Most of this body is still human. The brain is human. Mostly."

"You—I didn't—you didn't tell me," I said haltingly, looking Minji over from temples to toes, unable to demarcate what differentiated her from human. Questions frothed. I had a hundred things to ask, a thousand memories to dissect and interrogate, but my tongue sat leaden in my mouth, heavy as a gravestone.

"You didn't ask."

"Fair," I said again. It wasn't a cop-out if it was true.

Minji sank into the armchair with me, her leg sliding over my thigh, an entirely sororal gesture, as was the arm curling around my shoulders. She rested her head in the hollow of my clavicle and despite recent epiphanies, I closed my eyes, glutting myself on the sensation, on the somehow clean salt smell of her. You'd think a lifetime alone would inoculate you against touch starvation but then you're proven wrong.

"Hivemind or weird alien creature?"

"I don't want to talk about it," she said, finality in her tone.

Because I did understand boundaries, I dropped it.

We sat there for an indeterminate period, time macerating, ablating cohesion, softening enough that past and present and future seemed to accordion together, and it felt both like the instant when it became clear we were becoming friends and like we were standing at the other's funerals, eulogizing the dead like we were just girls, miraculous in our mundanity. The air rippled with heat.

"She was dying."

I didn't have to ask who.

"We asked. She said yes." Minji's voice was low and confessional. "They'd been experimenting on her."

"Who?"

"She didn't say. We wish we remembered but we don't."
She nestled closer. Unburdened of her—its? Their?—need for
subterfuge, her voice developed and discarded accents seemingly at random, rising and descending in octave, increasing
in tempo, slowing, the changes occurring sometimes mid-
sentence, resulting in an utterly schizophrenic listening experience. I might have been unnerved if the last twenty hours
hadn't already been so bizarre. "That is a lie. We remember
some things. We remember begging. We remember the laboratory. We remember being unwound, measured."

As she said this, Minji palmed her stomach.

"And someone talking about profit margins and patents, of
course." Laughter squeezed out of her, ebbing in a moment.

I stroked my hand over the shining expanse of her black
hair. Easy enough to pretend we were sisters, that she was just
here to confide a nightmare, and I wasn't frightened by the
fact I couldn't parse which part of her was human and which
part of her was not. Flesh lied, it seemed.

"Of course," I said gently and because it felt important, I
asked: "Do you know *why* they were . . ."

Minji nuzzled even closer. "Because no one would notice if
she was missing."

It wasn't the question I asked but maybe it should have
been. History ran red after all with missing girls, forgotten
girls. Sluts and martyrs and everyone in between. Of course,
Minji's vessel had been one of them. I squirmed until I could
look her full in the face. Her eyes were very nearly black even
in that rich peacock light.

"Why did *you* choose her?"

"Because she was alone," said Minji in someone and
something else's voice, each word laid down like it was glass,

like we'd both shatter if she spoke too loud. "Because she asked."

Then her face hardened, locking like a door.

"Because of all these things, we're going to protect her, you understand. With luck, we'll figure out something before we have to kill each other. But if it comes to it: no hard feelings, Alessa. We can promise it will be quick, at least."

"I wouldn't expect anything less."

Minji smiled thinly and we sat then in a new silence, aware we had, very companionably and without a shred of animosity in our hearts, declared, in fewer words than perhaps were merited, that we would eventually be at each other's throats. Whether such a time would come to pass was irrelevant. The words couldn't be taken back and a sliver of me would always regret our honesty in that moment. Minji parted her lips, was beginning to speak when I saw a face crane around a corner.

Ford.

"Get fucked," I told him.

He had a court once, a smaller one than what Adam or Sullivan had kept, but there were people who'd whored themselves for his guidance. I wondered what he told them about graduation. If he'd lied, if he read them false futures, if he gilded those lies with their biggest wants. Or if all this had come out of left field for him as well, a possibility I didn't like entertaining as it opened the door to other worries, like how many others of his prognostications were false, and I was full up on anxieties and heartache at the time.

"I seek the love of my days, my promised one, she who will live in my heart and she who will survive in your flesh," said Ford, eyes only for Minji.

I knew that look. There wasn't a woman anywhere who hadn't, at one point or another, seen a man drape his arm over a sister's shoulder and thought, *If I let you out of my sight, this is the last time anyone will see her alive.* Looking at Ford then, I *knew.* I knew what was coming. I was almost part of that statistic before.

"Out," I said.

"My beloved, my light." He half moaned those words. They were an offering, a sacrifice he made of himself. "You said you had use of me."

Minji unstrung from my arms to stride toward him, her expression flat as polished tone. Her hair, previously orderly, writhed and shuddered, rising from its coiffure to float through the air like she was moving underwater. I thought, *There you are. It was so obvious. I didn't understand how I could have mistaken her for human.* Going on tiptoes, she gently tucked his damp curls behind his ears, a gesture that would have almost been tender if not for how opaque her face was: she might as well have been an engraving, or the flat of a sharpened blade.

"I do," she said soothingly, tone ritualistic. "And you will give me all of you?"

"All of me for all of you."

It wasn't ever Minji who'd been the one at risk. She bent her head to him, pressing her mouth to his glistening cheek, and there was such a lost look in his eyes, the surrender of a calf in a killing chute. To my surprise, I pitied him. Kissing my fingers to the pair in salute, I left my armchair and the alcove and Ford to whatever justice waited for him in the blaze of that strangely quiet afternoon.

BEFORE

I could smell the garden dying as I raced away, a sweet vegetal rot that clogged the nose and coated the insides of my mouth. Flowers bloomed with sudden frantic energy and died with equal zeal, lining my escape with a crisp carpet of graying petals. Alarms blared. I couldn't tell if it was because of Rowan's antics or because Hellebore had been alerted to my attempted escape, but the bells were tolling and the best-case scenario would still likely involve someone looking around and going, "Where the fuck is Alessa?"

I increased my pace.

No one stopped me as I hit the roses' broad-leafed shadows; no one came to intervene as I wormed into the foliage, pressing into the thorns with abandon, hoping they'd take their pound of flesh and *let me go.* I was nearly sodden with my blood when the ozonic scent of open air overtook the roses' stench. A second later, my vision flooded with a white glare.

I was free.

Free enough, at any rate. Free to travail down the bluff and whatever other obstacles would surface along the massif, to die in the process: to get my head smashed open, have the splinters of my bones bake in the sun once the birds had their way with my guts. Most people might balk at calling that freedom, I guess, but at that moment, it was to me. When you have had your every freedom pared from you, you learn to hoard the manner and time and method of your death: it becomes the only thing that is really yours.

I blinked until my sight welled back: everything still a little too bright, limned in phosphorus. Birds wheeled through the air, unperturbed by how I clung to the roses, half of me flung outward like a ship's prow, my weight balanced on the ball of my right foot. A childish part of me half expected an applause of heroic music. What I received instead was an echoing scream as somewhere a rabbit was dragged out of its burrow and eaten.

Welp, I remember thinking.

Gingerly, I repositioned myself for the downward crawl, going to my belly and heaving my legs over the edge. I dug my toes into the cliff face, levered myself lower, lower, and—

There was the weight of a hand settling on my left shoulder, and then, polished floor under my feet. Before I could sufficiently process either of these sensations, the pressure on my collarbone increased. The air stuttered; a sharp taste of tin, like bloodying my tongue along the lid of a can. I was being pushed down into the deep cradle of an emerald armchair, sinking into its cushions, but also I was falling, hands losing purchase; my grip slackened, the mountain howling up, hungry.

"Miss Li."

My head ricocheted back into the cool velvet. I blinked twice, mouth still syrupy with magic.

The room I was now in was bedecked in cold jewel shadows: furniture in onyx and night-dark emerald, crushed satin curtains the color of old blood in a back alley. Portraits filled the walls in serried columns, the subjects in school colors.

They regarded me with the same phobic wonder as the woman standing before me.

"Headmaster," I said, flashing her the sunniest *who, me?* grin.

Divested of her mask, she looked even less human than she usually did. There was something of a coyote to her features, an elongated quality to her limbs and jaw, like there'd been a muzzle there before it had been hammered flat: the bones cracked and configured to simulate personhood. Between her and Professor Fleur I was beginning to wonder if the entire faculty were even human.

A plait of ivory hair draped over the headmaster's right shoulder. She wore a cassock—absinthe green where the light shone on the fabric, the material patterned with the school crest, padded at the shoulders—like the people in the paintings behind her, who I could only assume were headmasters past. Incense wafted through the room—her *office,* I corrected myself, as I took in the plinth of a desk squatting in the middle of the space, the folders stacked high on the surface. Beside it stood one of the masked servitors, trembling.

"Your complete attention when you're speaking with me, Miss Li." She took my chin very lightly in a gloved hand and angled my face, dropping to a knee so her eyes were on the same level. Her touch was cool.

"Just taking in the sights."

"Focus," she said, both hands on my cheeks. "When you are spoken to, you focus. Do we understand?"

"Sure."

The headmaster could fuck herself with her pointy, buttercup-buckled boots.

"Hellebores," said the headmaster. "Like the school."

"What?"

"They're hellebores," she clarified, the ghost of a smile wafting over her predator face. This close, she smelled animalic, carnal. "Not buttercups. You should know better. Your father was a man who loved nature, wasn't he?"

My blood went to ice. "Can you read my thoughts?"

"No," said the headmaster, winking. "But I can see where your eyes are looking."

She rose then, letting go of my face. Despite her platitudes, I remained suspicious and watched as best I could as she circled around to the back of my chair, until she coiled both arms around my shoulders.

"That wasn't very wise," she chided.

I had too much dignity to feign innocence. We both knew what I'd done and I wasn't going to give her the pleasure of seeing me cower from punishment. So I tipped my chin up at a rebellious angle, earning a low chuckle.

"Nor is touching me without consent."

"You lost all rights to consent when you enrolled—"

"*Enrolled?*"

I started to rise only to feel her nails puncture my skin, feel her push down, holding me in place. The headmaster might have looked like a length of bone swaddled in jacquard, but she was strong. Monstrously so. I could *not* move no matter how I writhed; the mountains around Hellebore would have yielded before her grip did. Unable to glare at her, I settled for glaring at a portrait of a wizened man who leered at me from across space and time and pigment, his mouth crumpled in a way that made me think he wore fedoras whenever he could. Something about the consistency of his skin, an odd shiny glutinousness, that made me think he was related to the current headmaster.

"I was *kidnapped*—"

"Is that how you see our charity?" asked the headmaster in a tone of false horror, erupting into a guffaw. The alligator snap of her laughter had the servitor flinching so hard, it went down to its knees, arms clasped around its legs. "As a kidnapping? As an act of violence? Goodness me, that will never do."

At the *never do,* the headmaster released me, allowing me to spring to my feet and move a comfortable distance away from her reach, aware that the foot of space stretching between us would mean nothing if she decided she would be a bitch about it, but as with a lot of things, it was the thought that counted.

"It was an act of grace, my dear," said the headmaster. "A stay of execution, you could say."

A downy chill settled over me, sinking through skin into marrow.

"What are you talking about?"

"My girl," she said, flowing to her desk. Her fingers ran over the manila folders—each of them unmarked and a lightless indigo—until they arrived at one in particular. She pinched one corner and pulled, freeing it, before extracting a sheaf of papers from its mouth. I caught a glimpse of a face in the documents, and another frisson of cold worked down my spine: it was a photo of me; a younger me, a mugshot from when I was found with my stepfather's corpse, thirteen with bad hair and acne-pocked skin and the thousand-yard stare of a child who hadn't quite come to terms with the fact that not only was she a murderer, she didn't dislike being one. "You have been under our observation since the day you tore your father in half."

"I was cleared of all charges."

"Only because of incompetence," she said cheerfully. "And sentimentality, really. People never know how to react when a child is on trial. I had it on good authority that at least half of them were convinced of your guilt but they felt bad about sentencing someone so young and sweet. *What a lovely girl,* they said to one another. *It'd be wrong to destroy her life.*"

The headmaster fanned out the papers and gestured me closer. Reluctantly, I complied, studying what she had on display. It was everything. My school records, printouts from CCTV footage, witness testimonials, rental agreements, pages from a journal that I had kept between the ages of fifteen and twenty; pages I knew had been burned down to cremains. I swallowed, raising my gaze to her once I'd taken stock of her trove.

"What do you want?"

"I don't want anything," said the headmaster. "Well, no. That's a lie. What I want is for you to know that if Hellebore had not intervened, you'd have been lobotomized. You'd have had your brain sliced up before they shipped you off to do some governmental dirty work. I promise, you don't want to be part of that."

"So you want me to be grateful."

Her smile lengthened by an eighth of an inch. "No, no. I don't want that. I don't care if you're grateful. I want you to know that Hellebore has enough power to circumvent the ambitions of entire governmental bodies. That the word of God has less authority than my signature. And if you think you can escape the school, that there is any way you can leave without graduating, you're not only a vicious little creature but a very stupid one."

The headmaster sat down behind her desk, fingers tented, her expression mild.

"Any questions?"

We're the wasps.

If she thought she was going to get a rise out of me, she was sorely mistaken. I kept my expression bored and tepid, with a slightly astringent sneer for good measure. I cannot count the number of people who have attempted to cajole, cow, and otherwise coerce me into doing what they wanted. It was one of the central reasons behind why I ran; my mother was no saint but she didn't deserve being subjected to that carousel of bullies tiptoeing up to our porch, half of which seemed to think threatening her would motivate me toward compliance. (Spoiler: it did not.)

Here now was another person, another *stupid* punter, gleefully trying to extort obedience from me. Briefly, I entertained the notion of testing my powers on the headmaster but a) I was angry, not stupid, and b) even if I successfully deposed the headmaster, there would be the rest of Hellebore to contend with and even I wasn't arrogant enough to think I'd survive that. Not yet.

She looked me over. "Some of you are the wasps. Some of you, like Miss Khoury, even rise to become queens. But you're not that. You're a corpse soaking in enzymatic secretions, hoping to be useful for the first time in your life. You're not a wasp, no. You're just raw material until you learn better. And for your sake," said the headmaster with the satisfaction of a dowager explaining she had spent her fortune and her vulturous children would inherit nothing but lifelong resentment, "I hope you do. What else do you want to know?"

"Threatening me isn't going to work."

"I'm not threatening you," said the headmaster with another effervescent laugh. She gestured the servitor closer, crooking two fingers in its direction. When it had shambled into reach, she wove one finger in a circle and the masked figure broke into sobs. As I watched, it went down first on one knee and then another, retrieving from a drawer in the head-mistress's monolithic desk the daintiest pearl-handled bone saw I'd seen in my life.

"A threat is a statement of *intention*. What I said was fact," she said, hooking a leg over the knee of the servitor. She propped an elbow on the armrest of her chair and set her chin in her palm. Almost imperceptibly, the headmistress nodded, the tiniest motion of her chin. In answer, the servitor ran the bone saw over its mask and around its skull, like it was a tin of dog food being roughly opened up. When that was done, the headmistress slid a nail under the lid of the servitor's skull and flipped it open, revealing an expanse of brain. "You are a vicious, stupid creature who thinks of nothing but surviving to the next day. Fortunately for you, I know what to do with food-animals. Which is to say, I allow them to live until their appointed time unless they fuck up, in which case—"

She hooked a finger into the servitor's skull, dragging it along the rim, before lifting the accumulated brain to her mouth. Her tongue was pale and gray as it lapped up the clot of gray matter, her smile languid. I didn't have a comeback to that, to any of what was going on. She took in how I was trembling: teeth gritted, fury radiant enough that I could pretend I couldn't see my own fear through the glare.

"Now get out of my office. You've wasted enough of my time already."

DAY TWO

I couldn't tell you how long I had walked in this agony of reflection, half hoping something, anything, would happen, and it'd all just end there. I was acutely aware the Librarian was there in the building with us, but where? I was no longer just physically tired; I was also emotionally exhausted. There was only so much trauma one could accumulate before the nervous system buckled under its weight. In comparison to everything else, being eaten alive felt simple at this point.

Mostly, it'd been Ford's eyes. As I was moving to leave the alcove, I saw the lost look give way, just for a second, to fear. He was in there. The lights were on but the doors were locked and the windows barred. Whatever else Minji had done, she had not—not fully, at least—disconnected his awareness from the world, which made me wonder if he'd been conscious of those hairs burrowing into him, if he'd been screaming inside the walls of his own mind as those fine strands punctured his corneal membranes.

I found myself wondering if it had hurt worse because he hadn't been permitted to scream.

"There you are. I've been looking all over for you."

I jolted at Rowan's voice. He slunk out from around a corner. I stared at his face. The deep shadows of the corridor had aged him somehow. I could see how if the years got to sap what little puppy fat he had it would crevice. I could tell where the weak jaw would recede into an excess of jowls. If he lived to be an old man, Rowan would thin to a long-limbed strip of ruddy-skinned jerky.

"What do you want?"

"Did you fucking see what happened to Ford? I didn't know Minji could do that. I didn't know a person could do that. I've seen a lot of shit but that was in a class of its own. Like, what kind of—" Rowan's hands shook as he patted at his pockets, his sleeves rolled up his bony arms. "Shit, where are my cigarettes?"

"Maybe because she's not a person."

Rowan stopped his search, wide-eyed as he said, "Shut up."

Long welts of blue shadow dappled the walls. I could still feel the weight of Minji's slender frame nestled against my side, hear those voices, and it'd been easy then to forget what she was with the salt scent of her skin in my nose, easy to put aside the fact she wasn't a human as much as she was a reservoir of parasites. I ground the nail of my index finger against the meat of my thumb, slicing at the skin until it was pared away, the pinprick agony enough to reground me in the moment.

"Between the teachers and the Librarian and Minji, I'm beginning to wonder what the hell Hellebore really is," I said. There was so much blood in the proverbial water, it was almost a clot in my lungs. "Do you remember what the Librarian said?"

Rowan didn't get the chance to answer. Gracelynn barreled in, relief washing across their features as they laid their velveteen eyes on us.

"Thank god," they said, hands outstretched for ours. "I thought—I thought—"

Neither of us intercepted that attempt at intimacy: Rowan installed his hands in his pockets and I took a step back, wary. Gracelynn slowed in their approach, hands closed into fists before they let them drop. Nonetheless, the relief did not abandon their expression.

"What did you think?" I said.

Their gaze ricocheted between Rowan and I, both of us smothered in shadows too dark for the sweltering afternoon. "I thought Adam might have done something to you."

"Can't be worse than what she did to Johanna," said Rowan before he let out a soft *aha* of pleased discovery, removing from a pocket a battered cigarette.

Gracelynn froze. I scowled at him.

"I'm sure there's something we don't know," said Gracelynn, licking dry lips. "I know Alessa. She wouldn't do anything like that for fun. We must be missing something and if—"

Suddenly, I thought of Gracelynn's spouse. I thought of them holding each other in the dark, and how Kevin had opened their veins to the shadows as the faculty surged toward us, how they'd kissed Gracelynn before they told them to run, told them not to look back, told me to keep them safe. Like Kevin, they'd absolutely die for someone else, counting themselves lucky the whole miserable time because it'd be a noble sacrifice they'd made, and it was all I could do not to scream.

"I'm an asshole. It's not that complicated."

Gracelynn's brow rucked.

"What are you talking about?" they began cautiously.

"Look, I don't want to talk about what happened," I said. "But I will say this weird little attempt at humanizing me? Totally unwarranted. I did kill her."

Something in their expression stuttered, gave up its last breath, and died. I'd be the first to admit they'd done nothing to deserve that. Their only fault was a suicidal amount of kindness but I can admit now what I refused to acknowledge then: I'd been afraid Gracelynn might think me worth martyring themself for. There were people I imagined were worth dying for, folks like poor Delilah and unlucky Sullivan, people like Eoan even, who played badly but had done his best with the rotten hand he'd been given. I wasn't one of them.

Not even close.

"Okay, okay, theydies and gentle psychos, please, come on," said Rowan, sidling between us. "Let's focus on what's important."

"And what is fucking important here, Rowan?" I said, teeth gritted. "Tell me."

"Getting out, obviously," said Rowan with far too much cheer, waving an unlit cigarette at me. "Hear me out. What if we all embarked on a nice trip into the stacks again?"

"What the hell for?" I demanded.

"Well, Eoan did us a favor. He overfed the Librarian before he, uh, went ahead and started becoming an all-you-can-eat buffet for Portia. This is the perfect time to go back in there and finally get the answers we want."

"Better plan. How about," I said, "we find Portia. Take Eoan's remains back from her and I don't know, smother Adam in the remains. Get her and Adam to kill each other."

"*What?!*" demanded Gracelynn, their repulsion so great, I could hear the extraneous exclamation mark.

"Sure," said Rowan. "But how about we table that as a backup plan and try my plan first?"

Some leviathan weight slammed itself against the wall so hard, the ancient oak moaned and cracked and broke. Dust fountained from above with every impact. *Whumph. Whumph. Whumph.* I backed away from the wall, an arm raised and laid across Rowan's chest, nudging him back. Six feet from us, one of the lights recessed into the ceiling seemed to stave into itself, its glow dimming, dying with a shiver.

"Looks like the Librarian woke up from its food coma," said Rowan.

"Then keep your voice down," I hissed.

The centuries-old masonry whimpered as it was climbed, a vast weight crawling into the ceiling above. More dust billowed down, veiling us with a fine white film. I touched my index finger to my lips, a warning. Then, nothing.

"We go now," I whispered. "Or we go never."

We heard something scuffle above us, like the world's largest dog turning in circles before it bedded down for the night.

"Well?" I said, staring pointedly at Gracelynn.

They scrunched their face at me. "Fine. Let's go."

The stacks were quiet when we crept back into the main hall and stayed so despite our paranoia. Hours passed in a fugue of surreptitious research. Despite our certainty the Librarian would find us, we remained undisturbed. Not that it mattered. None of the books, at least none of the ones in reach, yielded anything useful. And as night at last absorbed all color from the sky, it became clear all we'd succeeded at was moving the library's collection from their appointed shelves to a pile on the floor.

Sighing, I crumpled cross-legged onto the ground. I studied how the shelves sloped away into the darkness. The serried rows that had looked so beautiful when illuminated by the church light now made me think of teeth; the ceiling was a cavity, a throat leading to the black of an unseen digestive tract. The gold leaf inlaid in the blistered frescos of carnivorous deer and oversized wasps no longer gleamed. Instead, it was now the color and texture of boiling fat. It was almost ironic how absolutely banal half the library's contents were: it even contained annotated copies of every transaction the school had had with the outside world over the decades. We're talking hoarder levels of records.

There was still so much to read but we'd run out of time again.

"Alessa?" It was Gracelynn.

"If you're here to cry at me," I said, rising to see them standing on the opposite side of the shelf I'd been leaning against. "You can just—"

Gracelynn ignored my vitriol and instead held up what looked like a collection of crumpled, yellowing, coffee stain-mottled notes, all held together by a particularly hubristic paper clip. "I found something."

"Show me."

They circled around to where I was, riffling the pages with their thumb. I saw photos there, half-faded Polaroids. "I figured that if we were going to find a way out, we should maybe start by seeing who'd built what in the library. Figure out the bones of the place and all, you know? Fortunately, the school's kept excellent records. There's stuff here dating back more than two hundred years. I was looking through them when I found this."

Gracelynn handed over the hodgepodge of papers: students records, medical files, letters someone had written that the school I assumed had confiscated—but I only had eyes for the photographs, for the girl scowling up at me through the past. "Wait—"

"Uh-huh," said Gracelynn in a hushed tone.

I flipped through the pages again, checking each in turn. Much of the ink had faded over the years, gray now with time's passing, but the letters all had the same handwriting, a florid cursive all but extinct in this day and age, yet uncannily familiar.

"That's her handwriting but that—that isn't her face. That's not—how? I don't understand. It can't be." My voice stumbled as I stared down at one photograph in particular, of a woman, older now although not by much, in front of a mirror, painting her own self portrait. I knew the room she was in, had stood in it the night before. I knew the bend of her mouth and the tilt of her jaw, the shadows settled into the sockets of her eyes, knew the long gracile line of her throat: flesh changed but bones were eternal. I couldn't understand how it'd taken so long for me to realize this. "I can't believe that's her."

"It is."

My blood chilled to sludge. "Why did she change her face?"

"Maybe, she didn't do it herself. Maybe, the school made her transform." said Gracelynn. "Or the Raw Mother. I heard stories about others—they were changed too. Horribly. The Ministry had to take them away. I honestly don't know, Alessa. What I do know is that people would probably have questions about Bella Khoury not aging."

"I don't understand why she's here or how—" Except this *was* Hellebore and the idea that the girl I'd sort of harbored complicated feelings for had been alive for centuries didn't actually seem improbable. "She always spoke about Bella"—my voice trembled around the name—"like she was someone else. Why hide it?"

My voice died midway through my musings.

"Haven't you ever noticed that Portia's a bit . . . forgetful?

I can't tell you how many conversations I've had with her where she'd say one thing and then just not remember she said it. At first, I thought it was stress." As Gracelynn spoke, their gesticulations grew more animated though their voice did not, their Southern lilt made sweeter by their hushed tones. "But maybe, maybe it's because they broke her."

"I remember her asking me to go to a party. There was a card and it'd had a dozen signatures, but I was sure she'd faked all of them," I said, thinking of that first day when Portia had stood soft-eyed and smiling beside the self-portrait of Bella, and I wondered how you might torture someone to make them forget the work of their own hands. "I wonder . . ."

I riffled through the letters; they were all addressed to the same person: a lover that would not come to Portia, could not have come to save her even if she had every desire to, not with the missives here. I was struck ill by the thought that somewhere a girl had grown old waiting for Portia to come home. Swallowing, I said, "But what about the Raw Mother? What did she have to do with this? Why is she in the school? Nothing in this fucking place makes sense."

Gracelynn set the folders down onto the floor.

"Kevin and I, we researched for months before we decided we wanted to enroll here." They couldn't meet my gaze, could only stare down at their shoes as they spoke. "They're—I mean, they were so meticulous about it. By the time we enrolled, we knew just about everything there was to know about Hellebore. Except why all the graduates stay with the Ministry. I remember writing that down. I wanted to ask someone about that. Because that seemed off, you know?" They swallowed.

"But when I walked through the gates, something happened. Suddenly, I remembered seeing the graduates that the headmaster mentioned. In interviews. In person. Graduates whose names weren't in my notes. They do something to us here, Alessa. I don't know what or why. But they do."

Again, that chill, that feeling of my grave trampled.

"What are you saying, Gracelynn?"

An ichorous substance pearled down from the ceiling, an oversized amber droplet of something incandescently shimmery: like lava, or heated gold. It hung in the air for the moment and then landed on the tiles between with an audible *splat*.

The residue began to sizzle.

"Shit," I said. "The Librarian's awake."

BEFORE

I'm not ashamed to say I slunk back to my dorm room after being dismissed by the headmaster, starving for the comfort of the familiar. Like a child, I wanted to crawl under my blankets and cry until any urge to do so dried up to something more sensible, like maybe a devouring fury at my circumstances.

Unfortunately, my ambitions of being pathetically miserable were circumvented by the fact that not only was Johanna in our room when I arrived, she had her faithful friend Stefania in tow. If my roommate was a summer heatstroke in human form, Stefania was the dead of winter: porcelain skin and pitch-black hair, a mass of silver piercings along both ears, black clothes and platform boots that gave her the look of a nineties goth and at least three inches on the two of us. The two stared at me, expressions like those of teenagers caught passing their mother's best bottle of scotch between them.

"Well," said Stefania. "This is embarrassing."

It took me a moment to parse what the hell she was referencing and when I did, any desire to sit and feel sorry for myself went away, obliterated by indignity.

"What do you think you're doing with *my duvet*?"

Until they slipped out of my mouth, I didn't think that I, or anyone else for that matter, could fill the words *my duvet* with so much possessive fury. The two girls shared a look, eyes traveling guiltily down to the corners of the blanket they had in their hands: it seemed I'd interrupted them midway through housekeeping. Behind Johanna, a pillar of pillows slouched, denuded of their covers, a few feathers poking out of their skins. My clothes had been folded and shoved to the side, separated into two distinct heaps—handwritten *keep* and *donate* signs hastily hung above them—which made little sense as it was all school-issued but hey, sure, there's no accounting for fashion.

"We're . . . we—" Johanna started and stopped, dropping her gaze, the skin around her cheeks and the graceful curve of her nose bridge turning a liver-red, embarrassed, I guess, to be caught molesting my bed linens.

"We thought you were dead," Stefania said with much less drama. She had the thickest hair I'd ever seen on a person, irrespective of gender. She wore it loose over her shoulders, which made her appear even paler.

If I was someone more tedious and we were somewhere less dangerous than Hellebore, I might have said something to the tune of, *Why the hell would you think that?* Instead, I stared at the marauded nakedness of my bed and asked, "Yes, but why are you fucking around with *my* bed?"

"We thought, if you had, well, um—"

"Died?" I supplied. After several months together, I felt safe in saying I loathed her. Unused to dislike, I guess, Johanna had all but waged war on my dislike of her, ambushing me with presents, besieging me with compliments: it was a surgical effort, beautiful in its thoroughness. It did jack to improve my opinion which unfortunately just exacerbated Johanna's need for approval. Hell wasn't just other people; hell was living with them.

Johanna winced. "That, yes. We thought it would be an opportunity to, you know, move Stefania in."

"I told you it wouldn't work."

"*You* said it was because Hellebore would reassign the room share to someone else," Johanna shot back, one corner of my duvet dropped, the other woven into increasingly tight knots as she spoke. "It *was* a good idea."

"How about you two kill whoever Stefania's roommate is and move Johanna into their spot?" The pair froze, gaping at me. When neither of them moved to riposte or comply, I said exasperatedly, "Just go away."

"Is this because of Rowan?" asked Johanna with sudden deranged mischief, filching a long rectangular envelope from the inside of her cardigan. She thrust it at me, the previous conversation seemingly forgotten in the wake of this question.

"Rowan?"

"He told me to pass you this note," said Johanna. "Well, invitation, I guess. He wants you to meet him in the graveyard."

I took the envelope from her, turning it over, examining the luxurious cream paper, the debauched lap and its broken wax seal, the last a scintillant indigo, embossed with what I now knew was a warning symbol: a mark that said *here was a deathworker.* With a finger, I traced the ridges of the design: a headless crow with one wing spread and the other a bloody wreck. I frowned.

"When did he give you this?"

"He gave it to her yesterday. At lunch," said Stefania. "He said it'd make sense. So kudos to him, I guess, for being right."

I read the letter inside: it was brusque, to the point, the contents precisely as Johanna described. He wanted me to meet him in the school's cemetery at midnight. *For Reasons,* he'd written, underlining the words thrice, as though the unnecessary capitalization wasn't emphasis enough. I looked up to find Johanna staring earnestly at me. Preoccupied with the weirdness of the entire situation, it took longer than it should have for me to realize what she'd done.

"You read the letter."

"We thought you were dead!"

"This was private." I didn't care about Rowan but it was the principle of the matter. An oily warmth rode up my throat and spread out to my ears. I kept my voice a white-knuckled calm, saying, "If you ever touch anything of mine again, anything whatsoever, I'm going to unstring you over Hellebore like you were a ball of fucking yarn, you diseased little rat."

A cheap shot, a gun in a knife fight. I knew what I'd done but I couldn't help myself. Johanna jolted like I'd slapped her hard, her face angled to hide the psoriatic welts fountaining up from her collar. In the beginning, it'd been scarcely more than a discoloration, like she'd been kissed too hard by a lover. Over the weeks, the bruise grew abscessed and the lesions spread, a constellation of sores that wouldn't heal for love of magic or modern medicine. Johanna eventually took to wearing high-necked shirts and dresses, which worked until it didn't. I knew it killed her to be disfigured like such. I knew it was dickish to mention her condition.

But I didn't care.

I was angry. There wasn't anything in the room that belonged to me in any substantive way; I'd have been happy to burn all of it if it'd get me released from Hellebore. I had no attachment to any individual item. None of them carried sentimental value. Nonetheless, they were mine, and I hadn't consented to them being touched, or moved, or put aside so someone else could make themselves at home in the ruins. I

also most definitely hadn't agreed to have my personal corre-
spondences read.

"*Chill,*" said Stefania.

"Die in a fire," I countered inventively.

Rows of teeth cracked apart at her shoulders, the knobs of
her wrist bones, the long stem of her throat. Through them,
I could see wet muscle and a myriad of tongues, coiled in the
shadows like worms or a bulge of intestines. Stefania raised
one corner of her lips in a snarl, her dark eyes very nearly
black in the evening light. "We can see how much chiller you
get if I take off a limb."

"Oh, please. We're in Hellebore. You're *not* scary."

Stefania swaggered forward a step, the duvet forgotten in
a heap.

"I'm not trying to scare you," she said. "I'm just telling you
what'll happen if you keep fucking around."

I decided then that I wanted a fight. It'd been a long enough
day. I no longer wanted to cry myself hoarse but there was
nonetheless a welter of raw emotion that needed release or I
would implode. A fight, one full of literal teeth, with someone
who acted like they were spoiling for the same, felt exactly
like what the doctor had ordered.

But then, because she was that kind of sanctimonious
bleeding-heart showboat, Johanna rushed between us, arms
out and palms raised so we would keep separate.

"Please," she said, voice trembling. "It was an honest mistake. We thought—"

"I was only gone for a few hours!"

"Days," she corrected.

I paused.

"What do you mean *days?*"

"As in, multiple twenty-four-hour periods," said Stefania, a bit unnecessarily. "Three, to be precise."

"I've been gone for three days?" Any thought of violence died with the revelation. My interlude with the headmaster had felt like minutes. I could have understood it being actual hours, what with how trauma could smudge one's perception of time. But days? Small wonder that Johanna had given me up for dead.

"People die quick around here," said Stefania.

"In that case," I said. "I guess I'm . . . sorry for losing my shit."

Johanna spluttered. Stefania tensed like she'd expected me to sucker punch her. When it became clear I was being sincere, the pair dropped their own pretenses. Johanna collected herself; Stefania zippered up the mouths that had opened across her, faint red inflammations where the lipless maws had welded themselves shut the only sign they'd ever been there.

"Words I'd never thought would come out of your mouth," said Stefania. When I glared at her, she shrugged, unrepentant, and said, "Johanna is my best friend. I have heard all the stories."

"Look, it's fine," said Johanna, her smile brittle and bright as glass, a fever light in her blue eyes. "Things happen. We're all tense. Alessa, I hope you can forgive me—"

"Done," I said, not wanting to hear her flagellate. "As long as you can promise me you haven't given away any of my things."

"We were hoping to disinfect them first, so no," said Stefania.

"Under different circumstances, I could see us being friends," I said.

"Under different circumstances," said Stefania in return, "I could see eating you."

I shouldered past her to where they'd stacked my personal effects, leafing through the piles, still unsettled by the thought that the headmaster could *control time.* There'd been a glutinous hallucinatory quality to those first few weeks, a sense of being toyed with; of lost hours and endless afternoons steeped in a fatal dullness, the tedium such that it made me desperate to do crimes. Now, with this recent discovery, it felt like a definite thing, the implications of which terrified me in a way I wasn't at all ready to process. So I locked my abject horror behind a smirk, hoping neither of them would scent my new weakness. "And I wouldn't even need to ask? You're such a darling."

"Fine, I'm a *little* sorry we ransacked your side of the room." Her expression said this was the most contrition she was willing to show which was, well, fair. Anyone who'd ever met me knew Stefania was justified. Myself included.

I twitched a shoulder in her direction in acknowledgment, and Stefania rolled her eyes. Johanna sighed. I didn't blame her. There'd been progress in our relationship, something she had made clear she was overjoyed about, and it was evident that all of that would be set back by this confrontation with Stefania.

I glanced at the reading nook she'd cajoled me into helping her assemble: we'd scavenged furniture from across Hellebore, pulling it from shadowed corners and store rooms, even a standing lamp from the amphitheater where the headmaster performed her inaugural address. The armchair we recovered last week—last month, last year, *who fucking knew* with a time-bending headmaster—was the crowning piece: piebald for the most part but still beautiful where it wasn't, a linen-toned cream scarified by years of use, but so very comfortable from the weathering. It was into its seat that Johanna poured herself, knees to her chest, an arm comfortably wrapped around her legs. She stared at me, beaming sunnily, like we were girls at a sleepover and not trapped rats.

"Are you going to tell us what the story is with you and Rowan?"

I stared uncomprehendingly at her for a pathetically long time before what she meant clicked in my head.

"Oh," I said, intelligently. The thought of being in competition with Johanna for anything, least of all a *boy,* curdled my stomach. "No, it's not like that. I promise."

She pursed her mouth. "I'm not jealous."

The remark caught me off guard.

"Why would you be jealous? Oh."

Stefania rolled her eyes with so much enthusiasm, I briefly expected them to clatter onto the floor. "Everyone knows they're sleeping together."

"I did not need to be part of that group," I said. "Also, how?"

Johanna pinked winsomely.

"Barriers are a thing," said Stefania, tugging at the skin along her nose bridge, aghast to play interpreter in this frankly uncomfortable conversation. "It's basically magical herpes."

I mimed frantically hanging myself, flinging an invisible rope over the rafters and tugging with due gusto. "I did not need to hear those words. *Magical herpes.* Kill me now. Take my room. I want nothing more than to die. Don't let me live a life knowing those words have been said in sequence."

"Oh my god, Stef!" said Johanna.

"Well, it is. Anyway, they do a lot of hand stuff."

My roommate's cheeks deepened from an attractive

rosiness to a lurid, nearly purplish red. For once, we were in alignment: neither of us were happy to have the mechanics of deathworker sex outlined so thoroughly. Groaning, Johanna sank her head under her pillows, while Stefania looked dispassionately on.

"I interrupted. What were you going to say?"

"Kill me," I said.

"Me first," said Johanna and I was alarmed by how dangerously close we were to developing a rapport over this.

I studied the letter again in lieu of contemplating the logistics of avoiding *magical herpes,* affrighted at the concept I might be misreading a proposition. The triple underline could have been symbolic of sexual intent, I suppose, but I was practically illiterate in the habits of my own generation so who the hell knew?

"I don't want him."

Johanna sprang back up. "It's okay if you do—"

"He's a skinny weirdo. Sorry you don't have any taste."

"Speak for yourself," said Stefania, settling on the satin nightmare of Johanna's bed. Snacks were spread over the foliated duvet, the sight of which made me only nominally sorry for my own continued existence: they'd been planning a celebration.

I thought about this more. I didn't know yet what I felt about Rowan; had rarely, if ever, spent much time dissecting my feelings as a general whole, but I knew I didn't hate him. Something about him resonated: a sense of kinship, of recognition and being recognized.

"Look, the two of us are entirely too alike for there to be any kind of attraction," I said. "Just, no."

"Mutual interests are important for compatibility," said Johanna and then: "It's okay. Honestly. We're just friends."

"With benefits," said Stefania.

I chewed on my first response a dutiful twenty-five times before swallowing it down, smiling instead as Stefania broke into a packet of sriracha-flavored corn chips. "If you say so," I managed, and it almost sounded polite.

"What the hell happened in the garden that day?" asked Stefania. *Crunch. Crunch. Crunch.* She ate with her mouth open. "Fleur was furious."

"He was all the school could talk about for a day and a half. A deathworker *here* in Hellebore," said Johanna. "Most people weren't aware of this beforehand. Now they are, and well, I think that's a good thing."

Deathworkers were almost indistinguishable from folklore at this juncture of history. Most died while in the gestation phase, necrotizing their mothers' wombs within days of implantation: the poor women were inevitably found liquefied, sludge and rot and nothing more, their little embryonic murderers dead in the decay. The few deathworkers who survived to birth generally found themselves snapped up immediately, spirited away by cults and demon-possessed ministers, anyone with ideations of world domination. Rowan was a winning lottery ticket, an urban legend, and now, with the stunt he pulled in the garden, he was a target.

"I don't understand why anyone's surprised," said Stefania, a sigh in every syllable. "If there was anywhere you'd see a deathworker, it'd be here."

Johanna shrugged. Semantics weren't of interest to her, were rarely ever of any interest to her as they had a tendency to muddy the story, and it was the story Johanna loved best. She stared at me, unblinking, those green eyes of hers like tumbled malachite, deeper than Rowan's, richer in hue.

"Whatever the case, are you going to go see him?" she said a little breathlessly.

I reread the letter—*note,* really, but his overelaborate packaging of it was the stuff of Jane Austen romances, and the word *letter,* with its implications of careful thought and long meditations on content, felt like the only word that did the presentation justice—Rowan had sent for what felt like the umpteenth time, lingering on the *For Reasons.*

"Sure, why the hell not?"

Day Two

"Flesh-maker, dark-song, *food-animals*," sang out the Librarian as it spiraled down from the ceiling, a vortex of luminous scales, all wide-mouthed smiles, as its faces blinked shining tears down on us, like an Ophanim from the Bible. More of that gold splattered down: a drop hit my cheek, scalding me. I hissed from the pain. "I can hear them through the walls, talking about how they want to eat up, drink you up, devour you."

The Librarian lowered farther, becoming illuminated.

"When I say," whispered Gracelynn, "you run."

I shot them an incredulous look.

As if their words were a cue the Librarian had been anticipating, it accelerated. There was no time. No time to think, no time to breathe, to parse the thing's monstrous speed, its reaching hands, the sheer number of them, there were hundreds, gold-tipped, etiolated; all I could see was a centipede grown to a size of myth, with human faces where scales should have sat, lunging for Gracelynn, folding itself around them, cocooning them: a chrysalis opening in reverse, the insect swallowed up by its reconstituting pupa.

With Gracelynn in its grip, the Librarian, terrible and beautiful, almost human if you could force yourself to only regard it from the neck up, catapulted back upward. I heard them scream, a wet, thin noise.

"For before," sang the Librarian. "For when I asked and you said stop, for when I begged and you told me no—"

Through the dark of the shelves, I saw Rowan skidding toward us, then stopping. And I heard Gracelynn singing in their voice once again, that clarion silver voice that was as beautiful as the end of days and as terrible as creation. I couldn't tell you how they did it but their voice fractured into a madrigal, into a choir. Warmth oozed from my ears, my nostrils, my eyes: a liquid heat I recognized immediately as blood. I blinked twice, trying to un-gum my eyes as my tear ducts became clotted, but soon all I could see was a smear of crimson and blurred silhouettes.

Run, I thought I heard them scream through their song.

I was tired of running. Since arriving, that had seemed to be all I was doing but it felt worse to stay, to waste Gracelynn's literal swan song, and if I was going to be honest with myself, it seemed a waste to die there when I'd survived for so long.

And besides, for once, I knew where I was going.

It was the wet hiss of television static seeping down a corridor that stopped me in my tracks. Hellebore abhorred technology. Classes were taught with blackboards, lessons scraped painfully onto porcelain enamel. What Hellebore could duplicate with magic, it did, regardless of the cost. I had thought the library would be similar and for the most part, that guess had been right. Most of its knowledge was preserved the old-fashioned way, computers and other accessory technologies relegated to mentions in dust-covered encyclopedias like they were the ones who were relics of a bygone time.

To hear the sound of electronics, that familiar whine, that surprised me more than I expected. Light fed through a half-opened door in the darkened corridor. The walls were finned from ceiling to floor with shelves. On each shelf were video tapes. Hundreds of them. Thousands of them. Crammed into a little room was what felt like every production made for viewing on a home video system, all neatly labeled and alphabetically filed. It'd have felt quaint if not for the fact I could not stop imagining the Librarian here, snuggled into the interior, raptly watching old Westerns while the rest of us slept or died.

A single television radiated static at the otherwise unlit room. The cathode light from the vintage machine sheened the walls with an unwholesome pallor that made me think immediately of old horror movies. It was loud but it wasn't enough to disguise Gracelynn's song, which filled the halls: *Run, Alessa, run, run.* The couch had its color obliterated by the television's flickering glow, the palette of the room somehow flattened to the same eerie greenish gray.

"Alessa?" said a voice.

"Minji?" I said to the silhouette atop the couch. "Is that you?"

"Did you know the Librarian has an extensive collection of horror movies? Bad ones, good ones. It hoarded everything," came Minji's voice. "And it made notes."

My vision adjusted to the murk. Under different circumstances, I might have found the tableau before me hilarious. She wasn't sitting on the couch but was perched instead on the top of its central back cushion, straddling Ford's shoulders.

Her hair floated out from her in a nimbus, some of it cozied around the blades of the fan above her, some of it more ambulatory. I watched black tendrils feel their way over archipelagos of throw pillows stacked on each end of the couch; over armrests and across his shoulders, twinning around his neck like they were a lover drawing his throat close for a kiss; spilling down and over the carpet. *They look like they are searching for something,* I thought. I did not want to figure out what for.

Her voice grew fond. "Do you want to know what kind of notes?"

"I'm afraid to ask. Minji, I need your help. Gracelynn—"

"It's a good answer."

"Fine," I said, digging nails into my palms, wishing for different, wishing we'd all gotten better, her and I and them and every digested sob in the faculty's belly. "What kind of notes?"

"On dying," said Minji, patting Ford on the cheek. His head lolled away from her touch and settled at an upsetting angle.

"What did you do to him, Minji?" I asked, wincing. He wasn't dead. His heart still shuddered in its cavity, his lungs moved. But his neck. That was so broken I was surprised his head sat somehow still attached to his shoulders.

"You could say we made things easier for him. He was in pain before and it didn't seem right to keep him that way, you know?" She seemed to sift through her thoughts. "Life is a bitch and then you die. That's the promise most are given. You get to die eventually. You get to make the pain stop. But then there are entities like the Librarian, like the faculty, like me. We don't die. Not in any meaningful way. We dream about doing so, though."

"Maybe you can help with the Librarian then." I swallowed. "It has Gracelynn."

"No."

"Why the hell not?"

"Because we have more in common with the faculty than we do with you," said Minji with a gauzy, unselfconscious laugh, confirming what Rowan and I had suspected. "And because we made a promise to her. We'd protect her. The rest of you, well . . ."

She patted Ford on the skull like he was a puppy. It felt hypocritical to pass judgment, to be dismayed by this admission. Given what I was and given the place we were in, the company we kept and the cruelties we inflicted on one another, how could I hold any prejudice against monsters? Still, my stomach turned and I tried not to picture Ford *screaming* in his own head.

"At the end of the day, you're all just meat."

It's not the same, I wanted to say, but even there in the shelter of my own mind, the words sounded infantile, stupid, arrogant. Demands were made when there was a power differential in your favor, not when you were nothing more than steak in the freezer. I was livestock chatting up a rancher.

"And you? What are *you*?" I said, forgetting the urgency of the tableau outside, just for a little while, struck by the strange feeling I'd found something worse.

"What are *you*?" countered Minji, more convincingly a person, her eyes flashing with humor. She cocked her head at me as her hair spread to line the walls, the shelves, the floor, until I was standing on the very edge of a black box of pulsating keratin. "Can you tell us what's inside you?"

Outside, Gracelynn's song stuttered.

"Bones, muscle, organ—"

"What are those? How do they make you *you*?"

I eyed her distrustfully. "What do you mean?"

"What *are* bones?" said Minji, the air itself sheened with her hair, like the television had bled outward, filling our world with static. "What *are* organs? What *is* muscle? How does it all relate to the miracle of your consciousness?"

I was acutely aware I stood with my back exposed, and there was a thing outside with Gracelynn, a thing that could not die and only wanted to die, would do anything to die. And I wasn't sure anymore if there was time to run out of.

At that moment, Ford rose, swaying closer, first going down on one knee and then the other, head still bent at that eye-watering angle. Minji took his face in her hands, kissing him perfunctorily, tongue flitting into his open mouth. When she pulled away, a string of drool shone between their lips. Laughing again, she kissed him on his brow, his nose.

"If it helps, we suspect Gracelynn will be one of the lucky ones," she said. "They at least will just *die*. They will not be trapped in that mass of flesh outside screaming and scream-ing and screaming forever. Not like you. Not like Ford. Poor man. Shall we give her a show, darling?"

Ford moaned. He dug fingers into his solar plexus, clawing at the steeple of his ribs until the flesh tore and a wound like a mouth yawned open. He dug until the wealth of his entrails slopped onto the carpet, prying at the membranous tangle, pulling, pulling. I couldn't understand how he was standing upright still. Minji had made him carve his abdominal cav-ity clean. Ford was nothing but blood-greased bone and bare muscle, nothing but skin and a haunted stare.

"If it helps, we don't think the faculty *wanted* this to hap-pen. We think they'd have been happy if their work with Ford had succeeded. If they could have just filled him to the brim with their bodies and let him carry them out, none of this would have happened. This wasn't personal."

Down went Ford on his hands and knees, improbably alive, sifting through the still-steaming heap of his organs like a dog questing through the tall grass for a lost toy. He raised his liver to me, his heart, the desiccated sac of his stomach, his kidneys in succession. Then at last, the long coils of his intestine, which he nuzzled with his cheek, moaning. He had the soft dull eyes of a cow, like something that had never been taught to speak.

"We're afraid you were right. The universe does bend toward cruelty. For something to live, something else must die," said Minji. "Think of the school as the fig. Something must be done to extract value from the corpse."

"I don't understand any of this." I hesitated. This was torture. This was hell and one of its demons hard at work on a sinner. "Or whatever the fuck you're doing to him."

"Only what we need," said Minji primly, smoothing down her skirts. "Rude of you to think we would not take advantage of this gift, this eternally renewing source of magic."

With that cryptic statement offered up, Minji turned then to Ford and I saw her hair close over him like a funerary shroud, like flies settling on carrion. He vanished under the seething blackness. Before I could ask Minji what she meant, I heard the sharp *crack* of bone snapped along the lineation of a joint, heard muscle peeled into half, heard Ford gasp softly, as though surprised, and from that writhing mass of hair came a neat panel of calcium and flesh, raised up by a tendril of hair. Minji's face warmed with adoration.

"Tell me something." I said.

Crack. "Yes?"

"If you're like the faculty"—I knew the answer. I knew it like I knew the soft treasures of the human body, the wrinkled frightened edifice of the brain. I knew it like blood, like the roar of it in my ears—"why are you doing this to Ford? Can't you just walk out there?"

"Oh, yes. Most likely." *Schlorp.*

"Then why are you doing this to him?"

"Because. We hate him." Minji did not look at me, only at the meat her hair had now carefully set on her shoulder like a fragment of a pauldron. "And because we thought they'd like a gift."

Her hair was becoming more frenzied. Once again, that crack, that wet noise of human tissue shearing apart, the sounds increasing in volume, building in tempo. I took a step back. I could practically *feel* what she was doing, the excruciating dismantlement. Bone by bone, tendon by tendon. How Minji's hair was levering Ford apart, sectioning him, so it can reconstruct him as armor for her. I could feel his heart, panicked, seizing, wanting to die, wanting to stop, but being coerced to beat on.

"Adam would have kept him by his side until the last moment. The faculty deserve their toy back, don't you think?" said Minji very reasonably. The pieces were being attached to her more quickly now, and her hair was beginning to grout what spaces there were with clots of his entrails, packing it all down, tight as they could. "And besides, it's funny."

"You can't just walk out wearing him like a suit of armor."

"We can, actually."

She said this as the plates of Ford's skull closed over her face, his own meticulously flayed from the bone so it could be draped over Minji's like a visor. She stared at me through the sockets, her half-lidded gaze serene, and if there was any mercy in the world, the haruspex would be dead now but he wasn't. I tried to ignore the latter, the writhing evidence of his survival glistening redly in the light, keeping my eyes instead on Minji as she examined first one arm and then the other, the whole of her now entombed in Ford's remains. An unsteady laugh shook itself loose from my mouth: it was that or scream.

"Why are you making me witness all this, anyway?"

"Because when this is over, you're the only one we'll think fondly of." Then with a chuckle, she added, "Tell Adam we hope he dies screaming."

BEFORE

During the day, you'd think summer had an eternal stranglehold on Hellebore. From morning to the deep violet dusk, the air was as hot and wet as the inside of a mouth panting from a fever, and it stank oppressively at all times of floral pungence, the smell of green things in riotous growth. It was worse inside. Hellebore didn't believe in central air or breathable fabrics. We sweated through our classes, clammy in our uniforms, the reek of our sweat adding to the unpleasant atmosphere.

The nights, though, were much different. My breath plumed white as I passed the wrought iron gates leading to the graveyard, hands slippered in my sleeves, fingers cupped around elbows. To an observer, I probably resembled a disgruntled monk albeit an ostentatiously dressed one: rabbit fur trimmed every hem of my very festive velvet coat. On another person, someone like Johanna or Portia, who was tall and whose body had aspirations toward beauty, it might have maybe looked a degree of good. I wasn't such a person and we'll leave it at that.

Despite the growingly murderous reputation of the student body, very few of us made any habit of wandering the graveyards. (Really, few made a habit of walking unaccompanied through Hellebore.) Before this, I used to suspect it was out of collective and subconscious superstition, accrued osmotically through daily life in Hellebore, a life that seemed to frequently involve a lot of undue risk. But crossing the threshold, I felt a kind of primordial anxiety, something both bone and brain stem seemed to recognize, and I wanted to escape. I wanted to *run*. I never wanted to run. Not like this. Not with the desperation of a fawn losing ground to a pack of dogs. My head swam with adrenaline.

Rather than behave like a normal person, I stood there and breathed until the fear was gone, forcing each inhalation to last for eight counts and each exhale to do the same. Easier, yes, to cave to impulse: to run when and where it tells you to go. I had no idea if someone was watching me in the dark, but they wouldn't have the pleasure of seeing me disarmed by a particularly enthusiastic panic attack. Slowly, I began finding my equilibrium again: my pulse slowed, restored to its usual clop.

"Not going to lie. Kinda impressed, actually. Most people would have legged it. You've got more balls than I gave you credit for."

Rowan.

I looked up to see him slouching down a path, one of the many branching from the entrance like capillaries, headstones and grave markers jutting from the shadows. Here and there, a mausoleum loomed from between the tessellation of black fir, the leaves desaturated in the cold moonlight, not altogether barren of color but grayer than any healthy plant should look. He seemed at ease here and I realized then I'd never seen him so unguarded, his face gentled, *young*.

"What the hell do you want?"

"Help," he said plainly.

Rowan could make a funeral out of a Christmas party: the vivid red of our school-assigned winter coat was a cheerless vermillion on him, like blood that had begun to cool. He looked like a butcher, drenched through.

"I know, I know, I'm not really good at talking to people seriously. Snarking, yes. Being an asshole, *sure*," said Rowan, in visible agony at having to behave like a normal person. His lashes were iridescent with frost. I was very afraid he might have been crying throughout whatever had led him to the graveyard this late in the frozen night, and that it would be my responsibility to comfort him through his misery. "But this whole *being vulnerable about your needs* thing is really new to me so forgive me while I flail around a bit."

"You get ten minutes," I said pointedly. His boots, I realized, were damp with mud. All of him was crusted with dirt of varying levels of moisture.

"I need your help," said Rowan. "I have some books inside the library that I'd like to find but I need someone to distract the Librarian—"

"It's a library. You can just use normal channels to borrow said books."

"Come on, Alessa. You know that doesn't actually work. They don't really want you to make use of that enormous reservoir of knowledge."

I shrugged. "Okay. Find someone else to help you."

"You're the only person I can trust."

"Do you think I'm an idiot? Find a better lie."

"Okay, fine. No lies. No more prevaricating or whatever," said Rowan, his gloved palms offered up like an olive branch. His buzz cut had grown into a fleecy stubble, his curls beginning to tuft along his hairline, and it gave him a curiously puppyish look, an impression compounded by the fact his hair was the deep copper of a poodle's coat. "You're right. You're not the only person I can trust. It's more like you're the only person here who doesn't have vested interest in the school."

"I find that *incredibly* hard to believe."

"You're the only person who has ever given me the time of day without trying to stab me in the face."

At this, I had to laugh, a short bark of noise that curled his mouth into a hopeful smile. It went away when I said, very nonchalantly, "I'd buy that. Still, no."

"I'll help you escape the school."

That caught me off guard. I'd lost three days to a head-master who had openly threatened me with a lobotomy if I stepped out of line again. I was cold, and it was dawning on me I was risking said procedure for a boy who shouldn't exist and who I barely liked—just for a very tenuous *maybe*.

"How?"

"I have ways, okay? Trust me," said Rowan, for whom being difficult wasn't just a habit but a higher calling, a compulsion equal to his fondness for cigarettes. On cue, he attempted then to light one, only to have the wind pinch out the flame a second later. He tried again a second time, a third, before calling it on the fourth try as the wind tumbled the cigarette from his hand. "Just give me five minutes. I have also not smoked in two hours and it's *not* helping my mood."

I stared at him. Rowan stared at his cigarette, very plainly evaluating the cost-benefits of retrieving it from cold graveyard muck.

"Sure," I said when it became apparent he wouldn't be use-ful until his bloodstream was replenished with more nico-tine, another cigarette removed from its packet. He hunkered against a nearby memorial: a very traditional-looking angel that had long gray arms stretched out to nothing, like it was imploring a soul to come home, its bow-shaped mouth so lovingly sculpted you'd think it was modeled on the memory of a first kiss. The air soon smelled of cloves and tobacco. It was under its half-furled wing that he stood, face in silhouette. Feeling generous, I added, "I'll help you."

"Really?"

"Yes," I said, cursing inwardly a second later when a finger-gun was cocked in my direction. Irreverence was contagious. "Just try not to make it weird."

"I don't know if I can promise that," said Rowan. Still in shadow, he waved his cigarette as he spoke, marking punctuation, the cherry a tangerine wisp bobbing in the dark.

The chill had begun to pool in my joints, less an interpretable temperature than an ache, like a haunting. I rubbed my fingers, blew on them, and that did nothing except spread the cold around. Rowan was smoking his cigarette like it could save him, and I wondered when was the last time he slept.

Then, he added: "Thanks."

Rowan spoke the words with uncharacteristic passion, with the libidinousness of a flagellant opened up for his god, his desperate heart offered on the platter of that single syllable. I took a step back. I was many things, but I wasn't stone and I certainly wasn't impervious to being the recipient of his focus, his feverish want. My cheeks warmed as the clouds shifted, the moon laying its light over an eternity of tombstones, and I thought about how lonely someone needed to be to worry so much about those already beyond saving.

"Now, let's get some knowledge!" he declared, tossing his head like a prize stallion. No stain of his earlier vulnerability, however faint, lingered. The Rowan I knew was restored: crass, swaggering, eminently punchable. It was nearly perfect, this facade of his, but having seen it set down, I realized now how friable it was and how thin.

But I was absolutely relieved to see it, anyway.

"Yeah, let's do it!" I said with more gusto than I'd mustered my entire life.

Rowan having sincere emotions was one thing. Rowan having sincere emotions about me *specifically* was another. Especially right then in the dark of the graveyard and after an indeterminable amount of time since my confrontation with the headmaster. I needed at least eight hours of sleep before I could conceivably process even the idea of a romantic confession, particularly given his association with Johanna. I didn't have an issue with nonmonogamy. I just didn't want to be in a toxic throuple with those two.

I noticed then that he was staring at me. "I guess it could be worth it."

"What are you talking about?" There was that look again, that intense attention.

"Ford said you'd be worth dying for," said Rowan, lighting another cigarette.

"Ford said what?"

His reply was swallowed by a scream that shredded the air.

It said a little about Rowan and a lot more about me that we simultaneously bolted *toward* the source of the howling, all without consulting the other or pausing to debate whether forward was actually preferable to escape. The scream was the baying of a cornered animal, it was the scream of someone who'd stared death in the eye and was now jonesing to break its neck. That guttural defiance, more than any subcutaneous sense of nobility, was what had me running for the source: I understood too well to turn away.

The screaming led us toward the back of the school library,

an imposing monument of gray-brown brick and gorgeous Palladian windows inlaid with church glass, traceried frames rampant with wasps and stucco deer skulls, because *of course.* A cyclopean rose window stared from above the double doors of the main entrance. On a plinth outside the front steps, the statue of a teenager resplendent in one of Hellebore's very twee uniforms, a gladstone bag in one hand, gazed admiringly back.

"*Give them back!* Give them back to me! You will *listen.*" The voice we'd heard was now screaming demands. "You'll give back my spouse. *Give them back to me.*"

"You feel that?" said Rowan as we slowed.

I nodded. Each time the voice roared, an answering twinge shivered through me. On some mechanical level, I wanted to please the voice. I wanted to return said spouse, do whatever it took to salve its anguished rage. It wasn't mind control, per se, but close enough to be discomfiting.

Rowan shouldered past a broad-leafed fern and there, banging their fists bloody against a service door, was a soft-figured femme in a confection of silks and crinoline, some of which I recognized as scavenged from the school's upholstery. Whoever they were, their skills as a couturier really were quite good.

"Hey," I said. "What the fuck?"

They whirled around to face us, expression feral and panicked. In repose, they might have been beautiful, cherubic with a kind mouth and heavy-lashed eyes, the irises a lightless velvet, but the whites were lacy with broken capillaries and their skin was a black ruin of makeup. Gore matted the wet tangles of their hair, which was the pink of bloodied spit.

"She took them," they panted, glancing miserably behind

them. "She took Kevin. We had *permission*. We hadn't gone over time. She had no right to take them."

"Who took Kevin?" I said.

"The Librarian." They pressed the heels of their hands into their eyes, their shoulders fluttering like trapped birds, like they would cry if they hadn't forgotten how.

"Oh," said Rowan. "Well, that's actually kinda convenient."

DAY TWO

I watched as Minji, enveloped now in Ford's carcass, walked into the corridor and the gloom, horror fluttering in my chest, like a dying sparrow beating itself against the glass of a window. I felt like a guitar string wound too tight, like a garrote tensed for use, or a hare in its burrow, knowing there wasn't anywhere else to go. My head hurt, my heart too. I'd crawled so far past fear and exhaustion, the world seemed differently luminated: the colors too saturated, the light cold and tinged with blues. And Gracelynn's song was ebbing, slowing, *dying.*

Half live if Rowan dies.

As if on cue, I heard him scream.

BEFORE

As you know, most libraries are meant for the unrestricted use of whomever is in need of their facilities: refuges for the shy and the unprivileged, the impoverished student. Reservoirs of knowledge staffed by the excessively curious and the professionally methodical. Libraries, as a collective, are where you go if you are looking for a place that can't conceive turning you away, especially not if you're eager for education. In my experience, most libraries were basically perpetually at the verge of kidnapping passersby, handing them a catalog, and breathily going, "What can we convince you to read *today*?"

The library at Hellebore, however, was different. Appendage to the main campus, it acted only in the faculty's interest, which seemed to revolve exclusively around fucking us students over. It disdained visitors. It delighted in being impermeable and I suspect in the knowledge that we all knew it contained every book ever written or that would be written, work we'd never be able to make use of as the library was a vault with no door. Access required navigating a byzantine amount of nonsensical paperwork: applications and forms that were often in contradiction with one another, often demanding a student go speak with a teacher no longer on the payroll, or report to an office on a floor that did not exist. Most of us, we didn't bother. The effort didn't seem worth it.

Plus, there was the question of the library's warden.

"If the Librarian's taken your spouse, there really isn't anything much we can do for you, I'm afraid," I said. "They're gone. You—what's your name, anyway?"

"Gracelynn. Gracelynn Wilder," said our new acquaintance, knuckling at their mascara-smudged eyes.

"Gracelynn, you should know as well as the rest of us that if the Librarian has them, your spouse is as good as dead."

"Please help me," they said anyway.

Rowan lit his fourth cigarette of the evening, eeling around us to gently rap his knuckles against the plain metal of the service door, its hinges, testing the lineaments with intense curiosity. The cold hadn't improved remotely.

"Is this a trap?" asked Rowan.

"Test me," Gracelynn said immediately, a sleeve rolled to bare a soft forearm. "Trap? No. Look. Bleed me. Ensorcell me. Put me under. Dig in my brain. I don't *care*. Do whatever. Just help me. I need to save Kevin."

They inhaled, sharp, like the name had cut their tongue, like they'd stuff it back down their throat anyway if they could even if it gashed them in the process. Gracelynn's eyes were wild with a terror of calculations. But then, with a noiseless sob and a sudden loosening of their shoulders, they said, with a shame I didn't entirely understand, "Kevin can get you out of here."

That had me careening to a stop.

"Does everyone know about that?" I demanded. "Did a school newsletter go out? The hell's going on?"

"You were gone for *days*. Either you had died, which would

have been so sad." He made a jerk-off motion with his hand at this. "Or, you'd done something to piss off the school and generally, Hellebore doesn't give a shit unless you're trying a jailbreak," said Rowan.

I didn't like the thought that the whole of Hellebore was potentially aware I'd failed at escaping, or how it might adjust the school's esteem of me. I wondered how many people now saw me as weak, as *prey.*

"Keep talking," I said, outwardly ignoring Rowan.

"Kevin—they work with shadows." Gracelynn swallowed. "They can use them to let you travel anywhere. It's quite easy for them."

It was no secret that half the campus had enrolled out of desperation, hopeful that Hellebore might illuminate some technique for domesticating the terrible things inside them; to quiet the voices, calm their hungers; to stop the brood of ancient gods they'd been involuntarily nursing in their ribs from waking up and flossing with adjacent cartilage. But three months in, I couldn't imagine most not regretting those innocent hopes. The school didn't care what we did to one another. I was poleaxed, unable to reify the idea of someone like Gracelynn choosing to stay when escape was an option.

"Why are you two even here then?" I exhaled and there was hurt there that I wasn't expecting, a rawness in the question. Gracelynn's throat, I saw, leprous with scars: claw marks and knife wounds, fingerprint-sized indentations like someone had tried, at a loss for better weapons, tried to sink their hands through Gracelynn's skin and *tear.* "If I could get out of here, I'd have run ages ago."

"This is the only place where the shadows can't..." The hyphen of skin between their very straight brows rucked with concentration. "Well, let's just say it's safer for them at Hellebore than it is for them outside. They can sleep here. They can rest."

"What do you *mean* they can sleep here?" said Rowan, his investigation of the door concluded. He trotted back up to us, looking quizzical.

Gracelynn smiled, if you could call it that. It had the stretched idiotic quality of a skeleton's grin, an accident of biology, and so displaced from actual humor, even Rowan shuddered a little to witness it. The smile didn't last, thank god, brought down by a grief that seemed so old and familiar now, it might as well be a friend. Though their skin was unfretted with crow's-feet or laugh lines, buoyant enough to be called babyish, there was nonetheless a terrible sense of age, of Gracelynn having grown old before their time in the way people did when they'd kept vigil by a deathbed for too long.

"When we're elsewhere, when we're outside these walls, the shadows keep trying to get Kevin to go home," Gracelynn said with far too little inflection, a telling neutrality in their resonant singer's voice. Never had I been more convinced of someone's ability to belt out an aria with negative effort; never had I shuddered at the way someone said the word *home*. "And they badly do not want to."

Having offered that cryptic explanation, they turned to me again, a terrible dignity in their face.

"We're wasting time. Please help me get them back."

"I'm sorry, but we—"

"Actually." Rowan took an extensive drag from his cigarette, his spare hand cupped over the cherry to shelter it from the wind. Someone who wasn't looking for signs might have thought his expression bored. "I think we could help."

He waggled a gloved hand in the moonlight.

"Magic, turbo-speed syphilitic touch," said Rowan. "Also, three people are better than two when you're trying to distract something's attention. If you agree to help us, we'll help you."

"I didn't—" I swallowed my next words. I resented being volunteered but I resented being caged in Hellebore more. Here were two people promising me a way out and as much as the situation sounded like it was too good to be true, I couldn't look a pair of gift horses in the mouth.

"Yes, I'll help," said Gracelynn.

Gracelynn was now staring at Rowan not with pity but a pained recognition, the look of someone who'd had the misfortune of bleeding themselves on the same road.

Faced with compassion, Rowan did what I was learning was custom for him: he snarked harder.

I looked back to our new acquaintance. "Anyway, I think he's offering to kill the Librarian for you."

"Or just cause it a urinary tract infection. I could do that. I have no idea if our dear old curator of the world's knowledge is even capable of dying, but if it is, I promise you it's dilly-ding-dong *dead* as a doorknob," said Rowan.

"I don't need it dead," ventured Gracelynn.

"Listen, I respect your commitment to pacifism or whatever you'd like to call it," said Rowan. "But there is no reasoning with the Librarian. Trust me, I've done my research. It's the Librarian's way or the highway. Unless, of course, you kill it—"

"But can't we . . ." Gracelynn searched for the words. ". . . disable it? I don't know. This doesn't seem right."

"We're wasting time," I said. My brain examined *dilly-ding-dong dead* and decided there would be no commenting on the phrase for fear there'd be a repeat, so I turned the whole of my attention to Gracelynn. "Either decide you want to get your spouse out or let us go do what we need to do."

"It'll be fine, I promise," Rowan said. "Chances are the Librarian, being the learned being that it is, is going to know exactly what I am and go, *What? A deathworker? In my stacks? Heavens no! I will do everything I can to get him out!*" He grinned, strutting over to drape his coat over Gracelynn's shoulders, a kindness delivered with such remoteness, it was almost like his arms and hands were piloted by someone else, someone with no relations to the hubristic jerk in command of his mouth.

"Come on. I haven't drunk any scotch in weeks. *When* we get your partner out of here, I want a bottle of scotch. Hell, make it a whole goddamned crate."

I wish I could say that we did the intelligent thing of scaling the library and maneuvering to a higher level, finding access through the window of some obscure archive, which we opened by cannily picking the locks. Similarly, I wish I could say we dismantled the service door and walked in through there like competent thieves. While I've never felt any compulsion toward honesty, there's something tragic about a lie so blatant, you're too ashamed to give it air. Which is, really, a roundabout way of explaining we went through the front door.

"You're really making us walk straight inside. Like, straight in," I said, taking the stairs two at a time, trying to keep pace. Rowan had about eight inches of height on me, most of which seemed to have gone entirely to his legs. Gracelynn jogged stoically behind, bogged down by their endless skirts.

Rowan, oppressively lanky, did not slow for us. "Nothing says confidence like taking the front door."

"Nothing says *suicide* like taking the front door," I repeated, bounding up the wide, flat steps, and thrusting myself in front of Rowan, arms out.

He crab-walked three steps to one side and then three to another, rubbernecking unnecessarily around the top of my head. I mirrored him like an inconvenienced pedestrian before realizing the clownishness of it all, and stopped, a fist resting on my hip.

"Do you have a death wish or something?" I demanded.

"What? No. But, like, do any of us really have a choice when it comes to death? Do we not all eventually get folded into the arms of oblivion? It's really just a question of when, isn't it?"

"Yes, but did you want to die *today*?"

"Of course not. Come on," said Rowan, and it annoyed me to discover I couldn't convince my body to turn back. "If there were any other routes into the library, I'd be using those. Unfortunately, there aren't. I've looked, trust me. There's only one entrance."

"That doesn't seem smart, to have one way in and out." I palmed his breastbone and pushed lightly, leaving Rowan to pinwheel several steps back down. He was astonishingly light: bird bones under a wrapper of skin.

"Well, it's so heavily warded, we'd explode into chunks right here if we thought about trying a different way in. Hellebore spared no expense at making this a fortress."

Or a prison, I thought.

To my horror, he bounced back up to me and *chucked my chin*, his mouth coming so close to my earlobe, my skin warmed with his breath. "I promise if the worst happens, I'll say you two were my hostages, and you had nothing to do with this all, and you can run away and tell everyone I was incredibly sexy and you were turned on watching me be a hero."

Rowan pulled back. He smiled like whatever he saw in my face—his was sheened with the orange light gushing from the open and unwelcoming doors—was a benison, and resumed his march into the library's vestibule.

Gracelynn came gasping up to my side. They wore Rowan's coat like a mantle, draped over their shoulders, giving them the look of an overgrown robin, or a vulture gory with its last meal.

"What happens if he is wrong about this?"

"You run. Fast as you can," I said.

Gracelynn stopped dead. "And?"

"I run with you." I watched as Rowan's long, frayed shadow chased him through the doors of the library, and then looked back to Gracelynn's blanched face. "What?"

"You'd just let him die?"

"You really don't know me, do you?"

Whether it was my tone, the horrendous reality of the situation, Gracelynn's own wretched fears for their partner, I'd never know. Their throat bobbed a few times. They said nothing after that, only nodded once, a small terse motion, before they gathered their skirts and bounded up the stairs. I followed after, and we entered in time to hear a sonorous voice, a voice that went through the bones to the very marrow, a voice you'd think would sound unkind or vexed, but instead was girlishly elated, booming:

"You were not *expected*."

The vestibule of the library was as imposing as the rest of the structure: camphor floorboards, polished until they seemed a light source unto themselves and redolent of incense; a vaulted ceiling, with wooden ribs from which girandoles dangled, filled with wax candles the color of fresh bone; tapestries on each wall. Opposite the entrance: a brass counter of monstrous size, gilded, volutes on every corner, its main body dominated by elaborate marquetry depicting the death and consumption of a knight by several stags. Behind it stood a wall of keys and iron-ringed drawers and on each side of the counter, two doorways permitting entry to the rest of the library.

And there was the Librarian undulating down from the ceiling.

Picture a woman. Actually, picture one of those super-models from the nineties, who embodied the fashion world's belief that the body was just a hanger to drape fabric from. Picture the way their skin canyons where bone meets their socket, their exaggerated clavicles, the long ropes of their spines. Their faces, ghostly with malnutrition.

But lovely, nonetheless, in that way a near-death experience can be, everything human starved away.

From neck up, the Librarian resembled such a person: deep-set eyes haloed by a treasure of black lashes, cheekbones high and queenly, a mathematically perfect jaw, a mouth like someone's last wish. Neck down, however—well, the problem began with the neck. The Librarian's neck was as etiolated as a dying succulent, made of too many bones and too many things that could almost be called bones.

Emaciated shoulders yielded to the body of a monstrous centipede and honestly, that alone would have been upsetting, but its segments weren't just lacquered white chitin but tessellations of its *face*, its eyes closed and mouths serene, meticulously fitted together so there weren't any gaps, and its arms. God help us, its arms. Already utterly repellent, the fact it had literally hundreds of arms—colorless and elegant, long-fingered with scintillant golden nails, beautiful if not for the context of its existence—seemed like rank overkill.

Fearless, Rowan stood looking up at the Librarian as it turned its head a good three hundred and sixty degrees in its examination of him.

"No, but you have the love of Gracelynn's life in there, and I want them out."

"Mine," sang the librarian. "Calls-to-shadows, the dark-born, dark-loved, they're mine, from now until the day their heart stops its song. Mine, mine, mine. Thrice I was promised, twice denied. This one was the third and so they are mine."

Gracelynn whimpered.

"Keep behind me." I pressed my fingertips to their right shoulder and pushed, gently as I could. "When I say go, you run for one door. I'll take the other."

They nodded, trembling as they did just that.

"Yeah," said Rowan to the Librarian. "No."

"Who are you to say no to our covenant? Whelp, young-ling, embryo." It poured itself into coils behind the counter, towering over Rowan.

Rowan shed his gloves with less fanfare than he'd done before, a lifetime ago, it felt, in the gardens behind the school. Setting them delicately onto the counter, he held his palms out to the Librarian, as though pleading for a boon.

"Someone who can and will kill you with a touch—"

"Deathworker," said the librarian, awed, an almost sexual excitement kindling in its voice. "A deathworker stands in my library. After all these years of waiting, and waiting, and waiting, death comes in the shape of a *boy*."

The hair prickled along the back of my neck. Something was *wrong*. Neither Rowan nor Gracelynn seemed to have noticed as of yet, one busy committing rudeness, the other cowering behind me. Eagerness filled the Librarian's saintly face, which seemed much less ascetic now, more lascivious. Hungry.

"—so we can do this the easy way or the hard way. I just want this Kevin person out, that's—"

I could run. We could run. I could do as I had told Gracelynn. I could thrust them forward, trust the Librarian to be too ecstatic with having an appetizer and a main course to give a fuck about needing a palate cleanser as I bolted out the door. I owed neither of them my death. I tensed as the Librarian spiraled up, up, creating a knot of itself, still grinning down on Rowan like a white and alien sun.

"What's it going to be?" said Rowan like he was the one holding the aces.

"I have wanted to die for over a millennium now. They bound us here. She and I and them and all those who are now dead, dead, dead and gone, those of us whose names they fed into the machines, who they ground up and fed to themselves. They took my library and my books and they said—" It shuddered. "They said to choose. To serve or to see my books burn. So I served and I have served for a very, very long time."

"She?" said Rowan. "They? Who are you talking about?"

"But now that you are here, now that you have come, my beautiful death, my darling boy, my blessed final demise." It giggled as every one of its eyes opened and every one of its mouths began to shriek ecstatically.

I was lunging forward before my brain was informed of the decision my feet had made, running so fast, I could feel my heart rabbiting in my mouth. I leapt for Rowan, throwing both arms around his ribs, torquing him back. He tumbled, yelping; I didn't have time to think if his hands had grazed me, if I was beginning to fester. There was only the weight of him in my grasp, the Librarian's chalk-pale regard, its arms feathering upward in praise, its smile as it arrowed downward, reaching for Rowan, for us.

"And when I have eaten you, I will finally *die*."

Day Two

Rowan's scream pierced the air—and my heart—like a knife.

I chased his wailing back to the main hall, every thought of Gracelynn beaten down by the screaming. His wailing pummeled the air in the library, filled every corner: I could hear him beg, in sobbing gasps that then lengthened into an animal keening, nearly too high-pitched to be something to claw out from a human mouth.

When I reentered, the air was swimming with embers. If I didn't think too hard about it, I could admit to its eerie loveliness, the fluorescing cinders like fireflies, and I did not want to think too hard about it because why the fuck did I come back? I owed Rowan nothing.

"You're back!" said Adam, meeting my arrival with a genial smile. "It'd be nice to get some help around here."

The screaming tapered again to sobbing: it was lower this time, more guttural. Rowan was a splayed mess of limbs on the floor, panting. A rill of blood traced the corner of his mouth as his head lolled in my direction, eyes wide at the sight of me. His hands were broken, fingers snapped, all bent the wrong ways. Adam looked fondly down at him and then he gave Rowan such a kick. A gasp tore itself out of Rowan's lips and the sound wasn't loud enough to hide the crack of bone, the noise of his breastbone caving onto itself. Rowan spasmed into a protective ball.

"Some people really don't know when to just die," said Adam lovingly.

"You can't," I whispered. "I need him."

"I can, actually," said Adam.

Whatever color Rowan's face had had before, it was gone now. Rowan's breathing had texture. I could hear him wheezing, his lungs bloodier by the moment, filling with liquid. He was dying, I could tell. I couldn't do much about that but I inched over to him nonetheless, careful to keep as far away from Adam as I could. I reached out a hand, grazed my fingers over his chest, and disconnected the part of his brain that could register any tactile sensation. If I was better at what I did, I might have been able to unhook him completely from his pain receptors, but my magic amounted to blunt trauma. His breathing smoothed. It was something, at least.

"Besides, you deserve better than him," purred Adam.

He smelled of incense, clean; he smelled like a temple, like something holy. I stared into those blue eyes of his as he crouched beside me, wishing they weren't so bright and that I wasn't so human. This close to Adam, I couldn't help but burn for him like any fool. I wanted him. Gods above and below help me, I craved him. Rumors used to abound about how Adam had a carousel of lovers who survived only as long as his interest and after he was done with them, no one ever saw them again. Yet like Bluebeard from fable, he continued accumulating paramours. I hadn't understood how. Now, skewered by his attention, I was reminded the brain only thinks itself in control.

I wet my lips with my tongue and Adam grinned, the bastard

fully conscious of his effect on anything with a functioning endocrine system.

"We would be good together."

"Go fuck yourself," I said.

"I *see*," said Adam, the smile melting from his expression, the warmth from his words. *This is his real voice then,* I remember thinking. It'd been my stepfather's voice too and the voice of so many men I'd met before, all of them charming until privilege crashed into reality, then out came this aggression, this meanness. He reached into one of Rowan's pockets, procuring a cigarette, which he lit with a flame from the tip of his right thumb.

To my shock, he then lowered the cigarette to Rowan's lips.

"You're lucky I'm a generous man," said Adam. "I'm not going to take offense at what you said. I'm not even going to ask you to be grateful when I save all our asses. You can have that for free. It's called courtesy. My mother taught me that."

"I thought Miss Kingsley died when you were a baby," wheezed Rowan, smiling unrepentantly up at us. "You never talk about her. Is she hot, by any chance? I want to know if she's Mrs. Robinson hot or—"

Adam's smile collapsed. It wasn't a secret that he, like every good Patrick Bateman wannabe, hated his mother. He thought of her as weak. The story was she died giving birth to him and he had held the fragility of her humanity against her ever since. Now it seemed like that was just apocrypha, fiction Adam fed the world for reasons unknown. Despite myself, I was interested in seeing if he'd biopsy that mystery for us.

"The Ministry is all about making deals with the right people," said Adam in conversational tones, not turning, his eyes for me and only me, and if I had been anyone else, I might have been lost, a moth eaten alive by the fire. "And they made a deal with the Abrahamic Devil, who I'm told is very different from some of the other devils that exist in our blighted universe. Better because he prefers presenting as a beautiful white man. They promised my father they'd help him impregnate any woman he wanted on one condition: they get to own the leftover children, the ones who don't become the Antichrist."

"Why?" said Rowan, preternaturally calm.

"What does *anyone* do with test subjects that can't die?" said Adam. "They experiment."

We'd been right then. This was a holding pen, a processing center, a laboratory all efficiently rolled into one. The only question left now was why.

But maybe it didn't matter.

"Sully never did appreciate his good fortune," said Adam, his expression brittle. No wonder he loathed Sullivan so. Two sides of the same coin, one coddled and the other commoditized. Never mind that Sullivan, rest his digested soul, hated his predicament, that Sullivan was just as desperate to crawl from his destiny. Adam saw him as favored, a golden child. Ironic given how Sullivan's narrative resolved but then again, Adam seemed the kind to nurse a grudge from cradle to crypt.

"Anyway," he said. "If you ever bring up my fucking mother again, I'll burn you to ashes."

I was saved from having to answer when a familiar voice uncoiled through the air, low and eager and breathy.

"Deathworker, darling, dearest death," said something in the gloom above us, in echo of words spoken so many strange months ago. "I've found you at last and when I eat you, I'll *finally* die."

"Oh," sighed Adam, standing. "Hello, beautiful."

He was wearing the excitement of a child at a circus, one ready for a harmless spectacle or at least one where he had no stakes. No, that wasn't right. His was the face of the gore hound, the ambulance chaser. He wanted the crash, wanted the six-car pileup mess of body parts and screaming people.

"Give him to me. Give the deathworker and I'll give you the cursed song, a favor for another, a gift for a gift in return."

"Gracelynn," I whispered as a shape peeled out from the darkness.

High above us, the Librarian emerged, looking for all the world like a hand puppet being thrust out from behind a velvet curtain. It was smiling with every single one of its mouths; it was practically porous with good faith. Most of its hands were steepled, all but two: one held Gracelynn's sagging frame by their nape while the other gestured toward its captive. Blood sheeted from their face like a mourning veil, and maybe it was a good thing we were all going to die here or I'd spend the rest of my life dreaming of bloody hands.

Gracelynn blinked their eyes open.

"No, no," they panted, looking like a sacrifice. "You were supposed to run."

"I fucking tried," I shouted and they laughed, a long and hollow noise not unlike a coyote's sobbing call.

I felt fingers try to curl around my ankle.

"Alessa," said Rowan, spitting what was left of his cigarette out. "Now. Now's when."

"What—"

"It's happening. What Ford said," he said, each word costing him more than he had, every syllable syruped with blood. "It's okay."

"You're so gorgeous," sighed Adam, his eyes only for the Librarian. "But you don't have what I want. Keep the bitch."

"I can hold it," shouted Gracelynn from above. "Take Rowan and—"

"What are you talking about?"

"My death," said Rowan and it was sweet somehow, that red-gummed smile of his, fierce and sure. I remember thinking *oh* as I stared down at his face, beautiful in its fatalism. "He knew you'd be worth it. You're going to make this worth it because *you'll make him fucking pay.*"

Ford also said half live if Rowan dies. He didn't say *how* Rowan needs to die. I turned to the Librarian and shouted, my voice loud as the snap of a breaking bone, despair sanding away whatever self-preservation I had left. Fuck all of this. *"You can have him!"*

"Alessa." Adam's voice gleamed with warning.

"Take him."

"*Yessss,*" sang the Librarian, accelerating across the ceiling, unfurling, Adam and his threats and flirtations forgotten, its eyes only for me and Rowan as the latter wincingly propped himself up to meet his end. "Finally, I'll die. I'll die, I'll die, I'll die at last. At long last."

Snarling, Adam blanketed the air with a bright blaze of blue flame, earning a wail from the Librarian. It fell back, crawling halfway down a wall again with its myriad hands, Gracelynn clutched like a childhood charm, screeching what I suspected were curses in a language dead and old as compassion.

"He's *mine,* you fucking centipede."

Adam erupted into a star. I could almost see a humanoid shape in that terrible whiteness: it'd been cauterized of any extraneous fat; it was barely more than smoldering bone. Still, he rose into the air, still he bellowed. "So stand the fuck down."

"No," sang out the Librarian. "No, I think I will not."

I kissed Rowan then as the Librarian dove forward, through the inferno of Adam's refusal, immolation hardly a significant obstacle when one's long anticipated death was waiting there with an exhausted smile. I kissed him not full on the mouth but on the leftmost edge of his lower lip, where a scar ran to his chin. Carefully, because he'd been hurt enough. And softly, because I could. Because I'd rather remember him this way than broken, his blue eyes as clear as the winter sky. It wasn't technically my first kiss but it was the first that I'd offered of my own free will and Rowan tasted of ash and blood and too many things unsaid.

My hand closed around his jaw. He pressed his cheek into my palm, his eyes softening. When we broke apart enough, he was smiling at me with heartbreaking sweetness, every capillary in his eyes burst. Rowan was dying, dead already, really. I didn't love him could barely say I even liked him, but he'd always been in my corner and I was tired of losing everything.

"Go."

And it was strange he was so at ease with his death, but maybe he'd spent months acclimatizing to the thought and maybe he had been waiting for this: tenderness without condition, affection without restriction; lips against his, hands around his face. If you'd never had a choice about your life, maybe there was a comfort in knowing your death, especially if you knew it'd be the softest thing you ever experienced. Gracelynn screamed again, an animal noise cut short by the shatter of bone, and I didn't think I had enough of a heart left for anything else to be broken but you learn something new every day. I didn't turn to see Gracelynn's death.

Instead, I bit down.

His lower lip began to shear from his jaw, blood gushing

over both our chins. I would never get used to the *bounce* of human lips, not their texture, the slight gelatinous nature of it all. When I tried chewing, it resisted my molars. So I swallowed Rowan's lip whole, even as his eyes rolled up in his head. I kissed him on the brow for good measure, breathing his scent in—cigarettes and old books—and mouthing *goodbye* against his skin.

He pushed me. With more strength than I'd ever imagined his thin frame would conjure, he pushed me, just as the Librarian crashed down like a comet, carrying him into a wall, its laughter filling the world. For a moment, I could see through the fire, looking like a biblical lithograph, and my magic found the small bones of Rowan's neck, and I broke them, every last vertebrae, even as white swallowed my vision, my last sight of him his eyes as the light winked out of them and the Librarian's jaws closed around him like a secret to take to the grave.

Then it was over—for whatever value of *over* could exist with the Librarian shuddering over what remained of Rowan, gasping in the agony of its pleasure, short-breathed by its dying; if I'd ever wondered if it would regret its suicidality, those doubts were gone.

But the Librarian had not been joking. In all my years, I had never heard anything die with so much pleasure.

BEFORE

"Shit," said Rowan rather eloquently as the Librarian surged toward us, all of its eyes open and bulging, each and every one of them wet and blinking and gold, weeping runnels of red slime down its carapace. Its many mouths kept up their shrieking chorus, passing a triumphant *I will finally die* between themselves with increasing volume, until all I could make out in the happy cacophony was the word *die*.

"I can't fucking believe this is how I'm supposed to die—"

"Stop," came Gracelynn's voice. "Please."

And the Librarian did.

We all did.

Their voice itched inside my skull: it felt like Gracelynn had unstoppered my skull and reached in to dig their fingers into the folds of my brain, work them deep enough that I could feel their nails scrape over the hot fat. *Stop,* Gracelynn said, and the word felt like a vise, a pincer: it squeezed like a choke collar. I gagged on the sensation. I was nauseous from it. My vision doubled and swam. The light in the library went liquid and slippery, and it hurt to look at the world, hurt to do anything save obey. Even my breathing shallowed, eager to accede. *Stop,* Gracelynn said, and for a single dizzying moment, I wondered whether her word was enough to break my heart's promise to my continued health.

The Librarian hung slack from the ceiling, a puppet de-gloved from its owner's hand. Staring up into that galaxy of arms, no longer outstretched but heavy along the sides of the creature's blood-slimed centipede body, a part of me won-dered if it'd have been better if the Librarian had stared at us with hate in its multitudinous collection of eyes. But instead of vitriol, there was a childlike petulance, a pout echoed by every mouth it possessed.

"You," it said to Gracelynn with a shiver, the motion bringing with it a wave of noise not unlike a hundred casta-nets being clacked in unison. "You don't understand what it is like to be alive for so long, to be alive when even your books have forgotten your name and there isn't a page in the world to hold a memory of the syllable, to be alive now during the death of wonder."

Slowly, impossibly, its head creaked to where Gracelynn stood trembling on the side. A fine sheet of sweat glowed along their skin. Blue veins stood against the white of their throat. I could see their pulse quavering in the pale meat, like a bird struggling to loosen itself from a net.

"I want to die. I want to die. *I want to die.* Let me eat him and it will be done."

Another shiver, the air crackling like small bones broken.

"No."

"I will give you the tithe."

Gracelynn froze.

"Oh, that's not fair," said Rowan, still cocooned in my arms. It was pure fucking luck that none of my flesh was making con-tact with his exposed skin, not his hands, the nape of his neck, his scalp. He laid pillowed awkwardly on my chest. For all that I'd come to associate with him with necrosis and violent death, Rowan smelled of neither: only shampoo, a faint whiff of smoke, and something like old books and sandalwood. He wasn't wrong. At the offer, Gracelynn went rigid, what light there was in their expression draining.

Seeing its advantage, the Librarian continued hungrily. "We will give them back. Calls-to-shadow, your dark-born, dark-loved. The tithe for something so much better." Its voice smoothed to a creamy purr. "Because they are mine now, they are mine to give back, mine to do with as I please. Hellebore itself cannot stop me. Take your spouse. Give me the death-worker to eat. Give him to me as they gave her to the Raw Mother. Give him *now*."

"I am entirely bones and probably taste bad."

"Then I will choke on you," trilled the Librarian, much too happily. "Your spine will needle my throat. Your skull will suffocate me. Your scapulae will catch and I will stop breathing, and I will at last die."

"You can't," said Gracelynn, proving that some people did indeed have integrity. It was clear how tempted they were to say the reverse, however, each syllable spoken like it had to be dug out from concrete. In their tremors wracking their soft frame, I saw how they wanted to say yes instead to the Librarian, how the word ate through their tongue, the bowl of their jaw. "They're my friends."

"We just met!" said Rowan, unhelpfully.

"Jesus Christ, shut the hell up."

The Librarian's head lolled back in our direction, its expression no longer as put-upon. It had regained its pyrexic excitement. It licked the circumference of its mouth with a gorily red tongue, and blinked its many eyes in an undulating wave that shimmered up into the darkness of the ceiling.

"Just him," it said. "All others can walk free. Cursed-song, dark-born, *murderer.*" Its attention was for me alone.

I would have stiffened at the title if I wasn't already skewered in place by Gracelynn's command. "What did you call me?"

"I seeee you. I see what you are. I see it clear. Like the sun in the last hour on the last day of the universe. I see what you are. I will name you as they've named us: murderer, butcher, monster," trilled the Librarian.

Its devout gibbering seemed to have a secondary effect; as it prattled gigglingly on, the Librarian's movements were regaining their sleekness, and if before it had seemed like the creature was fighting unseen but very constrictive fetters to even twitch a look one way and the other, it now appeared like its bondage was beginning to loosen.

"Hey, Gracelynn," I said. "Whatever you're doing, you might want to consider doing more of it. Or something different. Because it's starting not to work."

"Don't you think I know?"

The leering visage of the thing Hellebore had named Librarian lurched a foot closer to Rowan and me. It had so many teeth: rows upon rows of molars tunneling into the back of its mouth, stubbling its tongue. From a distance, that excess had been invisible. The surplus dentition was the color of its gums, its tongue. But they were definitely there, a textural horror that made me abruptly glad Hellebore, with its endless murders, had killed any nascent trypophobia I might have had.

Gracelynn sang out then: a single mercury-bright note that shone through my bones like a flame held to paper, and I burned in its light. I was dying; I was euphoric in my dying. My vision mottled with silver, dripping rivers of it, diffusing every detail.

And then slowly, that argent began to gray as everything in me shut down: heart, lungs, the factory of my digestive system; blood slowed, went sluggish, began to still; it was like falling asleep almost, a pleasing cottony nothing lulling me to unconsciousness. I felt Rowan slacken too, his weight becoming an anchor, pulling me down into the dark. We slumped into a pile of inert limbs; still Gracelynn sang. They'd have sung me into death's arms if not for the Librarian's surprised laughter unfurling through the air.

"If only, cursed-song. If only, siren-sired. If only, sings-to-the-nothing."

Gracelynn faltered. It was a mistake on their part. A desperate, understandable mistake. A mistake anyone in their rarified position might have committed. I'd find out later that what Gracelynn had wasn't a gift for compulsion; they didn't have siren ancestry. What they carried was the echo of the words that calved the universe from nothingness and would one day put the cosmos back where it belonged. But some laws, it seemed, were older than creation.

"If only the song would take me. I wish so much to be sung into the dust and the dirt and the deep nothing. I want so badly to die."

The Librarian reared up, blotting the pressed-tin ceiling and what light there was with the spiral of its bulk. I could only see its smile, luminous somehow despite the rest of its face being in silhouette.

"And now I will."

It lunged. This time however I was prepared. Despite the headache I had accrued from being collateral to Gracelynn's attempt at unmaking the Librarian, a vertiginous sensation half like food poisoning and half like the worst migraine ever, I was on my feet and running before the creature's exultant declaration was finished. Rowan pelted after me, admittedly at an awkward stumble as he had about a foot of height on me and I had my fingers twisted at his collar, and was pulling hard.

"*Run!*" I snarled, not looking back, barreling for the exit.

Only to have the way blocked by a crash of coils, the Librarian barricading the exit with its own shimmering flesh. Letting go of Rowan, I reversed, slamming into Gracelynn, who went down in a spray of tulle. I didn't stop; I grabbed them by the elbow, dragging them forward.

"Inside!"

"Are you kidding?" wheezed Gracelynn, skidding to a halt. "That's the actual library. We're not—"

I dared a glance behind us as something came down with a *whumph*: it was more of the Librarian, more of its apparently infinitely extending frame, its arms everywhere, reaching for us, a nightmare forest of grasping hands. Given its size, the Librarian could have ended this long ago, but I had a feeling it either liked its games or we were being punished for cockblocking its plans for euthanasia. Either way, like it or not, we were being herded.

"We're out of options." When that didn't move our new *friend,* I said, "And your spouse is probably in there somewhere."

That did it. With a terse nod, Gracelynn gathered their skirts in both hands and sprinted past me with cartoonish speed; I could have almost laughed if not for the shrieking monstrosity thrashing after us, howling.

We fucking ran.

We tore into the library without even the barest grasp of its floor plan, pelting wild-eyed down its shadowed aisles, the

Librarian surging behind us like the ocean. It was *laughing*. Like a little kid. Like this was a child's game and we were all its pubescent friends being brought together for play in summer: nothing to see here, nope, nothing dire at all, no threat of being consumed by a monstrosity aching to die anywhere to be seen. In retrospect, from its perspective, this probably was *just* play, a moment of levity to be chased by light refreshments before it noped out of the mortal coil at long last: a perfect program for a perfect day.

"I could be a decoy, I guess," said Rowan without much enthusiasm as we zigzagged deeper into the library. "It'll be better than dying of lung failure. I bet she'd make it quick." The years of precocious lung damage were taking its toll on him. Despite his longer stride, Rowan lagged about two steps behind me and four behind Gracelynn, who proved an admirable sprinter despite their wedding cake of a dress. Rowan was wheezing so hard he'd begun to whistle with every breath.

"We're not *sacrificing* you," Gracelynn shouted over a shoulder.

"Where the hell did you last see your spouse, anyway?" I howled.

If we were being forced through the building, we could at least procure the catalysis of our predicament. Behind us, laughing, the Librarian brought a shelf brimming with leather-bound gold-inscribed texts crashing onto the carpeted floor.

"Oopsies." It giggled.

Rowan lost his footing, slipped, pinwheeling backward with a flail of his arms. I heard the wet snap of an ankle torquing out of alignment as he snarled in pain and without looking back, I reached out with a thread of magic, felt the frayed tendon, and *pulled,* glueing it to the mortise: it was a slipshod job but it kept him lurching forward, cursing but in limping motion.

"Kevin's area is penumbral anthropology—"

Rowan, irreverent until death: "Has anyone told you how weird it is that Hellebore has someone named Kevin walking—"

"Did we pass the *P*s yet?"

"Oh," came the librarian's voice from above. "A long time ago."

It descended on us like judgment, an alabaster delusion of grasping arms, its hands socketing around our faces, our shoulders, catching us; they positioned us to look up at it, like it was a solar god and us petitioners come to seek its favor. If I had had any doubts whether it was truly immune to death, that it needed what it claimed to need, I lost them then as the Librarian stroked Rowan's cheek with the ceramic back of one pale hand. The lamps lit the creature's profile in gold, plunging Rowan's terrified face into darkness. And briefly: silence.

Briefly: time to consider our repellent predicament. Briefly: an opportunity to study our environment in invasive detail because there was nothing else to do, no immediate hope for recourse. I glanced at Gracelynn, considering the morals of turning someone we'd agreed—tacitly, I suppose—to help into raw material for an escape plan, but even my rather minimalist sense of ethics balked at that level of villainy. There was cold pragmatism and then there was being an asshole.

"I promise it will not hurt. I don't hunger for your pain. I don't lust for it," said the Librarian, practically in a stage whisper, as it spiraled down like some nightmare serpent, curling around Rowan, coils tightening. In a second, surely, that would be that. "I only want to die. We will go into the dark together. We will be nothing together. We will die together. Just you and I, you and I, you and I."

I saw Rowan close his eyes and I recall thinking with a diamond clarity that this was, in fact, *it*. What surprised me was the utter absence of terror, every thought of self-preservation forgotten: it was with relief that I looked on the Librarian distending its jaw; relief as I watched each and every one of its blazing eyes open in excited witness; relief and maybe a tinge of apology as I looked over to Gracelynn, who was arguably the most unfortunate of our pathetic lot. They were pink from their exertions, their hair so soaked with sweat that it clung to their shoulders in a damp web, and they were staring for some reason at a point on the carved frieze wrapping around the balcony above us.

I followed their gaze to the lintel and to my surprise I saw, among the skull-headed stags and disemboweled knights, a very ordinary human face gazing right back at us.

"Sorry," said the face in a soft tenor, the vowels honeyed with a Dixieland twang. "This is probably going to feel very weird."

Then the ground opened up beneath us and something pulled us through.

We landed *elsewhere,* in a narrow corridor barely wide enough for one of us to stretch out in full, legs akimbo, arms flung everywhere, piled on one another in a jigsaw of elbows, cursing, and some panic about whose exposed skin was in contact with whose. It took us a minute to separate, longer to orient. The space we were in was pitch-black, and the air was silted with dust. I palmed the walls: on one side, I felt rough, unhewn stone and on the other, cold polished wood.

"Kevin?" Gracelynn's voice, raised up like a banner, a searchlight.

In answer came the click of a lighter and a small flame *whoosh*ed up to illuminate the face I'd seen earlier. Gracelynn's spouse was softly built in that way academics often were: kind-looking, their hair disheveled and their expression tottering between relief and for some reason, indignity. They had great nails.

"I said I'd be all right." Most of their weight seemed to be supported by a wolf-headed cane that looked like it'd been carved from the same block of polished birch. "Why did you come back? You could have gotten yourself killed."

Gracelynn didn't answer at first, rushing to embrace their spouse, and as palpable as the latter's ire was, it wasn't enough; it didn't seem to keep them from returning the ferocious embrace, albeit one-armed with a lighter still in hand. Kevin buried their face into the flower-colored wealth of Gracelynn's hair, the two clutching at each other like it'd been a year, a lifetime since they'd been together.

"I thought it was going to *kill* you," wailed Gracelynn into Kevin's shoulder, crying without remorse or care for the fact the lovely paisley shirt that the latter wore was getting soaked black from the tears.

"I think it just wanted to watch some shadow puppetry. The headmaster said I wouldn't have to—"

"The Librarian said you were its—wait, the headmaster?"

"I was going to tell you but I didn't have time. Everything was suddenly happening all at once. Regardless, I swear it was going to be fine. The Librarian's actually quite sweet once you get it to stop showing off," Kevin mumbled. "I'm pretty sure we could have worked something out. Admittedly, it was very abrupt, what happened, but—"

"Ahem," I said.

The two separated immediately, Kevin rather subtly crowding their beleaguered, still-snuffling partner behind them, the cane re-angled into a light warning. They inclined their head. "Who are you?" they said, their tone warm but somehow also affectless.

"Your rescue team, I suppose." I flicked my eyes over to Gracelynn. "Although it looks like you didn't need rescuing."

"In my defense," Gracelynn began, then stopped; they let out a breathless, giddy laugh that had as much to do with humor as their partner's voice had to do with friendliness. Their shoulders dropped, and they wrung a handful of their skirts in their hands. "In my defense, I was worried. The Librarian, it's . . ."

"A lot," finished Kevin. "Thank you for coming to help."

"I like getting undeserved credit for things," said Rowan amiably, striding forward, shooting out a gloved hand for Kevin to take.

Kevin, still holding on to their cane and lighter both, studied Rowan's hand for a minute before nodding, curt. "Glad to be of service."

"Thank *you* for saving us, by the way. We'd have been dead without you," I said and some of Kevin's reserve grudgingly thawed into real warmth.

"It was nothing. I wish the three of y'all hadn't come." They touched their cheek to Gracelynn's as they said this. "But you were clearly trying to help my darlin' here, so."

"They lured me with the promise of escaping Snake Island," I said.

Kevin's gaze flicked to Gracelynn. "You told them I could do that?"

"I'm sorry! I know I shouldn't have!"

"It's all right," said Kevin and they looked over to me then, guarded in their subsequent explanation. "I can't. I don't think I can, at least. And you should know it isn't without risk. The shadows don't mind me. Other people, on the other hand, they take them sometimes. I couldn't promise you'd make it through, and that's too high a risk to take."

"But maybe it's better than nothing," I said. *No, no, no.* My hopes of escaping Hellebore were running through my fingers like so much sand. I was willing to be unmade, shredded by the shadows, at just the smallest chance of getting out of here.

"If you didn't need rescuing, though," Rowan said, "why are you here instead of out there?"

"Ah, well. I'm going to let the reason for *that* explain herself."

The reason in question stepped meekly out of the darkness from behind Kevin: Johanna.

"Jo," said Kevin, earning my instant fondness, "was caught sneaking into the library without permission. Obviously, the Librarian took offense to that."

"Listen, I did absolutely nothing wrong. I came here to research an assignment!"

"Without permission," said Kevin levelly.

At this, Johanna crumpled. She'd been lithe once. These days, she was just emaciated, eaten up by the rigors of our curriculum, by what was increasingly looking like a rigged game. Shadows—bruises or something worse, I couldn't tell then—flowered along her arms, filled the undersides of her eyes. No faculty member would give an assignment that needed access to the library, not even Cartilage. The fact she was here said everything. Johanna was just behind, like the rest of us. Underwater, with no oxygen left in the tank.

"You're lucky I was there," said Kevin.

"I wasn't expecting secret passages for some reason. How did you know this was here?" I asked.

Kevin shrugged a shoulder. "I didn't. There was every chance that Jo and I would have found ourselves inside a rock face."

"If you were wrong, wouldn't you two have been . . ." Rowan drew a line with his thumb over his throat, finishing with a little choked noise, as though it wasn't clear what he was alluding to.

"Big time," said Kevin, kissing the top of Gracelynn's head.

"*Anyway,*" said Jo loudly. She extricated a prettily filigreed wireframe from a jacket pocket, put it together, and set it down on the dust-smeared floor: a smokeless flame leapt into life a second after, radiating a pleasant bronze warmth and enough light to show that the ceiling was about eighteen feet high. The corridor in which we stood seemed to go forever in both directions, a narrow channel of space barely wide enough for us to traverse it single file. Johanna picked up the lantern, its light casting a fan of multi-jointed shadows over one wall. "Can you please just use the shadows already? The Librarian's going to look in here at some point and I'd rather not be here when it arrives."

I scanned the path in both directions as the others argued about how to get out of here. I couldn't fathom the purpose of this space: it was too narrow to be an escape route, too ill-lit and too badly engineered to expedite the movement of staff or servants. I couldn't imagine the Librarian needing this crawlspace either.

Worryingly, the passage reminded me of when I was eight; my mother, in a weird fit of charity, had taken me to a farm to see its myriad livestock. We petted horses and doe-eyed calves, fed the ducklings at their algae-thatched pool before finishing the day with a trip to the abattoir, where we watched cows urged down a killing chute to their deaths on the other side; the owners had promised us steak to take home. I cried. My mother had chuckled, not unkindly, reminding me that life was eat or be eaten. The surfaced memory left me cold to the marrow.

"Okay," said Kevin, loud enough to make me jump. "Okay, if anything happens, that's on you. Y'all are lovely company, but I don't want to keep you any longer. We can all go. If you're open to it, anyway."

"Open as a—" began Rowan gleefully.

"Don't finish that sentence," I said.

"Finally," sighed Johanna.

"Ready," said Gracelynn, softer than the rest of us, their fingers twining with Kevin's.

Kevin gestured for all of us to link hands, then pressed a hand to their sternum and the world was bending in eye-watering ways. I thought I saw their hand reach through strata of realities, passing through bone to where their lungs nested; I thought I saw a wrought iron edifice of chains and barbed spires suspended in nothing; I thought I heard something scream just out of sight; thought I felt something brush my cheek, something with teeth and too many fingers; and I thought I felt a mouth close over the pane of my right shoulder, curious. It was like dying of the cold and burning alive at the same time, my tongue molten in my jaw. I felt past and future concatenated. I listened as the syllabary of time expanded into a thousand dead languages and then shrink into a single word and that word was *now*.

BEFORE

That last night before graduation, before all hell broke from the gates, Johanna woke me as the first eerie blue light of dawn crept through the sky. I startled at the weight of her settling on the corner of my bed, jolting from unconsciousness to wide-awake dignity.

"The fuck did I say about—"

"I just need someone to talk to."

I looked over to the mass of fabric on her bed. Lately, Johanna seemed unable to get warm: she spent her days practically mummified in every article of clothing she could find, all pretense of aesthetic sloughed like old skin. Even then, she still shivered constantly, her fingers and lips blued, her skin dark with bruises. It was worse during the night.

Worse still that early dawn. I could hear her teeth chatter and clack.

"What is it?" I said.

"Do you think." She panted each word. "We're actually bad people?"

I couldn't help the laugh that rippled out of me. "Well, I certainly am."

"You're a kid, though," Johanna said loftily, all of seven months my elder. "Kids aren't good or bad."

I jammed the heel of my right hand into an eye, tried to

scrub the sleep from it. Johanna didn't smell right either, hadn't in days. Weeks. A sweet stench wept from her skin, like dying roses. "I don't know about that. The things I did should have definitely gotten me a life sentence."

She squirmed out of her blankets. Johanna had been beautiful once and you could argue that she'd become ethereal in recent days, like some artist's rendition of a tortured saint, nothing but cheekbones and jawline and a smoldering pyrexic light that seemed to have burned her eyes into their sockets. But to me, she only looked unwell, eaten through by disease or despair.

"Do you ever think about why we're here?"

"No. I got kidnapped." I hadn't forgiven Hellebore for that.

"Stefania and I—we." She paused to cough. "Did we ever tell you about the Skinless Wolf?"

I shook my head.

"The Skinless Wolf," said Johanna, nodding, tone didactic, distancing. Almost at once, I knew what she was doing: when you phrased a memory as a story, it became easier to pretend they didn't gut you in the epilogue. "He—I don't know what he is or was. He could have been a god, I suppose. A small one that history eventually forgot ever had an address in the heavens. Who knows? By the time Stefania and I were born, he was just a curse, one that our families fed with all their spare daughters. We became his mute of Hares. And he hunted us when he felt like it. When he caught us, we died horribly."

I said nothing.

"We didn't want . . . we wanted to *live*. The death of the Hare isn't, um, it's not a good one. When one dies, they linger for a long time. Even if they're carved up. Especially if they are. They spend eternities screaming, begging, even as a forest grows out of them. I didn't want that."

"Who would?" I said, thinking throughout I should reach for her shoulder, bare and white and cold in the dim light.

Johanna spoke the next words with neither contempt of her past nor shame. In fact, she said them without anything but a chilly factualness, her eyes as they held mine unweighted by regret. "But there were ways you could distract him from hunting you or killing you, though. He'd give you reprieve if you gave him an evening. Do you understand?"

I swallowed.

"I do."

"I liked Rowan," said Johanna quietly. I didn't like that it was in the past tense, the decisive finality in her tone, its gauziness. Here was someone done fighting, beyond pain. And another person might have said *stay*, might have said *let me help*. But I was sorry anyway we weren't good enough friends for me to wrap my arms around her pain, hold her close, to tell her I understood morality and survival couldn't always exist in the same room, and to beg forgiveness for being frankly a judgmental bitch. Because we weren't, we sat awkwardly together instead, knees almost touching. And she was cold. I remember that still. "He's not a bad guy."

"I guess not." This was goodbye, I could tell. I just didn't know where she was going yet.

Johanna's eyes blazed like a pulse, like flint struck over and over again, a white spark in the black of her pupils.

"Anyway, like I was saying, we didn't want to end like that. We didn't just want to be hallowed soil. Food for a new universe. And there's only so long you can put off the Wolf. Eventually, you get too old for him." She laughed, a tissue-paper noise tearing into a pained cough. Johanna daubed at her mouth with the back of a hand, wincing, and there was blood on her skin, the corner of her lips now so dried, they weren't much more than wounds. "So we told our keepers and they said to go, to come here, that if we think our lives are worth more than our cause, we could go. But they said it wouldn't happen. They said everyone comes back, head bowed, arms out to embrace their fate."

"Sounds like the Amish rumspringa except cosmically worse," I said.

"Except none of the classes make sense. I tried to make them make sense. I did all my coursework. But it doesn't teach anything. There's nowhere to go, no way to advance. Unless you kill. It's all about how many people you murder. That's all it is. They want us to kill each other. I don't know why. I don't, I can't. *There's something wrong with this place.*"

"What do you want me to do about it?"

"I need you to keep Rowan safe."

"We graduate tomorrow morning. It won't matter."

Johanna stared at the wall past my head, eyes unfocused. Whatever she was looking at, it wasn't in this room or even this stratum of existence. "I don't think we're graduating. I'm not, anyway. The Wolf's coming tonight and I'm done. I don't want him to touch me. I don't want that future. I don't want what's waiting for us out there either."

"Johanna—" I broke, fingers reaching for her sleeve. She flinched from me, like I was a grasping flame, or teeth searching for her throat. But her expression remained unchanged, still that abstracted nothingness.

"I have a theory," said Johanna. "That the Wolf needs us for power. That's why it hunts us. But if I'm going to die, I don't want it to be for him. I'm not going to be his kindling. I'm not going to be his soil. I won't feed his belly. I won't, I fucking won't. I didn't come all this way for it to end like this."

With care, she took my hand in hers, twined our fingers,

brought mine to her throat. I felt her pulse shiver against my palm. Then when I had so gripped, Johanna drew down her collar, exposing the lesioned skin.

"I don't hate you, by the way," said Johanna and it was her in her entirety, with that softness I'd so loathed in the beginning.

"Thanks? Also, that's pretty hardcore. I guess I shouldn't be surprised that you and Rowan are into that—"

"It's the Wolf," said Johanna, tracing a crescent of sores that trailed from her collarbone, abscessed. "Was always the Wolf. That's how we know he's coming. He leaves marks. Warnings. But I don't want to talk about that right now."

I released my grip on her. "Please don't tell me you want to talk about Rowan."

"I just need to clear the air here, okay?" She hesitated. Her cheeks went maroon, like something had ruptured under the surface. "I don't hate that Rowan likes you. We didn't have that kind of relationship."

"You two were still hooking up, though. I'd assumed—"

She cocked her head. "That we had feelings for each other?"

"Not quite." The topic of Rowan felt more intimate than the galaxy of wounds spread over her chest, the mess of us more abhorrent than whatever the alleged Wolf had visited on her. "I'd rather we not talk about this."

"Oh, that I have feelings for him." Johanna laughed again. It cost her. "Because I've got stars in my eyes and I can't help falling in love with everything, being the manic pixie dream girl that I am?"

"Your words, not mine." If I'd been a better person, I might have hated myself for my own flippancy, the malice razoring my words.

"I absolutely have feelings for him but I meant what I said all that time ago. I don't care what he does with his time when he isn't with me. He's his own person. He's allowed autonomy. Besides." Johanna smiled, the expression small and luminous and unexpected in its beauty. "You seem to make him happy and I'm glad for that. Rowan's not as bad as everyone seems to think he is, you know?"

The smile died to a memory. "He deserves more than the world's given him."

I was almost sorry when I said: "Sadly, I don't like him that way."

"Your loss." She laughed again, that strangeness drawing over her once more like a shawl. "But yeah, I don't mind at all. I like thinking that there's going to be someone watching over him when I'm gone. I want there to be."

Johanna slipped from my bed then, even more a wraith than I'd remembered somehow. What I could see of her body through the layers of winter wear were bone and skin gone dull, sallow. She looked rubbed-out, aged, like a stain someone had tried to erase but lingered still in the fabric, a god forgotten, a ghost. Gently, she struggled loose of whatever was left of her clothing. The light caught in her eyes, and they glowed white for an instant.

"Kill me."

A part of me was surprised when I responded with, "What?"

"I need you to kill me."

"I heard you the first time, but why the fuck?" I struggled out of my duvet, grabbing at the clothes she'd discarded. "Also, Jesus, put some clothes on."

All of her was profaned with wounds, some deeper than others, some wide enough to bare bone like teeth; it was all putrid too, puddles of greenish shadow and yellow-veined gray. Her skin had thinned to near translucence and I could see the black rivers of her veins beneath the surface.

"Kill me. Please."

"You know," I said, "there was a time when I'd have given anything to hear you say that."

"We don't have time."

"Put your clothes on." I draped Johanna's shirt over her like a pashmina, struck by a sudden aversion to her bare skin: it had a repellent shine to it in that near light. "And go to bed. I don't know what fucking—"

"The Wolf is coming."

I paused.

"When he's here, I'm going to die," said Johanna. "He's going to eat me up. Unless *you* do it."

I didn't watch to touch her but I palmed her shoulder nonetheless, trying to steer Johanna toward her bed. "Goddamnit, Johanna. Go the fuck to sleep."

"I have a theory," said Johanna and she did not move under the pressure of my hand, green eyes brittle as glass. "I have a theory about the Wolf and the Hares and all of it. I think he needs us. They need us. The world, I mean. Our power."

"You're babbling. Seriously."

As I watched, her throat became scalloped with bite marks, the indentations deepening, until the flesh sheared away and blood spouted from the ruin.

"Shit." Instinctively, I wadded the shirt I'd thrown over her shoulders and pressed it to the wound but Johanna shrugged away from my touch, oblivious to her hemorrhaging. There wasn't enough in her to restitch the mess, nothing to pull from, nothing left.

"I think we are batteries, generators, reservoirs," said Johanna. "They build the future out of our bones."

"Johanna," I tried one last time.

"I don't want to die for him," said Johanna. "I'm not getting out, either way. At least give me some dignity."

And it might have been the wind, the low keening that blew up to our window, a sound like howling but something else too: older, crueler, more eager. At the sound, whatever light remained in Johanna's gaze extinguished.

"Please," she said as the door blew in.

A thing like heat haze, that my brain could acknowledge as quadrupedal but would not otherwise describe in any way that memory would capture, could only flinch from like it was a flame, like it was teeth, crawled in through the hallway.

It growled. The Skinless Wolf.

All at once, I was struck by the sense that it existed not just in multiple dimensions but in multiple times, in multiple bodies, in fur and fang, as a long-boned man, grinning with more teeth than there ever should have been; as with a forest erupted from the corpse of a screaming girl, which is all to say, it looked like a migraine. Blinking, I looked over to Johanna, who glowed now like a candle, our room clotted with shadow.

"Alessa," said Johanna, my name a prayer.

"Yes."

The Wolf leapt, crashing into us like grief.

You probably will not believe me but for whatever it is worth, I made sure it didn't hurt. There wasn't anything to do about what came after, no justice in what followed, but it didn't hurt.

I owed her that.

I collared Johanna's throat with both hands and she bent her head as if it were a blessing I was endowing. Maybe it was.

When I touched my brow to hers, I could almost convince myself this was a mercy. Her skin was like silk under my fingers, like tissue, ephemeral as memory.

"I'm sorry," I said, not fully knowing why. Maybe it was because of how we got there. Maybe it was how she had to simper through her life. Maybe it was because we could have saved each other if I had less spite and she some certainty I wouldn't bite her head off just because. Regardless, I was sorry. I don't care if you believe that either.

I broke her neck.

When she died, it was with the briefest exhalation, a small cut-off gasp. There was relief in her expression as the light in her eyes drained like a slit throat, emptying until there was nothing, until she was just meat and soft blond curls. Johanna slumped into my arms, and I might have wept then if not for her wolf crashing into us, bearing us down onto the cold floor. I couldn't quite *see* the thing pinning me down: my mind wouldn't close over the sight of it, refused to do more than acknowledge that there was a monstrous weight astride my breastbone. I could smell the rotten-meat stink of a carnivore's breath, feel its boiling saliva hit my chest; I knew it had mouth and teeth and eyes. If I focused hard enough, I could almost feel the slickness of bare muscle. Not that any of it mattered.

I held Johanna as the wolf panted above us.

She was mine, I heard it say in my mind.

"Fuck. You."

She was given to me.

My absolute terror evaporated. It was old, yes. It was ineffable too, a thing like a god and like what lurked in the cinerous bones of the place where Portia made her bed; I knew I should be afraid of it but all I had in that moment was contempt.

"She's dead." My voice sounded like an ache. "You can't touch her anymore."

Something like a man's laughter rumbled into my ear; almost a wolf's chortling growl. I felt hands reach past me, and it was then I realized I was clutching Johanna's body, skin warm enough still to be mistaken for living.

I don't need her alive.

It began to peel her from my arms. Tried to, at any rate. Laughter clawed out of me, a rasp of noise that broke then into shrieking. I tightened my grip. Teeth sunk into my shoulder, a warning. Pain rippled across me like a grease fire.

Mine. My body to use. My body to bury in the orchard. Mine.

I saw again the wolf's forests and the bodies beneath its branches; the wolf as a long-legged man, sitting on the soil, teeth digging into the white flesh of a girl's leg as she kicked, *screamed.* We were meat to them, I remember thinking. Just meat. To the wolf, to you, to everyone else.

"Hope you have a bucket then."

While I had no idea if I could stop the Wolf from doing what he wanted, I certainly could keep it from being easy.

DAY TWO

I tried to ignore the noises emanating from the Librarian's coils, tried to ignore the ache that was beginning to spread from my throat across the length of my torso; a sensation like ice and heat both, like a sentient fever traveling into the bones so every joint twinged. I tried to ignore all of that and rise to my feet instead, wincing.

Because there was Adam, smiling like it was Christmas and naked as his namesake, dragging Gracelynn along the ground by an ankle, their hair so matted with gore that it trailed red over the floor like a paintbrush.

"My father," he said in wondering tones, "he once appeared to me in a dream. And in the dream, he showed me my inheritance should I prove myself worthy: a hell of mewling sinners. It was the most beautiful thing I'd heard."

"And?"

"And I'm looking forward to hearing Gracelynn do an encore."

"Not to be that person, but that isn't how you use the word," I said in lieu of anything useful, preoccupied with maintaining focus, wondering the whole while if this was the root of Rowan's irreverence: easier to act like everything is okay if you're focused on something else. I forced a smile to my mouth. "Did he tell you he loved you at the end of it?"

Adam cocked a sympathetic look at me, guileless and compassionate; it made my skin want to writhe off the muscle. Where was Portia when you needed a fucking spider monster?

"Were you two friends?" he asked as if he hadn't seen Gracelynn give it all up for us, hadn't heard them scream for me to run, hadn't seen me come back, desperate. As if he hadn't been witness to their kindness and my refusal of such. The absolute sincerity in his voice suggested two things: either this was a trap, or he hadn't cared to pay any attention up until this moment.

"If I'd been a better person, we would have been," I said after a moment, a eulogy of a kind in the declaration. An odd epitaph, I guess, but a better one than I was liable to receive, which was to say when I was gone, there'd be no one to say I was here and that I mattered.

I ran my tongue over my teeth. One of my molars had loosened unexpectedly. I wiggled it, abruptly fascinated by how I could feel the tether of its root.

"Let them go. Please. You can have me instead," I said impulsively, my mouth filmed with a fresh wash of blood. "Let them go. Please. You can have me instead."

"And why's that?"

"Because you'll have way more fun with me. Let them go."

He laughed. Adam remained offensively attractive despite our shared deprivations, his hair tousled as opposed to ruined. I wanted him to touch me, wanted him, wanted to nuzzle into his shoulder, let him lie to me about whatever he wanted.

"No," he said. "No, we can't do that—"

"Adam, please."

Years spent around men who believed that their dicks were reliquaries taught me how to smile despite the wave of nausea rolling through me. I sweetened my expression as best as I could even as the world swam, every object becoming haloed by a soft light of its own. I blinked hard, salt stinging my eyes, nails cutting crescent wounds into my palms. My own stigmata, my own punishment for this weakness, this greed for life.

"Maybe," he said, raising Gracelynn's limp form so he had them suspended by the hair, their legs swaying. There was so much blood on them, I couldn't see the patterns on their skirts any longer. Their head hung slack, chin brushing their chest.

At the word *maybe,* I couldn't help the surge of hope. Adam's smile told me he saw it too, that misguided optimism of mine, and the smile widened like a slit throat as he said, "Maybe. If you'd been kinder to me, if you'd cooperated, I might have considered it. But none of these things are true and I need you more than I need her, *so . . .*"

He gave a philosophical little shrug, lifting Gracelynn so their face was level with his. "No hard feelings."

I was on my feet.

"I won't let you," I said. Blood shone down my chin, my hands, through the beds of my nails; I felt it trickle from my nostrils, thickening. My mouth tasted hot and coppery and rank. It might have felt less like a nightmare if Adam wasn't still fucking naked and utterly unselfconscious of his bobbing erection.

He was enjoying this. I might have felt rage if I wasn't dying too.

"How are you going to stop me?"

"Not sure," I said, reaching out with what little of me wasn't consumed by the work of staying alive, fighting against Rowan's deathworker magic coursing through my body. I traced Adam's bones, the line of his spine like a subtle question mark; there was his heart, his liver, that corrupted fire he'd inherited from his father, burning like a star. "But even if it kills me, I'll do it."

There was no warning. Adam's smile stayed genial as he transferred his hand from Gracelynn's collar to their neck, fingers coiling around their throat, and I watched the flesh begin to blacken. The only mercy of the moment was they couldn't scream. Gracelynn let out a soft gasp as Adam's fingers closed into a fist, the butter of their throat and the bones of their neck melting under his touch; it looked like it hurt. It looked like it was *excruciating*. And I am still ashamed of the relief that filled me when Gracelynn's head toppled from their shoulders, although not as much as I am of the childish solace I found in how I could not see their face, matted as it was with the gore-soaked strands of their hair.

"Too slow, I'm afraid."

"You're a fucker, you know that?" I managed, astonished by the tears running down my cheeks. I might have wept for them as Gracelynn had wept for the world if it wasn't taking all of me to keep myself relatively together. Adam stared soft-eyed in fascination at me as I trembled from the noise, from the work of surviving. I gritted my teeth, sinking then to a splay of limbs, mopping at my face. "Why are you keeping me for last? You don't like me that much."

"I'm not keeping you for last," said Adam. "I'm keeping you for Portia. And then I'll kill her when she's done with you."

"Why are you *doing* this?"

He released Gracelynn as if he were a child and they a toy that had lost its luster, letting them fall into a heap atop the soiled floor. Adam strode toward me then, his smile bright still. If I'd had any reservations about what I intended, they were gone now, like a last breath spent.

"Because I told you I'd make you fucking regret this."

"Is this about your fucking hand? The hand that you fucking healed in, like, a second?" I tried to laugh but hacked blood instead onto the collar of my shirt, taking an odd consolation in the fact there was no way to further despoil the damn thing: its original color was lost wherever our innocence had gone. I flashed him a red-gummed smile; all it provoked was laughter.

"A gentleman keeps his promises," said Adam, crouching down to fuss at my hair, tidying the strands, tucking blood-matted clumps behind my ears. "You have to respect that."

I reached for him and he let me. I twinned my hands around the back of his neck, pulled him to me. I kissed him. I kissed him with Portia's loneliness and Rowan's shocked tenderness, like this was the last time I would kiss anyone, which I guess wasn't untrue. I kissed him like fury, like grief, like a kiss could undo all of this, give us back our dead, make us young again, make death someone else's problem once more, make us whole again, innocent of all this pain. Adam froze against my mouth, his lips softer than I anticipated. He tasted warmly of copper when I bit him but also strangely of incense. I'd expected brimstone, but not this, not this smoke that bled down my throat like a memory. I cupped both hands around his cheeks, pulling his head even closer, devouring in my insistence, surprised at this unexpected energy. He sank obediently to my level, kissing me now in turn with a matched ferocity, his cock hard against my side.

His hand sank into my hair, fingers threading through the wild mass. He pulled, surprising a soft moan from me and he laughed at the sound, transferring his mouth to the column of my throat, where he kissed a path to my collarbone and then sank his teeth deep.

"Necrophiliac," I hissed even though there wasn't a part of me that did not recognize that he was beautiful, that did not hunger for him with his body in such close proximity.

Adam withdrew, blue eyes through his golden lashes like a caged sky. "It's so much better when they can't run."

My shoulder ached where he'd bitten me; burned, really. I ran fingers over my collarbone, and found scars instead where the teeth marks had cauterized. It seemed like a courtesy at first but I realized it was a branding. Adam watched me with starved eyes and a half smile that might have been beautiful on someone else, but on him resembled something stolen. Given his nature, it probably was. When I did not move, his hands found me again, palming my breasts, finding the buttons of my shirt. I closed my eyes. He undid them slowly, savoring the release of my flesh, and so intent was he on my disrobing that I don't think he even registered the moment the burning sun in his heart began to die.

Although, at that moment, his attention was pulled elsewhere.

"*M i n e.*"

A shape embroidered itself into the air. An outline at first, a suggestion of a body. Slowly, the shadows of the figure filled in. The light found the bladed lines of a leg, the still-lovely geometry of a woman's torso, denuded of its breasts: pale freckled skin save for the scabbed-over wound running down its breastbone. It wasn't *not* Portia, for all the alienness of her anatomy, for all that she was missing her head. Her skull was just gone. But she didn't need it. Her ribs had cracked apart and scythed outward, piercing flesh. I could see her mouth—clever, crooked—through the gore, grinning at us through what remained of her chest. She lurched a series of quivering steps forward.

"Ah," said Adam, turning away from my body. "There you are."

"*M i n e.*"

Adam stood. "When I'm done."

Portia skittered closer, a stop-motion horror. The constellation of her eyes traveled my skin and there was enough pity there for me to sneer back at her; instinctive vanity, at this point. I wasn't anything anymore, not really, just a dead girl sitting, a corpse that didn't know she was dead. The light shimmered along Portia's carapace like oil on water, and she was still grinning at me.

Her gaze flicked back to Adam, who'd begun to smoke, a black haze pouring over his skin. He smelled like a crematorium, like fat burning and bone cooking. Dismissed, I inched backward until I had my back to a wall. My shirt hung open, the fabric hanging like a flap of skin pared from a rabbit's corpse. The buttons felt like bones under my fingers as I straightened myself, watching as Portia let out another low growl.

"*M i n e.*"

"No," said Adam again. "She is not."

I watched my breath curl through the air, white. Thought of Rowan in the graveyard, his face in the dark. Thought of Gracelynn, my hands in theirs, telling me to go, *run.* Thought of Johanna that last night before, telling me about the Wolf. Thought about how she'd said, *Sometimes, we do terrible things to survive, don't we?*

And despite everything, I smiled.

Before

When we emerged from Kevin's shadows, zodiacal light had begun to soften the night's blackness, staining Hellebore's horizon with a dim whiteness. A lone figure waited for us in the jasmine-scented dark, illuminated despite the hulking corpse of the burnt-down building behind her: Portia.

The darkness suited her. In its tepid glow of the predawn, there really wasn't any color save for the deep carmine of her hair, like she was hiding a head wound. I was coherent enough to be surprised by the sight of her. Then surprise became suspicion. Portia likely had the ear of the faculty, and if she had their ear, it made sense they would have their hand on the collar around her neck.

She glanced disinterestedly at us as we appeared. Her expression, illegible at first, became one of faint disappointment. But then a small smile creased her face, her attention swimming through the dark to rest on me. She smiled and my breath snagged in my throat at the sight.

"You shouldn't be with these people. It's not safe," she chided, slinking up to loop her arm through mine. "You should know better. Especially after—"

"Her jailbreak?" chirped Rowan, taking hold of my other arm. "Yes, that was definitely something. We should probably get Alessa home."

All the warmth oozed out of Portia's voice. "What were *you* doing out here, anyway?"

"Enjoying the fresh air."

"You know better."

"I can neither confirm nor deny that remark."

"We should probably get going . . ." Kevin announced but Gracelynn dug their feet in, mouthing at me, *Do you need help?*

The two descended into an argument conducted half in shorthand and half in choppy gestures.

Johanna sauntered up to Portia, as if she were a long-lost friend and this a pre-arranged meeting. "We were *just* telling Alessa how she needs to be more careful on these grounds!" She drove a shoulder into Rowan's ribs, sweetly smiling throughout, charm laid on so thick, I could have scraped it off with a knife. "Hellebore will eat you *alive* if you're not careful," chattered Johanna, writhing between Portia and me, something she accomplished only because Portia, I think, wasn't expecting such an affront and because I wanted to escape this tug-of-war that Rowan and she had instigated.

"Leave me alone," I hissed at Rowan, who now clutched at me with both gloved hands, his smile glassy and manic.

"Come on," he said. "Johanna's clearly freaking out."

Had he said anything else, I might have gladly taken the excuse as an exit. Something about how Rowan spoke her name felt intolerably abrasive at that moment.

"I'm sure you can comfort her," I said, shrugging loose of his grip. I stuffed my hands into my pockets and withdrew several steps backward. I didn't like being touched even on the best of days and this certainly wasn't one of them; it didn't help that I was marinating in what felt treasonously like jealousy.

"—going to bite someone. I'm *worried*," said Gracelynn from somewhere nearby.

"—still not our place to stop that?"

"—is too?!"

"Free will is a thing, Gracelynn."

"I think Alessa and I might need some *girl time*," said Portia, the light catching strangely in her eyes, splintering into eighths for a second, except that wasn't possible, at least I didn't think so then.

I laughed at her use of the words *girl time*, the phrase so out of place it seemed code for something else, and even as that thought surfaced, a pang of warmth filled me. I swallowed.

"Is that you want?" Rowan asked me, something wary in his eyes.

"Yes."

"Well," said Rowan after a moment, nothing like dejection in his face, mouth fluttering into a smile. You'd think we had choreographed this from his nonchalant tone, the absolute complicity in his voice. "Let us know when you're done with your midnight rendezvous, huh?"

I didn't answer as he slouched away, arms flung out to drape over Kevin and Gracelynn's shoulders, who were caught out mid-argument and now were obligated to endure the rank overfamiliarity because politeness had been beaten into their very genetics.

"Are you sure you don't want to come with us?" asked Johanna, faintly strangled, a last-ditch effort in extending a lifeline.

"Incredibly," I said.

"Who wants to get some booze? Trick question. *Everyone* wants booze. Especially you," said Rowan, hip-checking Kevin so hard they stumbled.

Like some mutant border collie, Rowan began herding them away, sparing one last look before rounding the corner, worry in his eyes and something else, something like injury.

Portia and I said nothing to each other until the sounds of the four arguing trickled away, and the world was silent save for insect night-song and the waking verses of the first stirring birds. A little too late, I thought about calling out to them and as if she knew, Portia set a cold white hand on my wrist. I heard a creak of wood. I looked up then at the windows above us, and though perhaps it should have, it did not surprise me to see a light begin to grow there, begin to move; the glow the sickly yellow of old lymph.

"What you did was stupid," she said without preamble.

I shrugged.

"I know you think that the best way of getting out of this place is to run, but you're going to get yourself killed," said Portia. "There's only one way out."

"Guess I'm going to see if you're wrong," I said, withdrawing my hand, repelled by the clamminess of her skin. "Or die trying."

"There's another option."

Dawn had begun to pink the sky along the mountain line, a curiously fleshlike color. She spoke the possibility very mildly, but there was a portentousness to it that belied the blasé delivery. Every time I saw her, she seemed more tired, more distant, and if I was going to be honest with myself, less human, though in ways I couldn't easily index.

"I said no already." A filler statement. I was trying to buy time although I didn't know yet what for. Though I knew the air should be frigid, I was sweating profusely. The light now hung just outside Portia's right shoulder.

"The Raw Grail," said Portia like I hadn't spoken and

maybe, she wasn't speaking to me but to whatever was the reason for that sudden luminescence. "You could join us."

Her smile was as gorgeous as it was empty, like glass, like some perfect sculpture: wholly, utterly without true emotion. Portia regarded me with a lidded gaze and what I could see of her irises was a surprising mauve, almost luminescent, the purple fractured somehow, like light shone through a cracked mirror

"Still as unappealing an idea as it was the first time."

"You know, I was in your position once," she said. "She saved me."

My mouth was suddenly entirely arid. "Weird that you did not mention this even once before. I thought you were here because you wanted to be here. Not because you needed saving."

Portia licked bloodless lips and it might have been a trick of the meager light, but her tongue looked black in the instant it flicked into view. "I thought that when I was done, they'd let me go. But they didn't. They put me away. I was completely alone. I thought I'd have to die to ever get out. But she and I had a conversation. And she gave me a choice. She came to me and said there was another way, that it didn't have to end there in that room."

"What. Fucking. Room?" I said distantly.

Those freckled cheeks of hers grew dusted with rose. She was *shy*, I realized. Like a debutante being plied with attention for the first time, Portia could barely get her next words out, oblivious to my own horror. "All I had to do was let her change me. Just a little. Enough that she too wouldn't feel alone. Which seemed fair to me. Still does. She's been here for a long, long time. Always alone. Always left behind. So many girls made her promises. But they always went away in the end. I couldn't leave her like that. Now she's in me, and in me she will remain."

"I don't like what's being implied." Weird how obvious

that metamorphosis was now that she'd confessed to it. I saw it in the way the light broke in her eyes, in the black of her tongue, the new brilliance of her skin, like a bright membrane silvering the tributaries of her veins.

"To be loved is to be changed."

"I've heard that saying. I don't think they meant it in a non-consensual way." I sank my nails into my palm. The light had begun to move again, bored perhaps with my obstinance. "I don't want to be someone else's stuffed animal."

"She's not like that," said Portia in sad, sweet tones. Somewhere in the foliage, an animal screamed. "It's different when they love you. It hurts less. It means more."

Her voice softened.

"The Raw Mother doesn't hurt anyone on purpose. She knows what it's like to be trapped. All she wants is for us to be free," Portia said like she was a lamb brought up to a sacrificial altar, blinking prettily as she waited for the knife. I swallowed hard, trying not to picture that sad history: that sullen, dark-eyed girl on her knees before something older than our species itself, begging for a way out. "She'll keep you safe."

"Once again, thanks, but no," I said, wishing I had something more clever to riposte with. Later, I would tell myself it had been expedience, common sense that had me turning tail and running instead of coming up with a better repartee. But right then, I could admit that more than anything else, I was afraid.

When I returned to the dormitory, Johanna was awake and inconsolable, a towheaded wraith pacing in front of our shared room. She jolted a look up as my footsteps rang along the treacherous corridor, relief flooding her features. Her eyes were the deep green of the summer, the whites splattered with red: she'd stayed up waiting, it seemed, although for whom was anyone's guess.

"You're safe," she sighed with nearly theatrical relief, rushing up with arms spread. "I was so worried. I thought Portia would try to induct you, or—or worse."

"That should be a happy thought," I said, unable as always to help my own vitriol, resenting how this made us such a trope: she the sunshine-bright girl and I the unlikable grump who she'd win over with consistent attention and care. "You'd be able to move Stefania in like you wanted."

Low and obvious as that blow was, Johanna still winced. "That was a *mistake*, Alessa. You were gone. What was I supposed to do?"

"Wait for a body."

"Here? In Hellebore?" Gone then was her usual Pollyanna disposition. In its place, a ruthless clarity I hadn't expected of her, wouldn't even have imagined her capable of. Sunrise poured through the serried line of windows, burnishing the corridor with pools of yolk-yellow and wine-colored light. "Anywhere else, I'd have been busy calling the authorities, trying to figure out where the hell you were. But in case you didn't notice, we don't really have the option here. People disappear all the time. What was I supposed to think?"

"You could have had more faith I'd come back," I said, aware at this point I was simply being a bitch. "You could have gone looking for me."

"I tried," she snarled. "We tried. We didn't sleep for two nights. We *were* out looking for you. Stefania was about to kill me for that."

"You never told me." I was staggered. I didn't expect the

fury in her voice, how her face looked now that it was husked of what I finally recognized as a front, the glutinous sweetness no more than an affectation. Most of all, I didn't expect how much this made me like her.

"You didn't ask. You never ask, do you? You just go straight to being an asshole," Johanna hissed. Her anger receded with the next breath. She looked even worse for wear than before. "Look," she spat. She wasn't much taller than me but she loomed then in her righteousness, her grave dignity. Her eyes gleamed like strange stars in the bright tussled cloud of her hair. "I am *sorry* for whatever shitty situation you had to dig your way out of to be alive right now, but that doesn't give you fucking permission to be such a bitch all the time."

"You can't blame me for being impressed. I've been listening to you snore for months and this is the first time I'm seeing you have an actual backbone. I thought all you did was cry and run away."

"Who the fuck *hurt you?*" A surreptitious chorus of clicks in the hallway alerted me to doors being opened: we were beginning to attract attention, which was never a good thing in the school. "I'm sorry, Alessa, but you're not the only one who's suffered in this life. If you had any idea what I'd done to survive, you wouldn't be half as willing to be so mean to me. Not that it matters. I really just want to be your friend."

"*Why?*"

"Because people like us? We're all we have."

It should have come across as twee. It should have felt stupid to hear, like some prepubescent declaration of undying friendship or a little girl's vehement oath that she would change the world for the better, just you wait. But there was such sincerity to Johanna's exasperation, to her rage at being misapprehended time and time again, that the words developed force enough to drive me to a shame-faced quiet. I blinked in that new silence, chastened, flayed.

"I don't want to be your friend," I said after we'd both had time to steep in the aftermath of her tirade.

"Fine," said Johanna. "Can we be civil, though?"

That I could do.

"Only if you promise to cry less."

"Absolutely not." She gave a sniff. "Crying's healthy."

Her mask rose back up then, like someone pulled on a curtain's strings, even as the door to our shared room cracked open and Rowan emerged from inside, knuckling at an eye. He flashed me a yellow-toothed smile.

"Am I interrupting something?"

"Not yet," said Rowan, slinging an arm around Johanna.

She tittered at this, her smile doting. Johanna looked like she thought he had hung the moon and the sun in the sky. *You don't know what I've done to survive.* It dawned on me this was perhaps her continuing to survive, doing what was necessary. I'd never asked and at this point I suspected she would never tell, but I wondered then if he was insurance against what was hunting her. If all the scraping and fawning was just that. Whatever the case, I had a nagging feeling that of the two of us, Johanna perhaps was the stronger one.

"Do you two need some privacy?" I asked.

"No," said Rowan. "I was just keeping her company until you got back."

Another little giggle. "You're *so* sweet, Rowan."

You don't know what I've done to survive.

"In that case, excuse me." I shouldered past them both into the room, which smelled unusually of sandalwood and oud. Someone had put up candles everywhere: in the eaves, on the mantle of our unlit fireplace, the nightstands, the communal shelf now wretched with all the reference texts, half-filled notebooks, and books that Johanna and I had procured over the months.

Settling onto my own bed, tidied now to a catalog-quality condition, I said to Rowan, who stood there in the threshold like the memory of a nightmare, "What the hell were you trying to find in the library, anyway?"

"You were looking for something in the library?" said Johanna, voice girlish and piping, no more than a living doll again.

"Information on how to escape," said Rowan from the doorway and he was almost gorgeous silhouetted like that with the golden light tracing his profile. "And maybe some resurrection spells."

"Why the fuck for?"

"I owe a lot of people for being born."

"Fair enough. Welp, I'm going to sleep," I said, crawling under my duvet. It was unconscionable that we had class in a few hours and the world would continue to turn. Our midnight adventures would have consequences, I was so very sure of that. The headmaster was likely to have something to say. But then again, the Librarian had been desperate to die. Surely, that was a violation of its professional obligations. If so, perhaps it'd keep our misdeeds as secret as its own desires. Or maybe Portia, spurned, would rat us out.

Who the fuck knew. Either way, there'd be more classes.

"Classes are in two hours," said Rowan.

"Good night," I said.

"I'll make her some coffee, don't worry about it," said Johanna, fussing over the battered electric kettle as the pipes groaned and gurgled from being forced to do their plumber-given duty. The reservoir of essentials had grown since: instant coffee, tea, ginger chews, dissolvable packets of citrus-flavored flu medicine, saltines—whatever one needed to start a morning, soothe a hangover, and survive a minor illness.

"Anyway, we're on for a round two, right?" Rowan asked, a little too loudly.

"*Good night.*"

The biggest surprise of the night, as it turned out, was how quickly I could sink into a dead sleep even after all the nightmare fuel I had just lived through. I fluffed my pillow, and when unconsciousness arrived, it came without dreams.

Day Two

It is the nature of people to overcomplicate things: we want there to be nuance to evil and dimensions to good. The truth is often simpler than that. More often than not, it is about survival, making the pain stop. Looking at the wretched nightmare, the pieces finally together, I said:

"Were you that angry, Portia?"

I took in her ruin, her metamorphosis complete, and if there was any part of me that believed her capable of salvation, it was dead as the rest of our friends. I swallowed. Through the lattice of her ribs, I could see the line of her mouth, embedded in the torn walls of her abdominal cavity, flinch.

"Why didn't you just leave?"

There was movement there under the surface of the muscle: something pressing, straining to get free. So much said about the Raw Mother and so little known. I wondered—wonder still, will always wonder—if there were any other sisters in the sorority, if it'd been Portia alone, walking through that burned-down house, nursing this change. If everything else that followed was the god growing in her belly, stretching through her skin, wanting more, wanting someone else to connect to. If Portia had ever even existed or if it was the Raw Mother wearing her face, using her tongue, reaching with her hands for more, always more. Because if there's one thing I knew, it was that this world was hungry.

Portia struck the ground hard with one leg and the translucent chitin fractured. Out from it emerged a fresh limb, this one banded in pewter and white, robed still in the leftover molt. She shuddered, another leg writhing out of its molt. I couldn't tell how much of the girl remained, if it even mattered. After all, it wasn't like she even had a head any longer.

"*B o w.*"

"Dad tried that. Didn't work on me." Adam rolled one shoulder backward, then the other, a smile tipping onto his mouth, the expression nearly obscured by the smoke boiling from his skin. I couldn't tell which of the two sheened in the low and gilded light was the worse monster.

Portia let free a silken laugh and said, without any of its slurring lunacy, with such clarity and nonchalance that if I closed my eyes I could have believed it was Portia standing there, human and whole and unchanged.

"Then I'll make you."

If I had any illusions left of being either of their equals, they were gone the moment they moved: Portia blurring into motion, Adam erupting again into fire. Though she was the one to lunge, he was the one to strike first, bringing a hand scything forward. If Portia weren't just as fast, if her anatomy hadn't been so irrevocably changed, that might have been all she wrote, but she torqued midair to one side at the last second, and Adam's hand speared through her collarbone, bursting an eye.

Portia screamed.

The mouth in her chest widened farther, the jaws of her ribs spreading, and from the hollow sprung a second set of

jaws, spearing into Adam's chest. To my shock and his, the
fire did nothing. His expression went from one of insouci-
ance to surprise as the jaws sunk through his skin like he was
a pat of warmed butter. Then the blood came, a mealy gush,
entrails ribboning out, chunks pouring free.

Adam let out a noise, a gasp, really, and sank to his knees.

Portia stepped daintily over his smoldering form, her myriad eyes fixed on me. To my surprise, there was contrition in
her posture as she inched forward, in how she held her limbs
meekly to her chest, and the thing Portia had become felt irrevocably her again, for all that she was missing a head and
sporting a mélange of new bodily accoutrements. Inexplicably, she seemed sorry, not just for what'd happened, but for
all of it. The fact we were here instead of wherever she had
imagined us to be.

"You don't want to eat me, I promise," I said.

"It was easier." It was Portia as I remembered her, the words
gorgeously enunciated. I couldn't tell you how. She didn't have
the correct appendages for it, at least not as far as I could say.
"It was good for both of us. She told me this."

"Lots of abusive assholes say shit like that." I laughed,
blood fountaining from my lips. "Trust me."

"Touch me?" said Portia, skittering closer, claws reaching for
my hand, so much rasping hunger there that my breath snagged
in my rotting lungs. "Touch me. Make it stop. H-h-hold me. It
hurts."

They promised we would be fed, and they gave us carrion.

"Please." The word was moaned like a promise, like a por-
tent. Portia crossed the distance between us and folded herself
onto the ground beside me, her torso cocked so that she could
flash puppy-dog eyes at me, so miserable I almost felt sorry

for her, would have if not for the memory of her spooning meat from Eoan's severed torso like he was a soup bowl. Still, I almost reached a hand out for her.

"You're dying," said Portia.

But you will not; not you, not ever, wedded to us forever.

"No shit." Trembling, I took the cigarette pack I'd stolen from Rowan's pocket earlier, spun the battered cardboard in circles with a hand. "We all are. Well, some of us are doing it faster than others."

"Hold me?"

She is ours.

"Was it worth it?" It'd be so easy to retrieve the last cigarette from the carton, light it, let myself bask in the nicotine for as long as it was sustainable. Let a substance do the work of distracting me from my aches. "Giving it all up to her? Subservience instead of release?"

O u r s.

"I was trapped," said Portia. "I didn't know what to do."

"I get that," I said.

In her, we live again. In her, we grow again.

"Frightened," said Portia so very piteously. Gone were the pith, the facade, the polish. Gone was the monster, gone was the girl, gone was everything but an emptiness that ate through me like a disease. "It hurt. It hurt for years. It hurt. She made me hurt. *She hurt me.* She took away the pain but it hurt still."

She laughed then and the sound made me relieved to know I wouldn't grow old with that echoing in my skull.

"Lonely," said Portia like it mattered, and I guess in some strange terrible fashion, it did. "Don't leave me."

The words hiccupped out of me, a surprise.

"I won't."

So I gathered what might have been a god in utero to my

chest, trembling as Portia folded herself around me, and I tucked my chin into the nook of her collarbone, felt eyelashes against my chin. A part of me wonders what might have happened if I had said no, if I had rebuked her, refused myself this sentimentality. Would Portia have been inoculated against what followed? I think about that and other regrets a lot.

Adam rose up behind her, unfolding like a fable, the flesh melted from his bone. He was skin and charred tissue, grinning skull and those blue eyes still shining improbably through the mess. The hole gaped in his chest still, right where a heart should have rested.

"Fuck you too," said Adam, driving both hands into Portia's back. I could feel him pull. I could feel Portia coming undone, and I ran what was left of my magic into her, taking apart whatever was left of her that was human, unraveling her, even as Adam's fire blackened my vision. I must have screamed. I think I did. I'm certain Portia wailed, pinioned suddenly between the two of us, but at that point, it didn't matter.

When Portia was nothing but ash and clumps of meat on the ground, Adam stretched again to his full height, hands outstretched to receive the world's bounties. "And so the prophecy is fulfilled."

Except, of course, it wasn't.

"Actually . . ."

"What did you do?" said Adam.

And I smiled.

DAY TWO

"What did you *do*?" Adam repeated, thundering.

"You're a fucking idiot if you don't know that already," I said tiredly, daintily retrieving Rowan's last cigarette and striking the final match from the box he'd kept, the pornographic label lost under a crust of gore. I lit the thing as Adam went down to a knee, slumping under the weight of his own death. His eyes were bluer than ever as the skin along his cheeks blackened, his bones hollowing.

Then he laughed, a sudden ripple of sound that had my skin crawling despite everything we'd seen. "Ah. So that's why you kissed me."

When he laughed, it was in Sullivan's voice but when he smiled at me, it was Portia's smile beaming out of his decaying jaw. His teeth shone unsettlingly white; I thought of Rowan standing over the pyre of my old roommate's corpse and how pale Ford's bones had looked when Minji flensed him.

I took a drag from the cigarette, sagging onto the floor, wincing. It was good. I hated that it was good. I didn't like allowing myself vices. Too much risk. People have a habit of lionizing the human condition, describing us as exalted: creatures who can transcend our base instincts and ignore impulse in favor of community. I've always called bullshit on that. Even the best of us beg for our mothers when we're bleeding out. Point is, though, I've never trusted my body not to betray me when it wanted something badly enough, and the thought of being compromised because I was craving a smoke, because I so badly needed to have a drink, or a person; the thought of being sublimated by petty desire outraged me. Still did.

But given everything, it didn't seem to matter anymore.

"What did you *do,* Li?"

"Law of contagion," I said after my third puff. "Once in contact, always in contact. Do you remember that?"

Adam said nothing but watched me with those celadon eyes of his, now lashless, like polished stones set in the sockets of a holy skeleton. His breathing was tectonically slow.

I ashed my cigarette on the floor, the once gorgeous tiles scummed with dried gore. I couldn't tell any longer what had been blood, what was once organ: it was all the same reeking inkblot of clotted stringy black. "My saliva is in you now. I don't really know how it works. But some of me is in you, that's all I needed."

"Hot." Rowan's irreverence, Rowan's actual voice, coming out of Adam's ruined mouth.

"And a lot of Rowan is in me."

"Always liked a good threesome."

I didn't laugh, although Adam did in wheezing gusts, each exhalation causing more of him to flake away. Embers floated up through the late light prisming through the stained glass, and the air glittered gold where it wasn't a blood-tinged mirage of reflected saints.

"I can't take you apart for good because your daddy's the fucking devil. Gods know I've tried before. Do you remember when I blew up your hand?"

"Mhm. It's why Gracelynn died."

I didn't flinch. I'm proud of that, will die proud of my poker face then.

"You heal. You keep healing. So long as you're alive, you're going to heal from whatever I do to you." I wafted my cigarette over where the last of his intestines drooled from his belly, his abdomen mostly hollow now. His spine winked from what was left.

"Entirely." And this he said in his own voice, thank every god named by a desperate soul. I don't know what I'd have done otherwise.

"But deathworkers," I said. "They're something else."

"Oh, Li, you *didn't*."

"You probably know about rabies and why you should avoid touching woodland animals even if they seem harmless. If you get bitten by a rabid squirrel, you can, of course, take a vaccine and be assured that it has a one hundred percent success rate. But you have to take it within ten days. You have to be pumped full of it before the symptoms show up. Otherwise, that's it. Nothing to do then but keep you sedated and comfortable until you die horribly, sorry, good luck with your next life." This close, I could feel it: the nuclear reactor compacted into the very heart of him, the godlike power that would let him burn and burn and burn with life eternal until whatever destiny he'd been promised came to wed him. The thought made me faintly nauseous. "Any kind of skin-to-skin contact is the equivalent of being exposed to immediately symptomatic super-rabies."

"You killed us both."

His expression unwound from me the first real laugh I'd laughed in a year, and the sound tightened over the nacreous emptiness like a noose. Adam stared at me like a man who'd been expecting a birthday party but arrived instead at his own funeral. It only made me guffaw harder, which wasn't without its costs. I spat blood onto the ground when I was done, mopping the corner of my mouth with the knuckle of my right thumb; it left a cherry-red streak over the back of my hand.

Time can teach you such a fortune of things. Like a broken heart. Like rage. Sadly, it wasn't something I could sustain forever. Death was as hungry as grief and I was still human. With every passing second it seemed like there was more of it and less of me. I'd have to cede extremities soon—tracts of skin, whatever was extraneous—to this last furious Hail Mary I was making.

"Oh, come on, Adam, we're mortal. At least, I am." What good was all this if I couldn't gloat a little? "I've been dying for a while. And I know you'll die too because everything dies. If you don't, though, I'm counting on it being such a problem for you that you won't have the mental capacity to do more than keep it at bay—making you easy prey. Point is: either way, *I win.*"

The last I couldn't help but snarl before the world erupted again in immolating white, a killing heat convulsing toward me. But it didn't get far. I suffocated that torrential flame with the marrow from Adam's bones, wrapping him in spongy curtains of pink and fatty yellow until at last he yielded and the light spluttered out. Sweat drenched me. I tasted salt on my lips, although that could have been more from the internal bleeding.

When the glare died completely away, Adam said:

"I still don't get it, Li."

"Don't get what?"

"Your self-righteous act," he said. Adam seemed further diminished, no longer even an effigy of himself, but a shadow teased out in pen strokes. Only his eyes were unchanged, blue and lustrous as glazed ceramic.

"We're alike, you and I. We're both real monsters. There's a universe where we make that worthwhile." He laughed and now it was Gracelynn's soft, gauzy chuckle that wafted out of him. Even though it was crawling out of Adam's throat, it sounded as it always did: *kind*. If I hadn't loathed him before, I would have learned to hate him then. Our dead deserved more than this scavenging. "You and I, carving out a world together."

"You're wrong," I said.

"Oh?"

I finished my cigarette, flicking the stub into the bruise-yellow gloom, the amber like that of a contusion only beginning to heal. It was getting harder now to maintain my cavalier facade. An ache nuzzled through the bones of my fingers, up my arms, fanning downward over shoulder blades and spine to pool in my hips; it felt like what I'd always imagined arthritis to feel like, a dull yet consuming agony. *This is what old must feel like*, I thought.

And then: *I will never know for sure.*

"We are both *real* monsters, yes," I said, resenting his phrasing, the pride slicking the words. "But we're not the same kind of monsters. You do it because you love that bloody work. Because it makes you feel powerful."

"And it doesn't make you feel the same?"

I recalled vividly then how Ford had screamed when Adam fished the guts out from the man's belly: that high-pitched, panting, piggish shriek that went on even as he choked on his own blood. It had reminded me of my stepfather and how he'd wailed all those years ago as I broke him like a wishbone, my fantasy fulfilled in lieu of his own. Had I felt powerful then? Had I felt powerful each time after? There'd certainly been a kind of rightness, a sense that what was happening was somehow good and just: a fulfillment of some primordial promise, one made long before even the first microbe appeared in the first oceans. It was something you could stitch a life from.

"No."

"Then why do you do it? Why—" He gagged on the remnants of that sentence, ichor dribbling through his teeth, a viscid blackness that held clumps of what I knew to be tissue matter, bile and dark sticky bubbles of venous blood.

Ford's prophecy from so long ago drifted through my head. I got what I wanted. But it definitely wasn't what any of them deserved.

I stood with considerable difficulty, my right leg having gone numb in a way that suggested the nerves were mostly rotted away, a needling chill trespassing up my side. I didn't have much time left, which I somewhat resented, but I had no one to blame but myself. This was the gamble I'd chosen and the cards I'd played. "I think mostly it's because I've spent my whole life with this little voice in my head telling me that I never had any agency in the first place, that I'm collared and leashed to a hundred people, none of whom have even thought about offering compensation for partial ownership of me. And I hate it. You can't imagine how much."

Adam didn't answer, racked by sudden paroxysms, eyes rolling to whites. As he bucked and writhed, fire sheeted over his body in brilliant waves, like it was trying to burn out the infection, this death of mine I'd shared with him.

"Then again, maybe you can. It must be such a weight knowing your only hope for supplanting your bastard status is bringing about the end of the world. Nothing else. You're nothing but an implement, and I'm nothing but a thing to possess." I clasped both hands around the bone of his upper right arm and pulled, ignoring how the fire ate through the skin of my palm, how it glued the fat paddings to his raw tendons. It didn't hurt. You'd think it would but it didn't. "Actually, now that I think about it. Maybe you're right. We are the same kind of monster. All we've ever wanted was *control*."

I could hear the faculty coming down the hall to the library, the oily noise of their flesh thudding over the floorboards, the procession of their many feet, their gnarled hands. Nails *clicking.* Not too long ago, that cacophony had made me shudder. But now it was banal, mundane. I pressed my shoulder to the doors, these too gory with our past days, and pushed; the heavy wood screeched over the tiles and splintered. An eager murmur rose on the other side: the faculty must have seen me.

Like us, they must also relish the perfect joy of absolute control. Especially now that they were nothing but a wet mess of sinew and skin, threaded through one another like cords tangled in the bottom of a drawer. I couldn't imagine happiness in such a mélange. But they'd smiled, hadn't they? As they'd expunged every fluid from Sullivan's body, as they drank him down. And laughed. Some inflection of memory told me that they laughed, and it'd been in the timbre of good-natured grandparents, loud enough even to be heard over our valedictorian's screams. I think I remember those things, at least. Trauma has a knack for macerating the past so all that remains are the sharp edges of the agony you sustained.

It was hard work, maneuvering Adam's body through the four-inch crack I'd opened. I let the skin slough from my torso, what cushions of fat I still possessed; my hair, which loosened in rivulets along with the soft tissue of my scalp. Anything that wasn't immediately necessary, I surrendered, and I was glad I'd never really exalted vanity. Though both Adam and I were rotting by degrees, rotting with such speed that we smelled sweetly of what was coming, the air outside the library still cut through the putrefaction: it smelled like rain, like *ice*, like frost come too early to a world still dizzy with life. And I could have wept from my loneliness for the uninterrupted sky if not for the fact I was, well, *dying*.

There in the vestibule, the floor utterly eradicated of stains, was the cancerously lumpy silhouette of the faculty. They *stood*, I suppose, for lack of better terminology (because really how else do you describe that clamor of appendages seething under their mass?) in silence as I staggered toward them, burning and decaying in turn.

Upon seeing them, I thought there'd be some last confrontation, an opportunity for an exchange, for them to declaim their villainy and for me to tell them to go fuck themselves. Instead: the tense quiet of a hospital waiting room. Starlight flecked what little of the night I could see. For some reason, that and nothing else I'd experienced in my time at Hellebore had me wanting to sob for a father long deceased and a mother who might as well be the same, but doing so would require resources I no longer had: lungs that weren't mostly sludge, eyes that weren't losing their sight.

"All yours," I said when Adam's seizure had dwindled to a rabbiting pulse. The world grayed to a promise of sleep. Timing was going to be everything. "We're all yours."

I don't know if they heard or if they took their cue from my posture, my crumpling over Adam's body, the two of us now just wounds with faces. I closed my eyes, the trembling animal folded into my brain stem *screaming*. An atavistic terror nearly had me pissing myself as I bent over Adam, steepled hands pressed to my mouth like I was praying. But truth was I was counting instead.

One. The faculty reared up in preparation of the feast and I smelled them then: a greasy pungency like the windowless interior of an airless retirement home, sweat, and the stink of leftover student decaying away.

Two. They were *so* fast. I'd seen them come for us, of course, that first terrible night but somehow, I had since shed the memory of the specifics. That or my mind looked at the image scarified onto it and hid itself away, whispering, *We will process this later if we are ever safe again.*

Three. Of all the things I'd expected, tenderness wasn't one of them. Their fingers trailed softly over the back of my neck, nails grazing skin, worshipful in their movements. Their mouths traced the cord of my spine and if their lips were dry, their touch was at least ephemeral and I could almost pretend it didn't make me want to scream. I cradled Adam closer to me nonetheless, his poor heart, so recently re-formed, straining against its failing prison. There is a much misused, much misattributed line from the Bible that talks about how the spirit might be willing but the flesh is weak. With Adam, I suspect that was entirely literal. Whatever numinosity he'd inherited from his father would burn even at the end of the end of everything, but the rest of him would molder with everyone else. I pressed my cheek to his forehead, felt the bone soften, *break.*

Teeth sank into my back. I almost didn't notice, focused instead on what I had to do next.

What remained of my ribs bloomed ecstatically into a maw, into arms of shining bone. I enfolded Adam, covered him as the faculty covered us, held him to my bared organs, pulled him close until he was entombed in me, and briefly, I thought I could hear Rowan's shrill laughter brush my ear. He would have found this whole tableau hilarious. The pain worsened, keening through me, until it became the whole of me and it was difficult to imagine there'd ever been a me undefiled by this agony, this sensation of fingers burrowing through me like I was no more substantial than water, of being opened up and hollowed out. And gods, it hurt. I'm not ashamed to say I screamed.

Still, with the furnace of Adam's soul and the poison of Rowan's existence both interred in me, it'd have been a waste to give up there. I comforted myself with the thought that if there was an after, if some purgatory existed for little boy devils and brokenhearted girls, I'd find everyone who'd left me behind and I could go to them reciting the way Adam sobbed for reprieve. Maybe I'd find Kevin there too and be able to tell them how sorry I was I couldn't keep Gracelynn from watching them die. But that was for later. Now was for holding on.

Here's the thing: eaten without the intermediary of my flesh, Rowan would have simply been absorbed, disassembled too quickly for the malignancy of his nature to take effect. But allowed to incubate, to fester, to spread while the faculty was distracted with, say, an infinitely regenerating feast, a screaming thing they could gorge on in a thousand ways and know there'd always be more to eat? Well, that would change everything. With what I'd stolen from Adam, I made myself into a fucking horn of plenty, plying them with muscle, with marrow, with the myriad offerings of liver and lung, brain and bone. Whatever they slavered for, I fed them. And death grew in them like every cancer does, slowly and by degrees, until finally . . .

"Wait," came the headmistress's voice, scraped of its usual bubbling secret humor.

"Don't you love it?" I said with what I had left of a throat. "When the wrong person wins?"

DAY THREE

"That took far too long," I said tiredly as the doors heaved apart. The vestibule was tacky with the remnants of the faculty, no longer a tide of flesh-colored appetite but just meat, like everyone else was. I'd thought I'd be dead already but with so much flesh, so much meat around me, I could move my death around: store my soul where it couldn't reach and watch as it ate the faculty, emptied them, made them scream.

All said and done, I was proud. We'd done something historic: Hellebore was empty, its halls hollowed, its hopes ended. No longer would it feed magic to the starving world. No longer would eat it through generations of kids whose only sin was being born with a reservoir of latent power. Hellebore was over and the slow decomposition of our society, stunted by those brilliant governmental minds, would resume; it'd be a fucking catastrophe, I'm sure, but they started it: those bastards should have left me alone.

Because dear god, can I hold a grudge.

Sunlight blasted through the corridor, white and searing. The Ministry agents—I knew the symbol embossed on their chest way too well, seeing as Sullivan had been practically monogramed from head to toe with it—in their blue hazmat suits, faces occluded by their tinted masks, looked almost comical. Their shoulders were disproportionately widened by the plastic. Inversely, their feet, stuffed into black rubber boots, seemed hilariously petite. Maybe I was just tired. At that point I'd gone without sleep for three days. My perception had become glutinous; everything was softer now around the edges. I couldn't tell if the voices murmuring at the periphery of my consciousness were projects of my exhausted mind or the teachers chastising me for what I'd done. They were laughing then: lowly, like the sound of applause from an adjacent room.

"What happened to the school?" said one of the agents, inching forward. He, for reasons I couldn't conjecture, raised a handgun at me.

I blinked stupidly at the weapon, an animal faced with an unfamiliar death. Surely, they must have been informed about what Hellebore was. Or perhaps they were just that confident in the supremacy of firearms. I decided then this vanguard was American and suddenly, the world made more sense again.

"I happened."

BEFORE

The world spun and sudden as anything, we were in the gymnasium. Each and every one of us was in formal raiment, a mortarboard jauntily set at an angle on each of our heads. We were as pristine as if we'd spent the day in frenzied ablution: hair shining like it'd been oiled individually, faces beautiful. We looked like we were waiting backstage for our turn on the catwalk—like sacrifices, or saints waiting for the lions.

The air had an odd crystalline shine to it like it had been greased somehow. That or I was in the throes of a migraine. It was hard to be sure. I'd been plopped next to Gracelynn, who was sat between Sullivan and me, with Kevin on my opposite side. Bracketing us was a pair of twins I'd only seen occasionally but knew by reputation, the two notorious for the ease with which they procured reagents for whoever had the money to pay: they could get anything so long as what you wanted came from something with a pulse. A few familiar faces were past them to the right: Stefania, Minji, Eoan, and Adam, who slouched almost entirely out of his seat.

"What is going on?" Kevin hissed to me.

"We have to go," I said in lieu of an answer, standing.

The world stuttered.

I was back on the metal fold-out chair I'd been sitting on,

like my muscles had changed their mind midway to rising. Except I hadn't *felt* myself sit back down. Instead, it was more like the seconds had rewound, had flinched back from my decision like it was a hot stove. I tried again. This time, I felt it: reality slingshotting backward through linear time, not far enough to leave me discombobulated, but enough to have my ass on the cold, cheap steel. It hit me then that I was trapped. All my efforts, all those months spent trying to get out, and here I was with no place to go, a bunny with the hounds gathered all around.

The doors of the gymnasium opened, allowing our headmaster entry. She drifted down the aisle, splitting the crowd of so-called graduates, resplendent in a fawn-colored suit, the majesty of which was spoiled by the fact that her white hair was still in curlers. A clipboard was tucked in the crook of her left arm. She checked something off as she passed each student, her smile as it always was: slightly too wide for her face.

When she finally reached our row, she only said, with an effervescent giggle:

"Ah. It's time for a speech by the valedictorian!"

I have to confess something: the claim I didn't feel bad for Sullivan wasn't a lie, for all that I might have implied that it was. I don't. I doubt I ever will. I was positioned right in front of him when it happened, and I had a clear view of Sullivan's face as the faculty crested over the podium to blanket him in their flesh. There'd been the wet shine of grateful tears along his cheeks. He had smiled. He had looked relieved. In the half second before they reached him, before he was leavened into their mass, I saw Sullivan open his arms, and while he might not have enjoyed the process of dying, for a moment at least he certainly welcomed it.

I hope you've been paying attention, by the way. This wasn't a lie but some of the rest is.

AFTER

I have been dreaming of my friends. I can call them that now, I think: hindsight creates a kind of affection and besides, the dead can't hold anything against anyone, least of all grief. I dreamt mostly of Rowan at first; then it was Gracelynn and Kevin holding hands as they wandered through endless corridors; then Johanna, who no longer had a face, only a bleeding fissure where one should have been. I even dreamt of Delilah and Sullivan as he was before the faculty unmade him into bones and effluvium.

The night before this, I dreamt of all of them at the same time, coming together to sit in an open-air auditorium. The chairs were the color of fresh blood and the sky above was starless and black. Their faces were a bloodless white, cauled with a pink-tinged vernix. They looked like a wedding party on their high-backed, gore-red chairs, staring down at an empty stage. They looked like your judgment, a jury of dead waiting for the executioner to arrive.

If the arc of the moral universe truly bent toward justice, I'd be nothing but a honeycombed corpse right now. But such things like decency are nothing but human inventions. The cosmos bends nowhere except toward annihilation.

You showed us that.

By the time you read this paragraph, I should be at your door.

I advise you to stay there instead of evacuating. Otherwise, I will have to look for you and in doing so, I will have to eat through everything and everyone you love. I will devour all of it. And as they die, I will make sure they know you're the reason for their agony. So, for their sake, stay for me. Commune with whatever you hold holy. Leave instruction on what to do with your earthly belongings. Make peace with yourself.

Give me a moment and I will show you everything you taught us at Hellebore.

ACKNOWLEDGMENTS

As always, thank you to the fabulous team at Nightfire. Kelly, Kristin, Hannah, Jordan, Giselle, Michael, Valeria, Esther, and everyone else on the team, I wouldn't be able to do any of this without you. You are the reason I haven't run screaming into the woods.

Thank you to George at Titan Books for acquiring the UK rights and everything you're doing across the pond. You're a brazen, wonderful fellow and I cannot wait to hang out again soon. (Hopefully, it'll be soon instead of years.)

Thank you to Everett, you lovely clever man, you bunny of a human being, you softhearted delight. I don't know how you put up with me or my screaming through the creative process. Thank you to Ali and Kyungseo, sisters of another mother, who have also kept me from running screaming into the woods.

Thank you as always to Michael, my agent. I would fight God for you, my dude. You're stuck with me for life.

And last but not least, thank you to my darling Mouse, for another year of listening to me bang my head against the keyboard and talk wistfully about how I should run away into the woods. For being you. For always being in my corner. Catmouse forever.

Normally, this is where I'd end my acknowledgments, but

I'd really like everyone to know that there is a very good kitty by the name of Farrell who will be around nineteen when this book comes out. He is the best boy even though he is not mine, and he has a creaky meow and a slightly sad face in his old age. Please think of him from time to time. I need you all to know he is the best.

(And my kitties get none of the thanks because they're a bunch of assholes who keep me awake all night. But I love them, anyway.)

ABOUT THE AUTHOR

CASSANDRA KHAW is the *USA Today* bestselling and Bram Stoker Award–winning author of *Nothing But Blackened Teeth, The Salt Grows Heavy, Breakable Things,* and coauthor of *The Dead Take the A Train* with Richard Kadrey. They are an award-winning game writer.

Instagram: @casskhaw